Moment of Certainty

Moment of Certainty

Pamela Towns

Copyright © 2016 Pamela Towns

All rights reserved. No part of this book shall be used or reproduced in any manner without the written permission of the copyright owner.

ISBN 10: 1518613292
ISBN 13: 978-1518613296

This is a work of fiction. Names, characters, and places are the products of the author's imagination. Any resemblance to actual persons, living or deceased, events, or locales is entirely coincidental.

In Memory of

Melvin O'Neal McDowell, II

10/28/1982 ~ 8/5/2003

Acknowledgments

I'd like to thank, Christy Jackson Nicholas, Courtney Madden, Peggy Towns, Jennifer Wiggins, Carey Conley, Alexander Qi, and Dorrett Smith.

A special thanks to: Trice Hickman, Maggie Penn, Terry Benjamin, and Karla KL Brady.

Finally, I'd like to thank my wonderful husband, who has supported my literary journey from the start.

Chapter 1

Karen Williams had her butt raised in the air as she bent down under Mama's sleigh bed, sifting through the clutter of crumpled receipts, dated lottery tickets, and worn out pantyhose. Earlier in the week, she'd clawed her way through the grimy attic with boxes and bagged items, all of which were now a resting place for forgotten treasures. Giving in to defeat, she sucked her teeth hard, plopping down on the wooden floor next to the bed before releasing a set of twin cuss words.

She closed her eyes to calm her racing heart and thought about Mama saying, "Baby, just make somethin' of ya' life. Cut out all this silliness and act ya' age. That's all I ask."

But Mama was about as subtle as a derelict dropping his pants and peeing in the middle of a first-rate restaurant. She would take aim at the wall then throw a spoon or some other nearby object before spewing out a string of expletives. The scolding came when Karen strolled in late at night after hanging out with friends and hurling rocks off the overpass of the Davison Freeway.

Unsuspecting motorists swerved their cars toward other vehicles with near misses. Nonetheless, she joked and high-fived cronies, saying the way she saw it, she too contributed to the history of Detroit's oldest freeway.

Karen opened her eyes and gazed down at her clasped hands, dust covering her fingertips and palms. Her hardheaded ways, she knew, frazzled Mama's nerves, especially when she acted like she was deaf. That's when Mama started in, bunching her housecoat into her fist. "You betta' get right and stop all this foolishness," she complained, her chapped, bottom lip quivering. "You need to be in somebody's church, girl." Karen rolled her eyes so hard her closed lids fluttered. It didn't matter if it were Easter or Mother's Day. She wasn't about to get out of her warm bed. She also ignored Mama's beseeching hands and claims of nice young men being present because, up till now, the only "nice man" she wanted to get with was, Hershel Cummings, her best friend since childhood. But that required a whole other strategy altogether. Now that Mama was dead, Karen wished she could have taken it all back; the years of smarting off and stomping around the house like she was killing jumbo-sized roaches. Even so, all she needed to do now was stick to the plan . . . and find that doggone letter Mama was so secretive about.

Do it for Mama. You need to keep this job at Golden Walk Nursing Home, Karen told herself as she held her breath against the stench of Mr. Hamilton's armpit, which seemed a daunting task. She struggled to lift him off the checkered bathroom tile while his arm cradled her shoulder in a bear-hug. His feeble legs flailed about, but his hands managed just fine in finding security in grasping her breasts.

At the time, it seemed like a brilliant idea taking this second-shift job and proving to Mama she wasn't wasting her breath during all those talks. But now, starting work a month after her death in March, seemed a stupid thing to do, especially while she huffed at the weight of Mr. Hamilton's weak, wrinkled body against her small frame. They were both helpless on the floor.

"Mr. Hamilton, take your hands off my breasts, sir." Her upper lip arched with the request. What she wanted to do was drop the old fart on his wrinkly rump.

"What?" he asked. His voice was raspy. Then he had the nerve to look at her with a blank expression. His thin white hair stood straight up as if he'd stuck his finger in a socket and got a quick jolt.

She knew that he knew what he was doing, even if he pretended his hearing aid malfunctioned. Again, he latched on good to her breasts in attempts to stay lifted off the floor.

"Can someone help me, please?" Karen twisted her head and called out for another Certified Nurses' Assistant, hoping she didn't look as foolish as she felt. Still, she gazed out toward the opened door, awaiting someone to come rescue the both of them.

Moments later, the head nurse came into the room with fists connected to wide, wobbly hips. She appeared stern with an aura of dark clouds.

"Okay, Mr. Hamilton," Margaret Thornton said. "Let's get you up." She pulled him up with one swoop and positioned him in a wheelchair and dressed him.

Karen curved her bottom lip to one side as she interpreted Margaret's glance as a failing grade. There was nothing she could do at this point, so she turned to clean up the remaining mess Mr. Hamilton made in the bathroom, but not before she countered Margaret's narrowed eyes with a courteous smile.

"Thanks Margaret." Karen regretted the fact she needed help with one of her patients and from Margaret of all people. But when the head nurse left, she hurried to clean up pieces of toilet paper and droplets of urine that spotted the floor, which proved visually challenging as the pattern of the mustard colored tiles provided a camouflage.

After she'd scrubbed up behind Mr. Hamilton, she washed her hands and positioned his lunch on its tray.

"Where's that remote? I'm sure you'd like a little TV," she mumbled, as she lifted fishing magazines and glanced beneath the folds of the quilt lying across the edge of his bed.

"It's in the drawer of the nightstand." The loose skin under his chin jiggled as he spoke.

Humph. Hearing problem my behind. Karen nodded as she obliged him and placed the remote on the tray. "Okay, you're all set, Mr. Hamilton. I'll check on you later."

She left the room shaking her head, ready to grab her coat and purse, and smack her own behind then Cabbage Patch her way right through the exit doors of the building. Instead, she turned left down the long corridor, passing the fine dining area and lounge. While this was her first full day at work, she still had to learn her way around.

It didn't take long before she spied the nurses at the main station talking behind opened hands, their eyes darting in her direction.

"I heard you and Mr. Hamilton were doing a li'l floor dancing, huh?" One of the smirking CNAs asked as Karen walked up. The others joined in the laughter.

Karen took their grinning faces in the same fashion as coming out of a restroom with tissue stuck to the bottom of your shoe and your friends getting wind of it. In an instant, she thought of a way to wipe the smirk off their mugs and it involved ramming a thermometer up a hole on each of them.

A serious-looking young woman came from behind the station and introduced herself. "Hi, I'm Jessica."

"I'm Keekee," Karen replied, aware that she and Jessica were the only two with brown skin.

"What kind of name is that?" Jessica asked.

"The kind I like to be called." Karen rolled her neck left and right with each word after tolerating being laughed at, even though Jessica wasn't one of them.

"Fair enough. Keekee it is," Jessica replied, reaching for a clipboard on the counter. "Okay, Margaret wanted me to go over some basic procedures with you and then I'll show you your next patient. This is standard for all new employees."

Karen tried to listen as the young lady ran off a series of procedures: taking vitals, feedings, cleaning, obtaining specimens, admission documents and regulations, all the while watching Jessica gesture with her hands while talking.

"Of course we expect you to recognize S&S of possible physical problems, be prepared in the areas of CPR and first aid, and stay abreast of diseases from this list." She pointed to the paper on her clipboard. "Also, here are the names of your patients. You'll start out with six . . . eventually you'll work your way up to ten. Maybe twelve."

Karen's head started spinning. *Ten, maybe twelve patients? Was she crazy?*

Jessica flipped the papers to Karen before rattling off the lunch and coffee break schedules and the lowdown on Margaret. Then her voice waned from its rhythmic pattern when she said, "You don't ever want to be late for work or get on her bad side," Jessica concluded. Karen looked dead-center into her coworker's bright, hazel eyes.

Too late for that, she thought. She folded her arms under her breasts and pretended to understand the instructions. She didn't. Half the information went over her head because the ordeal with Mr. Hamilton had her reeling. Still, she watched Jessica as she multi-tasked her way around the station with ringing phones, visitors and managing a new employee with no incident. This impressed her. Jessica looked about twenty two or twenty three, which made her younger than Karen, who had just turned twenty four, a month before her mother died. It never mattered that her birthday fell the day before Valentine's Day. She didn't celebrate either date, which took on a whole new meaning of sadness. Flowers now reminded her of death and funerals.

On the whole, her mother's death had been the reason she took the job at Golden Walk Nursing Home in the first place. She'd done nothing with her life and now her mama was dead in the ground, never seeing one iota of success emanating from her. For starters, Mama wanted her to land a good paying job, settle down and get married. Karen wanted that too, but she had her own agenda. Yet, she felt unsure of herself and all the steps it took to get to those dreams.

Around her buddies she came off as fearless, but without Mama, she felt like a two-year old hiding behind a parent's knees. And forget going to Daddy. Mama and her big sister Val were mum on the subject every time Karen asked about the mystery man's whereabouts. Val didn't know her daddy either. Not that Mama was loose or anything, but she sure had her secrets.

When Jessica returned after answering a call, she guided Karen to her next patient's room, giving her a background of the patient's history and the medications she took.

"How is she?" Karen asked, walking alongside Jessica back down the long corridor with bulletin boards on both sides.

"What do you mean?"

"Well, how is she to deal with? What's she like?" Karen wondered if she should've refrained from asking the question.

"She's like a rose. Now, another thing," Jessica continued, not missing a beat. "Ms. Blout has Alzheimer's, so she may talk normal one day, and the next, not even know who you are. So, don't take it personally."

The tension that had settled between her shoulders earlier now seemed to ease.

"Right in there," Jessica gestured with her arm extended. "If you need anything just call."

Karen nodded a "thanks" and watched Jessica walk away before she entered Ms. Blout's room.

Chapter 2

The unrelenting knock at the door shook Val Williams out of her dream-state. She'd arrived home, dead tired, from a full day on the job not more than ten-minutes before the interruption.

"I'm coming," she called out, lifting from the side of the bed. Barefooted and still in her work clothes, she headed down the stairs. "Hold on. I'm coming." She stopped at the edge of the tattered steps, trying to peek through the faded, sheer white curtains covering the living room window. It was the UPS man holding a flat folder. When she cracked open the door, the tall man, clean-shaven and wearing a dark brown uniform and a fake smile said, "Hello."

Val released a soft, "Hi," and a weary smile.

The gentleman handed her a clipboard with a form to sign. When she completed her signature, he shoved a large envelope at her and said as dry as the desert, "Have a nice day," without breaking a crease in his face. It had already turned dark outside, she thought, referencing the man's parting words. She closed the door after watching him walk away then examined the envelope, mildly curious, yet, guessing it probably involved Mama's affairs.

She put on a pot of Maxwell coffee then opened the packet with her thumb. Inside she found papers from an attorney's office regarding the mortgage. *Oh, boy, this can't be good,* she thought. Her heart felt as if it were going to thump right out of her chest. The letter read:

Dear Madam:

This letter is to advise you of the loan secured by the above referred property, which may involve foreclosure proceedings against said property based on unpaid principal balance, unpaid accrued interest, escrow/impound shortages or credits, late charges, legal fees/costs, and other miscellaneous charges. Unless you notify us within thirty days from the date of this letter, we will assume that the debt is valid and will proceed with the process of foreclosing the above said property.

Sincerely,
James Johnson
James Johnson & Roy Steinberg, LLC

Val's hand shook to the point she'd knocked over her cup, spilling its contents over the table and the envelope. Every ounce of optimism she had about handling Mama's obligations drained from her body like air seeping from a balloon with a pin-sized hole in it. Her head began to pound. Everything seemed muddled with the thought of losing the house. She couldn't handle the debt by herself with her present income. Unless Ed McMahon came knocking with a winning sweepstakes, there was no way around telling Karen what was going on.

Val had managed a lifetime of mendacity, especially where Karen was concerned. She tried to spare her of the truth, hers and Mama's, in fact. She knew that Karen had gone through a barrage of emotions, starting a new job and all. Bills shouldn't be another thing Karen needed to worry about. So Val held her secrets as best she could.

Chapter 3

Right off, Karen noticed the yellow walls were bare and dull, like a dense fog ruining an otherwise bright day, partly because personal photos and magazines were out of sight. There was nothing cheery about the space. A TV hung from the ceiling, a small nightstand stood beside the bed, and a chair, furthest from the window, nuzzled the corner of the room. Karen placed her patient's lunch tray and linens down on their designated spots. She glanced over at the old woman as she stood in front of the window, aided by her cane. She looked skyward. Karen peered up, too.

    She cleared her throat before speaking. "Hello, I- I'm Karen. I'm your new CNA."

    Ms. Blout remained motionless as she stared out the window like no one had uttered a word, still showing her back to Karen. The old woman wore a beige scarf and blouse with dark brown slacks, dressed as if she were going to a function. Her short salt and pepper hair was neatly styled. She even wore a large decorative ring on her right pinky finger.

Karen spoke louder, figuring the old woman had a hearing problem like Mr. Hamilton. "I don't know if you . . ."

"What do you want me to do about it?" The woman snapped, still facing the window.

Karen's head jerked. "Do about what, ma'am?"

"The fact that you stand in my room in this . . . this moronic fashion . . . making this absurd announcement – It's obvious who you are." The old woman turned around in slow increments. She stopped then scowled at Karen as if she'd never seen a young woman before. Or, was she disappointed she was black? Perhaps Ms. Blout didn't like to deal with anyone who wasn't white like her, Karen assumed.

She bucked her eyes at the old woman. Ms. Blout had called her a moron without even looking at her first. Not that she would have been justified. Before she knew it, Karen tightened her fist. She thought about kicking the old bat's cane to the floor and punching her in the kidney.

"I suppose you're right, Ms. Blout," Karen said, fuming and feeling the tension return in her shoulders.

"A rose," was what Jessica had said when she'd asked about the temperament of the old woman. *A rose my eye.*

"Right about what, child?"

Karen moistened her lips. "What you just said. I guess you would know who I am."

"Why are you trying to have a conversation with me? I don't want to talk to you." The woman fanned an aggravated hand at her.

Karen's eyebrows sprang up. "Okay, then, I have your medication. Here . . . take these with some orange juice." Karen extended both items to the old woman.

Ms. Blout shuffled toward her, the cane steadying her steps. Again, she eyed Karen peculiarly, her face distorted as if she were constipated, then she took the two tablets and sipped from the small glass.

Karen hated being looked down upon. And the way Ms. Blout watched her, made her feel like the old woman thought she was superior.

As a child, Karen remembered sitting in the lobby of a doctor's office. She fidgeted and scooted in and out of her oversized chair while Mama sat next to her gritting her teeth and snapping her fingers. "Act right, girl. White folks is watching," she had whispered.

"Why do you look like that?" Ms. Blout asked.

"Why do you look the way you look?" Karen snapped before she could gather the words back into her mouth. "I'm black. I can't help how God made me, Ms. Blout, just like you can't change being white."

The woman's eyes glistened. "Hah." She turned and took her time as she walked to the bluish, paisley chair that hugged the corner of the room and eased herself down, grunting as she settled. "I mean, what is all that? You look ridiculous." The woman's arthritic hand circled the air, gesturing toward Karen's head.

Karen jutted her left hip as she stood in the center of the room. She rolled her eyes then counted to ten. She knew she had a quick temper and could draw words out like a sharpened blade. On top of that, Karen didn't want to lose her job on her first day because of this old bat.

"Why do you wear your hair like that?" the woman pressed.

"Thought you didn't want to talk to me?"

"I'm asking a question, child."

"First of all, I ain't no child."

Ms. Blout snorted. "What's the second thing?"

"W-what? Look, I wear my hair like this cause it's fly, that's why."

Ms. Blout snorted again as she tapped her cane on the floor, eyeing Karen's hair. "Admittedly, you do appear as though you're flying—the top resembles that of a chicken."

"I said 'fly' not flying. In case you ain't heard, chickens don't fly." Karen huffed and proceeded to replace the bed sheets, yanking at every thread. She snatched up the empty glass Ms. Blout had placed on the nightstand, and figured the old woman might top her list of people she couldn't stand.

"Haven't heard." She corrected Karen, after several minutes had lapsed.

"Huh?"

"I merely made reference to your poor attempt to speak the English language. You talk as though you've come straight from the alley dear," Ms. Blout stated. "How old are you?" she asked, lifting her chin as if it aided her perception to hear.

"Twenty-four."

"Where do you live?"

Karen tilted her head and smacked her lips before saying, "Detroit. I live in Detroit."

"And where did you work before you started working here?"

"Why? What's that gotta do with me caring for you, Ms. Blout?"

"I asked you a question?"

"I worked lots of places."

"Where? And speak clearly."

"Bur-ger King, o-kay."

Ms. Blout shook her head and tapped her cane to the floor. "Humph. Figures."

"Whatju tryin' to say? You never ate a burger? Somebody had to fix 'em you know."

"I'll have you know I've never eaten fast food in my life."

Karen parted her tight lips long enough to push out warm, deliberate words, "Do you want your lunch then, Ms. Blout? Or don't you eat that neither?"

"No, I do not."

"No, you don't eat food from the cafeteria?"

"I'm not hungry. I suppose your work here is done then, isn't it?"

Karen blinked long and hard at the proud-looking woman, thinking she should've offered her an enema instead, based on her stuck up manner.

As Karen turned to leave the old woman's room, her thigh bumped the sharp corner of the nightstand. The pain knotted but she refused to flinch. Instead, she stormed from the area, closing the door behind her, whether Ms. Blout wanted it that way or not.

She couldn't make sense of the woman's hateful attitude. At this rate, she assumed she would be fired within the next day or so for giving an elderly woman a beat-down. She didn't bear the patience to deal with these folks. Already, she'd had two loony patients back to back. What was she thinking when she took this course in school?

This type of work didn't suit her. Yet, she didn't know what did or didn't fit her life. She had avoided such questions when Mama was alive. She did her own thing, and sat back and watched her older sister Val take the heat for most of the crap she had pulled. Back in the day, it made her snicker whenever Mama slapped Val upside her head for neglecting her. After all, it was a big sister's job to watch after the younger sister as far as Karen was concerned. Now, she couldn't sneeze without Val hovering around.

Chapter 4

While the evening wind pushed against the flapping screen door, Val's attention zoomed in on the pile of bills which seemed to have mounted since she had last eyed them hours earlier. After the funeral, there wasn't any money left. And Mama didn't even have insurance which put an extra burden on her to pay for the coffin, headstone and everything in between. She sat at the desk in the den, rocking back and forth in the rickety chair which squeaked every time pressure was placed against its back. She began performing an unconscious habitual finger exercise, tapping each one to her thumb five times. This was done simultaneously with both hands as her thoughts drifted into oblivion.

Concentrating on even one subject proved problematic. She refused to complain to Karen, though. Maybe this meant a new beginning for them. With Mama gone, they now had each other to lean on. As a disability case manager, Val figured she could put in overtime to make ends meet. There were always caseloads that needed updating or files to be renamed. Although she hated living in the house, she still had to find a way to pay the mortgage and keep the water running and the electricity and gas on.

As if someone snapped their fingers and said, "Okay, when I count to three, you'll awake." Val shook her head and looked up toward the clock on the wall with the peeling wallpaper, aware that Karen would return home in another hour or so. She fumbled with the most pressing bill and decided to tackle that one. In the process, she knocked two blank pieces of notebook paper onto the floor.

Val's pulse accelerated. The formation of the papers panicked her. The top sheet shifted below the bottom one, lining up perfectly. She stared at the papers until her eyes burned. Her palms grew sweaty while reaching for the sheets. Her hands trembled. She stopped and turned to face the desk, but wanted very much to gaze back at the sheets on the floor. She could pick up both pieces together, or one at a time, if she wanted to. "It's just paper," she mumbled. "Frank has nothing to do with this . . . it's just paper."

Val bit her bottom lip and closed her irritated eyes as she bent to pick up the papers. She stopped before snatching them both up then tossed them onto the desk. Her eyes glistened as she clutched her chest, reaffirming that indeed, these were Frank's papers. His scent, his words, his preposterous dare . . . all Frank. In fact, every corner of Mama's house, at some point or another, reminded her of Frank.

She remembered it as if *that* day had leaked into her current one. She had come home from elementary school, happy that Miss Jenkins had given her candy for spelling all her words right. Frank questioned her on the number of words that had vowels and consonants in them.

"You aren't gonna trick me," Val said, licking her sucker with long strokes. Frank, who was a tall and slender man, came up with other ideas to trip her up.

"Well . . . what number comes after five? Twenty-three? One hundred?"

Her answers were all correct. Frank then thudded papers on the floor, testing her yet again, to pick them up. She giggled and plopped her green sucker on the kitchen counter, happy to meet the easy challenge.

When she bent over, she felt Frank's rough hand grip her butt then slide into the crease of her buttock. It happened so fast she questioned the incident. Still, she jumped straight up, speechless, her heart hammering madly against her chest. Spinning her head around, she'd taken in his expression. Her eyes widened while Frank's beady eyes danced about as he licked his lips with delight. In that instant, she raced to her room, leaving her favorite flavored lollypop on the countertop. Several days after the incident, her queasiness persisted. Part of her had broken off and died. Why did he touch her like that? It had been the first time her mother's boyfriend had betrayed her trust.

Chapter 5

Karen exhaled, relieved to take a break after the verbal spars with Ms. Blout. She wandered over to the cafeteria for a snack, paid for her yogurt and sat by a large two-paned window that opened up from the side. There were a few people seated at tables, either reading the paper or chatting on their cell phones. Karen blew out puffs of air every time she reflected on Ms. Blout. She couldn't believe the racism of that old woman. The nerve of her, she thought, as she dipped the white plastic spoon into her fruity yogurt. Maybe it was too soon with her working and all. But she had to. She had to start what she set out to do and prove to Mama she was making changes in her life. When she had finished eating, her head pivoted up to catch Jessica approaching.

"Hey, Keekee." Jessica emphasized her name and gave a half grin before she grabbed a chair and sat down.

Karen let out a dry, "Hey." She couldn't decide if she liked Jessica or not. Was she a coworker who smiled in your face before stabbing you in the back? Her looks alone warranted a grudge against her. She was pretty with long hair and hazel eyes, not the fake eyes that people purchased to bedazzle others with their so-called unique look. She spoke well, too. Karen knew Jessica would try to pounce on her look because she was a glam-girl, while Karen wore her hair spiky. She just blew it out with a blow dryer, the top sticking straight up, the sides straight out. No fuss. And Jessica, well, she looked like she spent hours at the salon.

"Why did you tell me Ms. Blout was like a rose?" Karen wiped her mouth with a napkin, still tasting yogurt on her tongue.

"She is. The long thorny part." Jessica gave a sly smirk. "Oh, you assumed I meant the sweet flowery part?"

Karen had to smile. "Yeah. You tricked me and you know it." She leaned back in the chair. "That prejudiced woman asked me why I was wearing my hair like this. What's her problem with black people?"

Jessica's eyes made a cheery squint. "Well, for one, Ms. Blout is a ninety-something-year-old woman who doesn't know 'cool' when she sees it. Secondly, you have Ms. Blout all wrong, you know."

"What do you mean?"

"She's not white, Keekee. She's black," Jessica clarified, glancing and waving at a passerby.

"Get out," Karen's tone elevated.

"When her family brought her here, her brother was as dark as a Hershey bar. But, now, she's all alone. Ms. Blout used to teach history at Lawston University of Massachusetts," Jessica said, folding her hands on the table. "And, get this: she was the first black woman to ever do so. And, she never married."

"Humph, wonder why?" Karen's sarcasm made Jessica's head snap back.

Karen thought about how sweet the woman appeared, almost regal. But she acted more like an evil witch on Halloween night.

At that point, Karen turned away from Jessica and shifted her eyes to the sizeable window and pedestrians with coats wrapped tight to their bodies. They took swift steps due to winter's sluggish exit, and spring's equally lethargic appearance. Even so, April winds kicked up and a swift breeze whistled through a tiny crack in the glass, alerting her senses, and forcing her to admit she didn't want to quit. She had to make this work. Karen wanted to try her hardest even if it meant dealing with crazy Mr. Hamilton and Satan's grandma, Ms. Blout.

The rusted gray Camaro puttered and shook for several seconds after being shut off. Karen only cared about the car taking her where she needed to go. She was happy to be going home after an exhausting day. Every muscle in her body ached. Second-shift would take some getting used to.

She exited the car and dashed through the night to her porch, eased in and closed the door behind her. Once inside, she craned her neck to the sound of the late night news on the TV. She wondered if her sister was still awake.

"Hey, you're home," Val called out to Karen, her head peeking around the high back chair.

Mystery solved, Karen thought. As usual, Val was ready to suffocate her with a bunch of ignorant questions. From what Karen could tell, she'd been loafing around, doing nothing. Her clothes were untidy and her hair looked like someone used it as a dust mop. Because Val had no life, she couldn't wait to suck up whatever she could from her.

"Hey." Karen responded in a flat tone as she took a stride up the stairs.

"Well . . . how was your first day on the job?" Val asked, entering the hallway and showing a full set of teeth.

"It was auugh-ite." Karen's words fell out in an ascending octave, with irritation settling on 'ite'. She leaned into the bannister, knowing full well Val would ask her another aggravating question.

"I'm just interested. I'm not trying to start a fight or anything." She threw her hands up.

"Whatju' still doin' up?" Karen asked.

"Just making sure you're in okay is all."

"Mm, huh. Sure you ain't just being nosy? In my business, as usual?" Karen twisted her lips.

"Nope. Promise. I saved you some spaghetti. I can heat it up for you if you want."

"Nope. I'm cool. I just wanna chill out."

Without another word, Karen continued up the stairs, closing her bedroom door behind her.

She turned on the radio, plopped on her bed, and grabbed her cell phone. Her fingers hastened with each punch to Hershel's number. He could have been her big brother because ever since they were kids growing up in the same neighborhood, Hershel, who was three years older, looked after her and beat up the boys who wanted to hit her for pocketing their water guns. Moreover, his protective ways continued even when they became adults.

He also understood her gripes about Val. "She's always in my personal space," Karen would share. "She's an old maid who doesn't have a life. She needs to get out the house and socialize. Heck, buy a friend or something, just stay outta' my business and gettin' on my nerves." As far as Karen was concerned, Val couldn't even blame her actions on Mama's death because she moped around the house long before Mama went to heaven.

"What's up, dude?" Karen inquired, her right arm folded behind her head.

"Hey, you know, just staying fresh like Tupperware, keepin' it real like Shaquille O'Neal. What's going on with you? How'd the job go?"

"I hate it already." Karen complained. "I'm not cut out to deal with wrinkled people."

Hershel laughed. "You ain't cut out to deal with no kinda people. Hang in there," he added.

"I will. There's only one other black worker there. Jessica. She thinks she's all that and a bag of chips," Karen said.

"Is she?"

"No . . . maybe . . . if you like her type."

"Say, let me call you right back, okay?"

"Why?"

"Just let me call you right back."

"Okay, but spray after you're done."

"You are sick."

"I'm right, ain't I?"

Click.

I'm right. After that, Karen shut her cell phone off and tossed it on the bed. No matter how long or brief, she always smiled when she talked with Hershel. In fact, she had considered the possibility of taking their friendship to the next level. She didn't have to pretend with him. Most men tried to change her. "Hold your fork this way," or, "Act more lady-like." Yet, in private, they were all smiles in hopes of getting up in her foo-foo.

In an instant, Karen became wired, no longer feeling worn out when a Lenny Kravitz tune came on the radio. If Hershel were still on the line, he would have teased her, saying she took after him liking the same music and movies.

"Oh, I want to get away, I wanna fly away, yeeeah, yeeeah, yeeeah." She jumped to the floor, now in her bare feet, holding her balled-up hand to her mouth and bobbing her head wildly when she noticed Val standing in the doorway, arms folded and shaking her head. Karen stopped cold and sat on the edge of the bed, her chest rising and falling in quick succession. She glanced at the clock on the radio because there had been, for the past few months, never-ending points of tension between them, always, always on the verge of a flare-up. That's why she stared at the secondhand as it ticked, steady and slowly. It allowed for a brief diversion . . . right before she crooked her neck to stare down Val.

"Okay, what's on your mind?"

"I'm just checking . . . you sure everything's okay?" Val's brows gathered inward. She walked over and turned down the volume on the radio.

Karen did a double-take. "Yeah, didn't you ask me that? Why you asking again?"

"I asked how your first day turned out and you didn't have much to say."

"I answered you, Val. What else am I supposed to do? Start breakdancing?"

"I don't know, talk about . . . your day. I'm wondering was it difficult seeing the patients in bed . . . you know . . . because of Mama and all."

"Are you tryin' to say I saw our dead mama, instead of the patients I tended to?"

"Well, I don't know."

"Look, I ain't gonna' stand for you sniffing around me like some doggone . . . asinine blood hound. I don't need you calling yourself tryin' to keep an eye on me. And another thing, don't think because I'm living under your roof, that I gotta answer to you neither." Karen's voice strained against the harsh words. With a short distance between them, the phone rang, and relieved Karen of guilt, but fueled her anger. She leaned across the bed to retrieve the phone, the springs squeaking under her weight. "Thank God. You always got something crazy to say, Val."

"Okay, okay, I'll leave you alone," Val said, standing in the same spot.

Karen clicked on the phone, although she held it before answering. "Please do, and get out of my room."

After Val threw her hands up and retreated from the space, Karen answered her phone. But in fact, she wanted to sting Val with her words.

"Hey, again," Karen said into the phone, her voice settled, but each word was plaited into snappishness.

"Okay, what happened now?" Hershel asked.

"Oh, brother. She's just flat out crazy."

"That's your sister."

"That's my crazy-whacked-outta-her-mind sister."

"Okay, then. New subject: I am proud of you, career woman. Making six-figures now, huh?" Hershel joked.

"Thank you, thank you. Yes, I'm rollin' now," Karen snickered.

"Well, I'm about to roll over and catch some Zs, know what I mean? I gotsta get up early."

"What? You called me back to tell me that?"

"I'm tired. Detroit Edison kicked my butt. I must get some sleep."

"I had something to ask you."

"What, Keekee?"

"Nothing, now. Good night, Hershel."

"No, what did you want to ask me?"

"I don't know if you can handle it," she said.

"I can."

"Forget it. I'll ask another time."

"You sure?"

"Yeah. Goodnight, Hershel."

"Goodnight, Keekee."

Karen needed more time to get her words together. After her conversation with Hershel, she thought about having to go into work the next day and do it all over again. She fell against the faded quilt, her body like bricks. She stared up at the ceiling while the table lamp now flickered with indecision.

Mama's words of reassurance would have been appreciated right about now. One thought folded into the next as she imagined her mother's hand lightly touching her shoulder as she chewed a piece of gum. Mama would push the sugarless wad to one side of her jaw and say, "It's gon' be all right. You have to think positive." She said that often, from the most serious of situations to the simplest.

"Mama, I think I missed my TV program."

"Oh, baby, think positive. It's gon' work out."

"Mama, I think my eyeball fell out."

"It'll be fine, baby. Just keep pressing on."

Even when she caught her mother in an irritated mood, Karen found it amusing. One particular time, during her younger years, she was talking to Hershel on the phone, and Mama had entered the room to hear the end of her phone conversation. "Okay, well, I'm gon' make a PB&J. Gotsta go." Karen hung up the phone with a thud. Mama had a broom in one hand and a dustpan in the other.

"What's going on, Karen? Why you talkin' in codes when I come into the room? I don't wanna' have to come up to that school again. I'm tired, girl, tired."

Karen grabbed her stomach and started stomping her foot. "Mama, PB&J is short for peanut butter and jelly. I'm gonna' make a snack," she said after composing herself.

"Oh," her mother replied, still holding a stern face then walking away.

Nonetheless, Karen accepted the blame for Mama being so distrusting of her. She'd gotten into more fist fights at school than she could count. Girls, boys, it didn't matter. She'd even hit a teacher in the jaw with the end of her cell phone once and had to attend a new school. Most problem-kids got it together by or during high school. But, Karen's behavior extended beyond her walking across the stage. She got fired from jobs for mouthing off at the manager or tearing up the place in a rage. And that Burger King incident landed her in trouble with the police, plus a fine Mama wasn't too keen on paying. Dumping out hot grease over the floor and breaking glass at the drive-through window didn't exactly make her employee of the month.

On rare occasions, she would watch Mama sitting on the side of her bed, gobs of tissue by her hip, removing her eyeglasses to wipe away tears. It was like trying to dodge a tsunami while standing right off the shore. You weren't going to get anywhere. That's how Mama was when it came to talking about her personal life. She was an enigma in every sense of the word.

Not even upon hearing the news of her mother's death, nor at the funeral, did Karen shed a tear. She couldn't bring herself to the realization of it all. Now, she wanted to drown herself in them, get lost and bathe herself clean from the emptiness she felt throughout her body.

Val called herself picking up the slack but came off as a nuisance. Karen let go a heavy sigh, and rolled over onto her side, pulling at one edge of the quilt and draping it over the uniform she was too weary to step out of.

Turning down Patton Boulevard would become Karen's daily work routine. She watched for the neighborhood kids, Jeffrey and Tyrone tossing a football in the street because they'd played hooky from class ever since starting elementary school. She also thought about her first patient, Mr. Hamilton. *Oh, I'm ready for yo' nasty behind*, she assured herself as she blew into each hand because her malfunctioning car heater proved useless in the chilling cold. When she drove into the nursing home's parking lot and killed the engine, on-lookers whipped their heads around to see who left the sputtering car. Karen acted as if nothing was out of the ordinary. And for that car, nothing was. She pranced on like she was walking away from a Jaguar.

After clocking her timesheet, she focused on achieving one single goal: do everything perfectly. Four of Karen's patients made that task easy. They ate their lunches and allowed her to clean the room and tidy their beds. And, when it came to Mr. Hamilton, she'd mustered up more confidence than she had on Monday.

"Hello, Mr. Hamilton. You need to use the bathroom or anything before you eat?" Karen asked in a louder-than-normal-tone.

He opened and closed his mouth a few times before responding. "I'm fine. How are you doing this afternoon?"

"I'm good, and you?" Karen asked.

"Oh, I couldn't be better. If I were younger, I'd take you out on the town. But, I don't think you'd be interested in going out with an old geezer like me, eh?"

"Nope. You got that right, Mr. Hamilton," Karen spoke truthfully. "You could be my great grandfather, so behave yourself." Karen snickered and so did Mr. Hamilton. His neck jiggled like Jell-O and that made her laugh harder.

After she checked around his room and made sure everything was intact, she left him to finish eating his chicken sandwich and a side of corn. Karen saw Mr. Hamilton in a better light as she grabbed fresh linens and towels and headed toward Ms. Blout's room. This day was going to work out after all. Besides, Ms. Blout's rude remarks could be ignored if she tried her hardest. After that, she would be home-free. When she stepped into the old woman's room, Karen smiled in a cautious manner.

"How are you doing today, Ms. Blout?"

The old woman said nothing. Again, she observed Karen's head as if squirrels were nesting on it.

Not today, ya' ol' bat. I got this. Karen placed the fresh linen on the nightstand and began to undo the old sheets and linens from Ms. Blout's bedding. She worked in silence and after she'd checked her room thoroughly and tidied it up, she said, "I'll be back with your lunch."

Satan's grandma snorted and turned away, sitting in the chair in the corner of the room. She waited only minutes before Karen stepped back into the room with her food.

"It certainly took long enough," Ms. Blout hissed.

"Ms. Blout, that didn't take long and you know it. Now, do you want this tray by the bed or over to where you are?"

"Don't be silly. Bring it over here." She started eating the pudding before any of the other items.

Karen began gathering up used napkins and tissues, tossing them in the trash. Without warning, the old woman began wheezing.

"Oh, no," Ms. Blout said after a couple of coughs. "Why are you trying to kill me?"

Karen rushed over to the old woman. She bent down to her only to feel a strong whack from her cane.

"Ouch." Karen rubbed her foot. "Whatju hit me for?"

"I can't have peanut butter. You stupid, stupid, girl."

Karen's nostrils fanned out. "Ms. Blout, I'm gon' forget you an old lady in a minute if, one, you hit me with that cane again, and two, you call me stupid. I'll check your chart. Besides, all you did was eat some pudding."

"Well, peanut butter can be in pudding. You should have known. How did you get this job anyway? At this rate, I won't survive your employment here." Ms. Blout turned and pushed her tray away and placed her fingers over her slightly swollen eye.

I ain't gon' survive it either, ol' woman. Karen checked Ms. Blout's chart and there wasn't anything on it about peanut butter. When she showed it to Jessica, she pointed out right away, "no peanuts or peanut products." Karen felt awful about the mistake. She didn't realize the pudding contained peanut butter. One of the licensed-nurses gave Ms. Blout an antihistamine. Karen felt grateful her reaction wasn't more severe. When her shift ended, Margaret called her into her office.

Karen, undoubtedly, felt like she had to pee as Margaret shuffled papers on her desk before looking up at her. To Karen, it seemed like hours, hearing only her heart beating like a bongo drum, and watching angry veins pop in Margaret's oily forehead.

Finally, she alleged, "I understand you gave Ms. Blout a food item with peanut butter. It clearly states on her chart she is allergic to peanuts and peanut products. That, of course, includes pudding."

For a split second, Karen thought about picking up the paper weight off the corner of her desk and throwing it square at her mouth. She couldn't stand the manner in which Margaret spoke to her. It was difficult to believe now, that during her final interview, Margaret had extended her hand and gave a firm handshake, welcoming her aboard and joining their "close-knit family," as she called it. On top of that, she had released a boatload of pleasantries about her nephew and neighbor's new puppy, laughing hardily and making eye-contact with Karen, urging her to join in the mirth.

Now Karen heaved a sigh against Margaret's sourpuss face. She then said, "I didn't know her pudding had peanut bu . . ."

"It's your job to know everything that goes on with all six of your patients. Around here, we take our jobs seriously. Do you take this job seriously, Karen?"

Karen pressed the lines of her mouth into what mimicked a smile.

"Is there something funny?"

Aside from your odd shaped head? "No, Margaret, nothing's funny. I'll watch it. And I do care about this job."

Karen drove out of the parking lot seething. The woman was a dragon. She didn't help matters any because Karen truly felt bad for not catching the mistake with Ms. Blout. She promised herself, she'd never let it happen again, mentally committing to her new mission to prove to Margaret, and to herself, that she could do this job well.

Chapter 6

By the time the weekend rolled around, the wind had subsided considerably, allowing tree branches to cease shimmying and shaking like a sixties dance number. If Val hadn't forgotten the barbeque sauce for the ribs, she wouldn't have had to go home again to get her wallet, and wouldn't have gotten caught by the red light at the corner of Wyoming and Six Mile Road; she may never have seen, Linda Pete, her best friend from Armstrong Middle School, at the checkout line when she entered the grocery store.

Val's eyes widened with familiarity toward the woman. Linda looked good after twenty years. Her creamy skin was as smooth as ever. She sported a shorter version of the hairstyle she wore well past her shoulders in junior high school. Now it nestled close to her jawline. Her figure seemed the same, Val guessed, as her fitted jacket hugged her hips.

Val had always told her inner secrets to Linda. And Linda spilled personal stories as well, like the time she'd caught her mother in bed with their next door neighbor, and later, making out with the choir director, all during her junior year of high school. Not once did they blab to anyone else. They'd always vowed their silence, even pinky swearing, if necessary. In spite of that, one dark secret Val knew she'd take to her grave, the good Lord being her only witness. She'd even tried putting it out of her mind, pretending it wasn't her who'd done the horrible act.

Instead of walking up to Linda, Val chose to quickstep in the opposite direction. Seeing how happy and together her old pal came across only magnified Val's dismay with her own miserable life. She tossed and turned at night thinking about bills and the problems that cropped up daily. And the creditors grew nastier by the day. Mama led her to believe everything would be all right, which made her resent the woman all the more.

She wanted to scream and cuss Mama for holding her hand and smiling weakly, saying everything was taken care of. There was no way she wanted Linda to see the pain that bordered her face. So she pulled at coarse strands of hair to cover her profile and flipped up her coat collar. She ducked behind a woman holding a little girl's hand. Right before she made it through the automatic exit doors, a voice rang out.

"Val Williams, it's been a long time."

Val's pupils dilated as she swiveled her head around and took in the sight of her friend like she'd laid eyes on her for the first time. "Linda," Val said. She forced a smile as if life had assigned her a personalized rainbow.

"Oh, my, didn't expect to run into you," Linda's pitch upturned. "Boy it's been a long time."

"Yes, it has." Val's smile dwindled. She felt uneasy. What could she say? *My life sucks and is going downhill every day?*

Val could only guess what went through Linda's head as she straightaway, and perhaps involuntarily, looked concerned, unaware her eyebrows knitted together as she gave her a glance over. Val was well aware tiny crow's feet had worsened around her eyes, aging her beyond her years. She hadn't seen the inside of a hair salon in eons and her hands and feet lacked pampering as well.

"Say," Linda said, "I'm in town for one more day. Do you want to get together, play catch up?"

"Sure." Val convinced herself the suggestion was a good one.

"Well, what are you doing now?" Linda rubbed Val's shoulder.

"Uh . . . well . . ." Val said, thinking about the remaining dishes she wanted to prepare. There was plenty of food for Karen, minus the barbeque sauce. Furthermore, she would probably be able to make it home before Karen anyway. "Let me make my purchases and I'll meet you outside in the parking lot."

Linda's face lit up. "Great."

Val shoved another bite of salad in her mouth. One side of her jaw protruded out when Linda shot in with a question. "This little café isn't half bad. How did you find it?"

Val gulped. She glanced at a large, frameless picture of soul food dishes which hung above a two-toned border. "Oh. I heard an advertisement on the radio about a new soul food place with homemade dishes." Val had already eaten lunch, though. Salad suited her just fine.

"Like I said, I'm visiting and will be leaving tomorrow. Just checking on my dad. He's been sick so I decided to spend some time with him. I'm living in Phoenix, Arizona now, or did you know that?"

"No, I didn't. I'm sorry to hear 'bout your dad."

"Thanks."

Val tilted her head, immersed in Linda's words as she went on about her dad and her travels over the years.

"You were never afraid to venture out," Val eventually said. "I've always admired that about you."

"Well, I've gotten a few bumps and bruises along the way, but I manage just fine. Still single, but the guy I'm seeing is such a gentleman, couldn't have asked for a better person. I feel he'll ask me to marry him at the appropriate time. He's not a game player."

"What's his name?"

"Daniel. He's a music teacher. So, girl, enough about my boring life, what's been going on with you? How's life treating you?" Linda probed.

It was inevitable, Val thought. She coughed out, "Fine. Fine. Trying to keep up with these bills and house payments. But, we'll make it somehow." She jabbed her fork into a tomato dipped in dressing, painfully aware of her comment now settling on the cusp of silence.

"Bills?" Linda asked after a few seconds. "Aren't you helping out your mom? That's the last I heard at least."

"Yeah I was, but she died in March so now everything is on me."

Linda touched the hand Val ate with. "I'm sorry to hear about Miss Dottie. She was a kind person."

Val blinked hard at Linda's last statement. "Well. Life happens, right?" She turned her eyes from Linda and toward a couple placing an order of muffins and fried okra.

"Do you feel you can ever forgive her, Val? I mean, I know it would be hard for me."

"I struggle with it, but, we have to forgive, right? If not, people and situations become like termites, eating away at you . . ." Val released an uneasy chuckle as she shifted in her seat. She didn't believe her words. Nonetheless, she hoped Linda fell for the fib. But feeling her own words fly right back in her face for her heart and mind to sort through proved both liberating and debilitating at the same time.

Val knew Linda sensed she had been putting on ever since they got together. Her exaggerated words and chest thrust forward didn't fool Linda one bit. Linda pressed in her lips like a mother does when they require a child to spill the truth after a string of lies.

Again, Linda broke through the quietness. "How is that adorable baby? Well, she's no baby anymore. How old is Karen now?" Linda asked.

"Twenty-four."

"Great. I know you're a proud and wonderful mom, so there. It turned out fine."

Val's head dipped near her plate. Linda stopped chewing and held Val's hand when she burst into tears.

"Oh, Linda, I-I never told her."

"My God, Val . . . Karen doesn't know that you're her mother?"

"Nope," Val sniffed, grabbing a napkin to stop her runny nose.

"Why didn't you ever tell her?" she asked.

"I just couldn't find the right time. Mama demanded, of course, in the beginning to make everyone think the baby was hers, but the right time to tell the truth never came. I couldn't shock her with something like that." The words made her throat tighten.

A handsome, young worker holding a dingy dish towel came over to the table. His cheap gym shoes made a squeaking sound across the linoleum floor.

"'Scuse me, everything okay?"

"Yes," Linda answered for her friend. The young man ambled away.

"Val, there is help. You need to reach for it. Find a support group or something, don't go it alone. But you must tell Karen the truth."

"I don't want to do that."

"Why not?"

"Because I would be ashamed for her to know I'm her mother. She thinks I'm her sister and I see the disgust in her eyes."

"Disgust?"

"You heard right. No matter how hard I try, she seems so disappointed in me. The times we do get along are few and far between."

Val caught Linda searching for comforting words, but they were devoured by the drawn out silence. When Linda found her voice, her comments were awkward and forced.

"Why didn't you return my calls all these years?"

Val looked away, still holding on to the creased napkin. "I felt embarrassed. You were doing so well with your life and I felt like a failure. Don't get me wrong. I'm happy for you. It's just that I didn't want to bring you down, like I'm doing now."

Linda knuckle-dabbed at her left eye. She batted it as if a small particle had made an invasion. "Nonsense. I love you, and nothing will change that. I'm not saying you should sit around and have a woe-is-me-party, but, you've been carrying a heavy weight far too long. It's not easy to bounce back from something awful. That's why I strongly urge you to get counseling, sweetie."

"I hate to even ask this question," Linda hesitated. "Whatever happened to *him*?"

"Who? Frank?"

"That would be the one," Linda said, her facing looking vinegary.

"Walking around free."

"Bastard." Linda sucked in her cheeks before blowing out air.

Both women held hands as they faced each other, eventually smiling at the other.

"You know none of this has anything to do with who you are," Linda said. "You are wonderful and deserve the best. Unfortunately, you had adults around you who didn't recognize how precious you were and . . ." with the last two words, Linda shook Val's hands and said, "still are."

Val bit her trembling lip and released a feeble nod as if she'd turned into a seven year old again. Even Linda's hand touching hers sent an unexpected trigger reminding her of Frank. He would hold both of her hands, taunting her and licking his lips. She could smell him still. His scent wormed past her nostrils and into the part of her brain that wouldn't forget; no matter how many early morning showers and late night baths she'd taken. Whether she'd indulged herself in Chloe, Beautiful, Liz Claiborne, Fendi, and all the numbers of Chanel, his scent, the unwelcomed thrust, superseded every last one of them.

Val eased her hands free and placed them in her lap. "I would . . . I would love to pack up and move away you know. Get a fresh start."

Linda released a soft smile. "Now that's a great plan. You don't need all those bad memories weighing you down. Sell that house. Move on with your life."

"I'd even like to leave Michigan. Maybe travel and settle down in North Carolina or Texas. Anywhere but here."

"Wow. Now you're talking. I think that would be great. Make it happen. If there's anything I can do, please," Linda patted Val's shoulder again, "don't hesitate to call me."

Both women held hands before parting ways, vowing to keep in touch. Val latched onto Linda's encouraging words. The sun had completed its dutiful shift and the moon stood in its stead, now illuminating a darkened sky, with shadows dispersed into nothingness. Val managed to get the house cleaned and have dinner done before she'd plopped down on the high-back chair. She hugged herself in self-pity, discounting Linda's earlier statement at the restaurant. She sized up the room, thinking how enormous the house appeared.

She anticipated seeing Karen walk through the door, eager to hear how her day went. Because Karen made a concerted effort to change her life, it filled Val with pride. Right then, she listened to the car idling in the driveway, and held her breath until the car's sputtering and knocking noises ceased.

"Hey, how'd it go at work?" Val asked walking to the hallway the moment Karen stepped foot through the door.

Karen glared at her with a sweeping annoyance and replied, "I wish you wouldn't ask me that." She pushed her hip into the door to close it.

"You don't want me asking how your day was?"

"No. Not all cheery the way you just did. Dang. Sickening, man." Karen glared at Val as she went into the kitchen. Val trailed behind her. "I can't believe you went to work looking like that," she said. Val glanced down at her wrinkled sack-like dress as she stood in the doorframe.

"Girl, you look closer to seventy-seven instead of thirty-seven. I keep telling you, you're gonna look like an old maid for so long, nobody's gonna want you. Skin all dry." Karen lifted lids to warm pots and sniffed. She continued on Val. "Your hair has no style. Clothes look like something from the sixties." Karen snickered after her last remark.

Val turned and walked away, locking herself in the bathroom. She ran hot water in the tub and poured in store-brand peppermint bath crystals. She'd managed to take Karen's remarks and stash them away, nice and neat. She didn't need to address them, she told herself as she wiped mist from the mirror over the sink, bypassing her own reflection. She didn't want to dwell on the words Karen used. She wanted to forget they'd come up against her from the start. Besides, she had more pressing matters to focus on, like going to the Water Department and making some sort of an arrangement. If not, they might be forced to wash in bottled water. Even that was an extra expense she couldn't afford.

Chapter 7

When she turned off Orchard Drive onto Finmore Street, which was on the west side of Detroit, Karen called Hershel to tell him to be ready. It seemed that her first week on the job ended at a snail's pace. As usual, Margaret eyeballed her whenever she could, and Ms. Blout found something to complain about and raise her cane to. Karen managed to laugh it off and ignore the old bat because prior to Mama's death, she would have cussed her and everybody else out and broke some glass. After the pudding incident, Karen felt Ms. Blout was good for nothing but sucking up air in the room.

Like clockwork, Hershel stood out on the porch, waiting for her to pull into the driveway.

She rolled down the window and yelled out, "What it be like, Hersh-Hersh?"

"Ain't nothing but a chicken wang." He stepped inside her car and buckled up.

"It is real good to see you, brother," she added while rolling up the window. "After dealing with all kinda mean folks, it's good to see your smiling face." Karen looked over at Hershel, grinning.

"Ditto," he said, focusing his attention toward finding a better radio station. He patted his knees to the beat of the song he settled on, The Rolling Stones, from the 60s, *Get off of My Cloud*.

As Karen drew closer to downtown, she continued to ignore the speed limit while merging onto the service drive of the Lodge Freeway. Saturday traffic downtown was a bit congested, but Karen didn't mind. She embraced the pockets of crowds rushing through the streets of Greektown. She searched for a spot and backed the car into a tight fit between a white Toyota and a blue Ford, then, she looked at Hershel while the car was still trying to turn itself off.

"Well . . ." She continued staring at him.

"Well, what?"

"Are you going to get out or are you waiting for me to come around and open your door?" Karen asked as she exited the vehicle.

"You were dropped on your head as a baby," he called after her while unbuckling his seatbelt. Then he flung the door open. Once outside of the vehicle, he stretched out his arms. "I was just waiting to make sure the car wasn't going to change its mind and drive off." Hershel closed the door with a thud.

In a playful manner, Karen slapped at his shoulder. "I'm thinking Fishbones. You wanna eat there?"

"Sure, Keekee. It's whatever you want. It's your world, baby, I'm just the squirrel."

After Karen had two margaritas, she mustered up the nerve to ask Hershel about dating but wasn't quite ready to let on she wanted to date him.

"Okay, spit it out. I wanna know the dirt. Why ain't you dating anybody? And don't try to say you saving yourself for me."

"Ha. Funny. What can I say," Hershel said. "I am saving, not myself, but my wallet. You women are crazy. Think a man's supposed to spend all his money on ya' and you can't call a brotha' until you need something. What's up with that?" Hershel held his hands up, but got sidetracked watching a game on the big screen TV.

The tables in the restaurant were set up strategically like pieces to a chess board. Loud chatter emanating from each table put Karen at ease. Even though Hershel was like a brother, she didn't know how to tell him outright that she wanted more. Hershel wasn't a bad-looking man. He had the kind of features one would say, "If his eyes were a little smaller," and, "If only his nose weren't so flat, then he'd be over-the-moon fine."

Karen didn't need *fine*. Cute maybe, but fine meant too many problems trying to keep up with their behind and the trail of women positioning themselves to be number one.

"What about you?" Hershel asked during a commercial.

"Men don't find me appealing."

"That's 'cause they all got wind that you'll try and beat 'em up."

"Oh, you Mr. Jokey man, huh? No, I don't know. I just don't have it in me to try and convince anybody to like me either. So, here I am, take me or leave me. I guess everybody can't be cool like you," Karen disclosed, fidgeting in her chair. "But at least I ain't homely looking like Val. Oh, God, she is pathetic."

Val had always been her go-to topic whenever she wanted to unload pinned up emotion. At this point, dropping hints to Hershel about her feelings made her a tad uncomfortable.

"What's she done to ya' now?"

"What hasn't she done? She just irks me to no end. She has weird habits too, always playing with this toy ring she wears . . . a grown behind woman, mind you. Earlier this week, she asked if I was getting along with everyone on the job. I told her it ain't my place to try and make friends. But no, Val gotta go on and on asking stupid questions. She's an idiot. Even Mama had to talk to her like she was crazy. I remember she got a beating because she told Val to do something . . . I can't remember the details, but it involved Mama's boyfriend, Frank. I was a kid but Mama was mad as all get out. She told Val to go upstairs and get the extension cord and whipped her tail good."

"Wow. What did she do?"

"I just said I don't recall. But it had to be awful for Mama to get so worked up because she didn't get after me. She gave a lot of lip service, but that's about it." Karen beamed then continued as she picked out her hair with her fingers. "So, aside from her walking around like a big klutz, I'm tired of her asking too many questions, always in my business, and just plain ol' boring. She doesn't do anything but work. She needs to purchase a personality."

"Ouch. Man, Keekee. Say what you really feel. Don't beat around the bush." Hershel took a sip of his beer.

Karen giggled a little, now feeling she'd come off a bit ugly, but it was too late to stop. "Well, it's the truth," she justified. "But, back to me. I still think about dating, you know." She rubbed Hershel's shoulder in a kidding way.

"Sure you do." Hershel took another sip of beer and nodded. "You'll be all right."

Karen's smile weakened. She allowed her hand to slide from his shoulder. It was the familiar words of Mama, echoing, and using Hershel as an avatar.

"So, what'd you have to tell me earlier in the week that you couldn't say over the phone?"

"Huh? I don't know whatju talkin' about." Karen turned her neck with a jolt.

"Yeah, right."

She knew full well what he was talking about. How could she say it? That she wanted him to be her man? When they were kids, before she'd stopped getting her hair pressed, she knew Hershel had a serious crush on her. She and a bunch of neighborhood kids ended up at his house. Hershel lived a few blocks over and offered to walk her home once the street lights came on. That's when she knew, even before the kiss. They all sat in his front room, goofing off and slapping each other's hands. Karen watched Hershel shift his gaze toward the corner of the room where rays of sunlight burst through the shadows. He spotted a tiny spider climbing down from its web then scurrying across the floor.

Karen stared at Hershel wide-eyed when he smashed the daddy longlegs with his opened palm. Years later, she learned that Hershel used to have to sit in that same corner as a child when he'd overstepped his boundaries lipping-off to his mom. And it was that corner in which he leaned in to kiss her.

There were two remaining kids playing *Twister*. He and Karen were on the same team and had lost. They had both fallen after she tried her best to place her right hand on the large, blue dot while reaching over Hershel's long torso. The rules had to be honored. Still, Karen sucked her teeth hard while Hershel puckered. He pressed his parted lips onto hers but soon after, snapped his head back when Karen dug her nails into his cheeks. There was nothing in the rules that said "tongue," which Hershel tried to use. Karen pretended to spit on the floor, after which, she smeared her sleeve across her mouth. She could tell her scrunched up face affected him more than the laughter from the other children. From then on, he never made advances toward her. She knew that he knew they were *just friends*. Who knew a corner could tell so much.

An hour later, Karen now waited on Hershel. By the time he used the men's room, checked out the game, paid the bill, got a tooth pick and went back to leave a tip, Karen began jiggling the keys. He shook his head and held open the door for her. Then they exited into the chilly night.

The sky, a hauntingly darkish gray, had no cloud visibility. Once inside her car, they drove around passing pockets of sports bars and ethnic restaurants until they found another parking spot, after which, they headed toward Hart Plaza.

The two of them strolled until they reached the Detroit River. She and Hershel stood at the boardwalk by the railing and stared out at the waves that swayed like a drunken sailor. Serenity draped over Karen as she took in the sight. Just across the water was Canada. She peered over at the Canadian neighbors and perused their hotels and casinos. The city's lights were starting to come alive on the streets and through the windows of buildings. Like a tipped paint can, Karen leaned further over the railing to gaze down at the waves lapping up against the concrete under the bridge. A ship hauling steel passed by, making its presence known. She wanted to reach out and touch Hershel's hand but fought the urge.

"Oh, man. I hope this weekend doesn't go fast." Karen spoke more to herself.

"It just started. Whatju complaining about? Learn to hang loose."

Karen thought Hershel spoke more to himself than to her.

She still sulked. "Hey, are you doing that thing next week?"

"Painting from a live model?" Hershel shoved his hands deep in his jacket pockets and tapped each foot to the concrete.

She gripped the railing with both hands and said, "That's the thing." She smiled cleverly, leaning back then swinging left and right.

"Ha, it won't be as sexual as you may think. We're all true artists, Keekee. We aren't getting off on the nudity of the subject posing for us, especially if it's a male . . . at least I'm not," Hershel said, with a side-eye glare. "We're trying to get our lines and color-blends precise. Besides, we don't know if the model will be male or female."

"Uh, huh. Whatever, Mr. Art Van Gogh. Count me in. I may bring my snooty coworker, Jessica. She's been trying to hang out with me. This is right up her little golden alley. So we'll go with you. Maybe we'll watch if it's a dude. If not, eh, I'll . . . we'll sit in on that writing class they always have. I ain't got nothing better to do with my time. I might as well go to your weird perverted workshop."

Hershel lifted one surprised eyebrow.

"Oh, yeah, I know a li'l somethin' somethin' about the art-world."

"First of all," Hershel corrected, "the artist's name is Vincent Van Gogh. Art Van is a furniture store."

"Whatever, dude. I'm going with you next weekend."

"Okay. It's a date."

Hershel's grinning face made Karen believe that, in time, she could get him to see that they belonged together.

Chapter 8

It almost seemed a rare sight. After days of gloom, the clouds took off and allowed the sun to take center stage. Its rays made pavements glisten and buildings look more impressive.

Val didn't have much time to return to work from her Monday afternoon lunch hour. As she stood by her car, she looked up from the door lock to see a man running out of the Water Department building waving his arm and yelling her name.

For a quick moment, her shoulders tensed. She scrutinized him like he was a bible salesman. But as he stepped closer, she recognized him and relaxed her shoulders. She realized she'd left her license and other personal information on his desk.

Working her story to the hilt, she told him how the bills and mortgage payments were dumped on her once her mother had died. It was the truth, which made it easier for her to tear up when she sat across from him. Her legs wouldn't stop shaking, even after he'd handed her a tissue. She hadn't planned on such a display as she gazed at her nervous hands, sniffling and wiping at her runny nose. The corners of the man's mouth turned into a sympathetic frown. Then with a last minute glance at the computer screen, he agreed to work out a payment plan. Now he was chasing after her in a congested parking lot.

"Phew. Not as young as I used to be," the man said, catching his breath and giving her a cheery smile. He handed over her items.

Val reached for her identification cards. "Thank you. I'm so sorry."

"No problem. If you want to remain indebted to me, let me take you out to dinner," the man said, pushing up his eye glasses with a knuckle.

His dinner proposition surprised her and made her heartbeat quicken. His face, cute and round, made him look younger even with his thin mustache. And he appeared self-assured when it came to second-helpings at the dinner table, judging by the overlap of bulge hiding his belt buckle. "Oh, I don't know." Val closed her purse after she'd secured her personal items inside. Was he being serious? she questioned. He knew she was in a pitiful state and here he was, asking her out.

"Are you sure? Look like you, eh, had a shred of doubt there," the man joked. "Naw, I don't want you to feel weird or anything. I just wanted to get to know you. I wanted to take you out the moment you walked into the office, but of course, that definitely would have been way inappropriate." He waved his hand when he said, 'way.' "I'll let you go." He gave a swift smile and turned to march away.

Val toyed with the broken costume ring on her right pinky finger and thought about Karen's ugly criticisms of her hair and appearance, which she did take heed to. She'd gotten the ends of her hair clipped and even bought a new multicolored blouse. Yet, she couldn't enjoy the new look or purchase because she felt conscious-stricken. "Wait," she said, sounding desperate. "Wait."

The man walked back toward her, his eyes sparkling.

"I'm sorry. I don't remember your name. Inside, all I heard was how much money I owe," she said.

The man laughed with his head tilted back, the braces on his teeth shining in the sunlight. "It's Mr. Taylor, but you can call me Brady."

"Dinner, huh," Val remarked, narrowing her eyes.

"Yeah, dinner."

"Okay. I think dinner would be nice."

Val released a nervous smile as Brady recited his number to her while she punched the digits into her cell phone. Her mouth went dry. Was she having a full blown nervous breakdown? She must've been for accepting a date with a stranger. It just wasn't like her. But then again, neither was getting her hair cut so she just went with it.

"So, tonight then?" he asked in a serene tone.

"Tonight? Isn't that a bit soon?"

"I don't have a problem with it. I'm not a game-player. If I see something . . . or someone I like, I let them know."

Val teetered. On one hand, she hadn't dated in God knows how long and felt flattered Brady noticed her. On the other hand, she didn't know this person. Although she would be at a public place, she rationalized. Val blinked in quick succession. "Okay." The word shocked her. "I'll meet you at . . ." she allowed her sentence to trail off.

"Oh. Applebee's, the one in Farmington Hills, off Grand River, 8 o'clock," Brady said.

"Applebee's it is." She lowered her lashes then added, "I'll meet you there." She allowed her eyes to pop up with her last statement. She studied Brady's face for a second then said goodbye. She swung her hips and resumed getting into her car, driving off, and praying he wasn't some crazed maniac.

By the time Val got home, she was so stressed she'd sweated through the underarms of her blouse and looked like she needed a touch up to her roots. She peeled off her coat and raced upstairs and stared at her reflection in the bathroom mirror, her lips mimicking an audible conversation along with accompanying hand gestures. Val stretched out an opened smile as she lifted her imaginary drink and nodded before taking a pretend sip. She talked to herself for more than five-minutes, conjuring up responses to potential questions Brady may possibly ask. She practiced how she'd respond, a laugh here and there, a hand motion to the chin. But the thought of going out on an actual date caused her to hyperventilate. With a swift resolve, Val left the mirror and stepped into the bedroom to call Karen on her cell phone. She wanted to talk about her date and in some small way, gain assurance that it was okay.

Val tapped her foot as she stood waiting, but Karen never picked up, so she ended the call without leaving a message. She assumed Karen would call her once she took her break.

With growing anxiety, Val fished through her closet for something to wear. She flipped out a pair of pants, then another and another, not feeling comfortable with any of them for tonight's date. She dialed Brady's number and then hung up abruptly. She did this a total of four times, still rethinking whether to go out with him as she questioned his motives. Out of frustration, she clumped around her room, both feet pounding the print of the tattered rug by her bed. She stopped long enough to hug herself as tears streamed down her cheeks. She rocked left, then right. *You can do this, you can do this, you can do this,* she repeated.

Once Val got her emotions under control, she found the perfect pair of black slacks to go with her new blouse. Prior to leaving the house, she did her hair, and applied makeup. She didn't want to feel anxious in any way so she left early and obeyed the speed limit.

When she met up with Brady, he looked handsome, in a nontraditional sense. He wore a blue striped button down shirt with black pants. His cologne made her inhale deeply. He shook her right hand then held the door of the restaurant open for her. Once they were seated at their table, a tall waiter took their order. By the time their food arrived, Val's rehearsed dialogue dissipated into a natural one, especially when Brady made her laugh. He did have a kind face. He was funny, too. She spent as much time covering her mouth with her napkin as she did eating her steak.

"Is it difficult?" Val asked Brady, tapping a finger to her front teeth.

"What? My braces?"

"Yeah. Is it tough eating with them?"

"Nah, you get used to it. I can't wait to get them off though. I've had them on a year now."

"Ah, I see. Well, I think you look nice in them."

"Oh stop," Brady said, wiping his left eye with an opened hand and lowering his head.

Val took delight in Brady's reaction as he chuckled with embarrassment, giving a little snort at the end. She liked him.

"I hope *Applebee's* isn't too casual of a place for you?" he asked.

"No, no, not at all. It's perfect," Val said.

"I figured it would be a more relaxed, cool atmosphere since this is our first date, eh, meeting."

Val shifted her backside in her seat and smirked at him.

Brady patted his stomach. "Okay, time for a joke," he winked at her and cleared his throat.

"Oh, boy," she said, now scooting her chair closer to the table.

"A teenage boy sits in the barber's seat and says, 'I want you to give me zigzag lines on the side, a Mohawk at the top with patches of missing hair from the left side and a dent right here at the hairline with wiggly lines coming from it.' 'What?' the man said indignantly. 'I'm a professional,' the barber added. 'I can't give you that.' 'Well, that's what you gave me last week when I came in,' said the teenager."

"Oh, that was awful." Val's shoulders shook as she laughed anyway. Somehow the stupid joke tied them closer together.

She now felt loosened up around Brady. His smile made it easy to copycat. He didn't ask personal questions, but allowed the conversation to flow.

But neither of them could have expected what happened next in the midst of the crowded, noisy restaurant. At one of the larger round tables, a man fell back in his chair and crashed to the floor. If that weren't bad enough, he took the tablecloth and all the items on it, with him. He left other members at the table with their eyes averted to their hands and the floor. Any place but into the eyes of on-lookers.

"What in the world happened to him?" Val asked in a concerned whisper as she leaned across the table.

"Don't say anything yet. I'm trying my best to keep my composure." Brady held his hand to his forehead and looked down at the table. His eyes and mouth countered each other like jumper cables with a negative, positive charge. He cried and laughed at the same time.

It took Val a second to catch on that the man was drunk and humiliated everyone he was seated with. It actually added spice to the evening.

Brady tossed his tip on the table after the waiter gathered the leftover dishes and collected the payment for the meals.

"Let's go, I have an idea," Brady said, reaching for Val's hand.

Without hesitation, she pushed her chair back and accepted Brady's hand. She caught another good whiff of his cologne as he came up behind her and pulled out her chair. It felt right and she welcomed the next phase of their date. "Where're we going?" she asked.

"Sightseeing. Let's take in the city."

Chapter 9

"Hey, Ms. Blout," Karen said, entering the room. "Think you might wanna take a brisk walk around the grounds since you ate already? It ain't too bad out for Michigan this time of year." This Monday felt good. She felt good. Good enough to be kind to Ms. Blout, even after she'd turned from the window and eyeballed her.

"Dear, I didn't understand a word you said. I'm not even sure you were speaking English." The old woman fanned a hand by her face, looking as if she heard something vulgar.

Karen tilted her head. "Ms. Blout, I know that was meant as a blow, but, I'm still not gon' let you get to me. I'm still gon' keep checking on you, and asking how you doing, and looking out for you, whether you want me to or not."

She smiled at the old woman and practically skipped out of the room, leaving Ms. Blout and her cane immobile. Whether it was the weather or a fluke, she felt great. Even after she'd swore on Jesus' robe she wasn't gonna' be nice to the ol' bat. Not even Margaret scolding her about forgetting to clock back in from lunch had dampened her spirits, nor did Val's phone call, which she had dodged on purpose.

Karen did, however, develop a tip-toe gait whenever she passed Margaret's office. She'd been in such a good mood that she went through with inviting Jessica to go with her and Hershel on Saturday to watch him paint. At the last minute, when reality kicked in later that day, she tried to talk Jessica out of going when she thought about how pretty she looks. Jessica was a prissy and proper, play-by-the-rules type. "Are you kidding. I'd love to go," Jessica insisted. So, Karen was stuck.

Hershel had no problem doing the driving this time around. He even seemed a bit more jovial knowing that he'd be in the presence of someone new. Karen warned him that she was cut from a different cloth. Of course, neither of them had anything in common with Jessica.

Chapter 10

Val peered out the passenger's window of Brady's navy blue Sedan, while her car remained at the restaurant. That was another move that surprised her. The entire evening held an element of charm. They'd driven around Comerica Park and Belle Isle while Brady joked about his upbringing with two older brothers and the spankings they had gotten up until their teen years. She couldn't remember the last time her cheeks hurt from laughing so.

She felt happy. Her senses were heightened to the elements outside, the soft interior of the car and the butterfly feeling in her stomach from sitting inches away from Brady as he drove. When he returned to the restaurant and her parked car, he volunteered to follow her to her house.

"Glad you accepted my invitation, Val." Brady walked her up the walkway with his hands in his jacket pockets.

"Uh-huh. Me too," Val said, gnawing into her bottom lip a few times. "Yeah. This was fun. Thanks for everything. You wanna come in . . . for some wine? Not that I'm trying to send the wrong message." She blushed, shocked at her straightforwardness.

"I don't drink . . . but certainly I'll come in for a bit."

Val lifted both eyebrows. "Oh, okay. I noticed at the restaurant that you didn't order alcohol," she said, leading him into the den. The same room that had witnessed intense conversations, hot meals and tired butts that plopped on the furniture.

"Sit here." Val pointed to the worn loveseat.

She excused herself and went into the kitchen, resisting the impulse to sneak a peek at Brady who was likeable enough to go out with again. She returned with a cold, sweating glass of cranberry juice and said, "I think this is probably your speed." She handed him the drink grinning then sat beside him and turned on the TV to a cable channel.

"Cozy," Brady said, making himself comfortable and taking a few gulps.

Val watched him look about the room in a nonchalant manner before directing his attention toward the TV.

"Oh, my, I remember this movie." His face lit up. "*Blazing Saddles*. This movie's hilarious," Brady said, releasing a chuckle.

Val's thumb was set to continue channel-surfing, but when his eyes grew wider and he started snickering like a pure fool, she laid the remote down on the cocktail table. She laughed along with him at all the funny scenes.

The only light in the room emanated from the TV and a small lamp on the corner of the writing desk. When Brady innocently placed his hand on her knee, still laughing at the movie, saying, "Oh, this is going to be good . . ." it triggered something inside Val. It was the combination: his hand, her knee, and the familiar words. Even the house played a part. Factoring it all in, Val let out a shrill that stopped Brady in his tracks. For a second, Val figured he thought she was joking, until he witnessed her opened palms strike her ears again and again.

He placed his half-filled glass down on the cocktail table. "Hey, hey, what's the matter?" Brady stood, taking a few steps back.

She took weighty breaths, repeating, "No, no, no, no."

Brady gathered himself before he approached her.

"Val, I'm sorry if I stepped out of line."

She shouted as though her voice reached the heavens, repeating the words, "Get out! Go!"

Brady's body twisted. He witnessed Val's eyebrows gather over deep-set eyes; eyes that, without warning, became hollow, dark and removed from reality.

Val looked as if she could have taken a blade to Brady's throat.

"I'm sorry, okay?" Brady moved toward the front door. He opened it and called to her, "I'll let myself out, okay? I'll check on you later. Sorry, again."

Val sat rocking herself back and forth, touching her fingers to her thumbs. She wasn't aware that Brady left the house. Her mind had already left the room. She now had to cope with Frank, who had once again, come into her bedroom in the night, speaking with composure and touching her on the thigh. "Don't worry, you'll love it," he said to her. "I don't want to," she pleaded, drawing her knees up to her chest.

"Shhhhhh," he responded, and took his large coarse hands and rubbed the inside of her thighs, allowing the tip of his fingers to graze her private part. Her small hands tugged at his fingers, hoping to counter his movements away from her private part. The part Mama talked about when it came to saving yourself like all good girls did. He grabbed her hand and made her touch his manhood. She sobbed uncontrollably and stopped only when Frank grabbed her shoulders and shook her until her hair ribbon came loose. He threatened to leave the family, causing them to be out on the street. "Now, you know your mama would be mad if she didn't have a house to live in. You see, your mama can't make it without me. So you betta' do as I say."

Tears became trapped underneath her lids as she squeezed her eyes shut and imagined riding on a merry-go-round, having the time of her life going round and round and round. It didn't ever have to stop. It felt safer than her four walls and Mama right on the other side, unable to protect her. That's when she decided to disappear. She no longer took pride in ribbons or bows. In fact, she stopped brushing her hair to keep it neat. Bathing and wearing nice clothes were reserved for special occasions and when Mama hollered, releasing a handful of disparaging words. But her plan faltered against Frank's will and strong stench of lust.

Val returned to the present and yelled out, ramming her fist into her belly. She did it again and again until her abdomen throbbed with pain. She allowed her body to slide off the loveseat and land onto the floor. She felt as though she were going mad because more than ever, Frank's intrusions on her thoughts were getting the best of her. She wished she could run away and hide from the constant thought of bills and past due notices and Frank's beady eyes and rough hands and his scent that couldn't be washed away. Something had to give . . . and soon.

Chapter 11

Saturday morning turned out to be a clear day with the sky vibrant enough to resemble a bright, blue ocean. Karen advised Jessica to drive to her house and the two of them would ride with Hershel to the workshop. She searched for some old poems she'd written. She looked underneath her bed, and pulled out a couple of boxes then sorted through the papers. They didn't sound as good as she thought they did when she'd written them in high school. Karen sat on the floor and re-wrote some of them in an attempt to spruce them up. Her efforts felt jagged and soon she placed all but a few papers back where she'd gotten them. As she was about to shove the second box back underneath the bed, a glossy image caught her attention. She lifted a stack of papers and saw a cluster of pictures of her, Mama, and Val.

In one picture, she sat on Val's knee smiling, showing two bottom teeth. Mama's hand was on Val's shoulder. Val actually looked attractive, Karen thought. Mama's old boyfriend, Frank, was in another picture. Karen always wondered what happened to him. She never got a clear answer because Mama would shoo her off and Val would look like someone burned cookies on her Easy Bake Oven. No one ever talked about him. Karen assumed that there was bad blood between him and Mama because he never married her. She had to find out. Maybe this time, Val would shed some light on the subject.

When Jessica arrived, Karen had her sit in the den alone. She pretended to busy herself by going from room to room looking out of the window for Hershel. Anything to avoid having to talk to Jessica. She was conscious of the dull furnishings they had and wondered if Jessica looked down her nose at her. What Karen didn't need were rumors floating around the job about her. She wondered what in the world came over her when she'd asked her coworker to join her for the weekend workshop. In any case, they had nothing in common. When Karen entered the room, she observed Jessica's seemingly genuine curiosity toward photos on the side table next to the high back chair. "This one?" Karen asked, stretching to see who Jessica pointed to. "Oh. That's not me, that's my older sister, Val."

"Oh," Jessica replied with a smile.
"So, where do you live?" Karen asked.
"I stay on Cherry Lane, off West Outer Drive, with my dad and stepmother."
"Off West Outer Drive, huh?" Karen said dryly.
"Yup."
Jessica seemed oblivious to Karen's cynicism. She figured as much, that Jessica would live in a nice, beautiful home. She carried herself like she had a good upbringing. Because of that, Karen figured that deep down Jessica thought she was better than her.
"So, how long you been working at Golden Walk?" Karen inquired, eyeing her up and down. This was the first time she'd seen her out of her uniform.

"I'd say about a year and a half. This coming semester I'll start my nursing program at U of D."

"Huh?"

"University of Detroit Mercy," Jessica clarified, picking up another photo to look at.

"Oh. I figured that's the one you were talking about," Karen lied.

"What about you, Keekee?" Jessica asked. "What school are you attending?"

To Karen, it seemed that whenever Jessica said 'Keekee,' it was used in a tone of mockery. She was almost tempted to make her start calling her Karen. But it was too late for that after she plainly told her Keekee was her preferred name.

"Well, I ain't . . . um, I'm not sure yet. You know. I'm still trying to decide my major and all."

"Well, I certainly hope you choose to further your career in the medical field. I think you're excellent with people. They need someone firm, but compassionate . . . like you. That's my opinion," Jessica said glancing at the papers in Karen's hands.

Karen looked at her incredulously, feeling compelled to announce why she had the poems. "Figured I'll bring some, you know, in case we end up at the writers' workshop."

"Cool, fine with me. I'm excited to go. It's a treat to be in the presence of creative people. I love it. They're usually so free in how they see the world."

"Yeah, whatever, girl, you are trippin'," Karen said, thinking it humorous how animated Jessica became, moving her hands about when she spoke. She even sat like a lady with her back perfectly straight. Yet, her shoulders were relaxed. The idea of how pretty and picture-perfect she came off sickened Karen. Deep down, she knew she could never measure up to Jessica's grace and style.

Three honks of a horn intruded on their conversation and they both stopped to gather their belongings. Karen went to the front door and opened it wide, holding up her first finger the way folks did in some Baptist churches when they had to walk during the service, then she closed it. She checked the stove and turned off the lights then gestured for Jessica to go first through the front door. Karen made sure the lock was secure before she tossed the keys into her oversized handbag. Her poetry and a notebook were also stuffed inside.

Karen shook her head at the sight of Hershel getting out of his Grand Cherokee to open the door for Jessica, smiling like The Joker, from the movie *Batman*. *Give me a break.*

"Jessica, this is my ace, Hershel. Hershel, Jessica," Karen said as she slid in the back seat.

"How are you? So nice to meet you," Hershel said in a peppered, deepened masculine voice. He followed that statement up with a series of civilities that made Karen want to jam her fingers down her throat. For most of the ride, she remained quiet, staring out the window at storefronts and office buildings, while soaking up their conversation and sizing it up for validity, especially where Hershel was concerned.

She knew Hershel's best manners were brought forth as he tried to impress Jessica. Karen also knew that this was only the beginning of something she'd wish she hadn't started. It had to have been a mistake because Hershel was already stupid, gaga over Jessica. Maybe she shouldn't have introduced Hershel as her 'ace,' she thought. She should have said, 'her man,' instead, but knew that was pushing it.

With her arms folded and confidence shaken, Karen hoped Hershel understood that just because Jessica came along, she didn't have to interfere with their relationship jumping to the next level. But then again, she had to get him to understand their relationship was about to undergo some serious revamping.

When they entered the art studio, there was an immediate vibe of eclecticism that made Karen bob her head and chime out, "This is da' bomb."

Jessica leaned into her ear and whispered, "Oh, Keekee, this is awesome."

"Uh-huh," Karen said, trying her best to display her pissed-off face. Her head nearly exploded from the nonstop talking from Jessica and Hershel. This went on the entire drive. Meanwhile, Karen decided she didn't want to have to look at Jessica's face once they were at their destination. And so she walked heavy-footed in front of her whenever she had the chance. By the time they'd passed through a small room with sculptures of varying sizes that stood on pedestals, Jessica caught up to Karen, practically bouncing with delight. Karen fumed and under her breath said, "Freak," because in her mind, no one could be that doggone happy. Next, they entered into the main area where artists sat concentrating on a relaxed and nude subject lying on a Victorian sofa on a wide platform in the center of the room. The female model appeared to be thirty-something and a bit plump. Her long, thick brunette hair hung in loose curls about her shoulders.

Hershel pulled up a stool and uncovered his paint brushes. He adjusted his blank canvas onto the easel and looked back and forth at the subject as he started with long thin strokes. In Karen's eyes, Hershel looked masterful with his paint brush, favoring oil painting. She also witnessed him give Jessica a quick wink, which seethed her insides. With that, she snapped her free hand to her hip and whispered to Jessica, "I'm ready to go sit in with the writing class. Staring at another woman's junk ain't high on my list."

Jessica giggled behind the hand that covered her mouth. They both resembled the Hunchback of Notre Dame as they ambled across the wooden floor, and went to the room next door. When they entered, all heads whipped around then back toward the instructor who was in the middle of lecturing about metaphors. Karen and Jessica crossed the back of the room with one wall filled with award-winning poems in frames and pulled out screeching chairs to an empty table. They glanced at each; Karen snarling, Jessica smirking, as they opened their notepads and began taking notes.

After forty-five minutes of hearing about interpretation, plot and character development, Karen started yawning. She wasn't interested in writing altogether; only in poetry. Even that was done sporadically. As if the instructor heard her thoughts, he announced, "Class, if any of you would like to share your work, feel free. Passages from a short story or essay, poetry, anything you have is fine."

Karen eased out her poems and eyed them, still uncertain which one she wanted to read. By the time the instructor pointed to her, she grabbed a poem from the middle of the thin stack. She smacked her lips, strutted to the front of the room, and threw her hip to the left while clearing her throat.

Your kiss makes me wanna scream, walk a mile on my knees, holler, Oh, please baby, please, I need you. Your kiss makes me wanna do right, stop hangin out all night. I feel your kiss in my

> *mind, my soul, and down to my toes. Your kiss is poison though, makes me wanna fight cause I'm up half the night, thinking about who else may be getting your kiss. Oh, please baby, please, I need you.*

Karen lifted her eyes but not her head. A few students clapped, Jessica among them. Unsmiling faces ricocheted off her upbeat mood. In her mind, this was her best poem, which she planned to give to Hershel later on. It was everyone else's fault if they were too stupid to get it.

"Thank you," the instructor said, making the comment sound more like a question. "Eh, this is the beauty of poetry: self-expression. There is no wrong way in free-verse, which means it doesn't have to be consistent with meters, rhymes and so forth."

When Karen plopped down in her seat, Jessica delivered a playful tug to her shoulder. If nothing else, she had her own "amen corner" with the girl, and as much as it pained her to admit it, the support made the speaking ordeal bearable. But could she trust Jessica's reaction? All of it? Here and at the house when she looked at pictures? A part of her wanted to snuggle beside it, accept her coworker's reaction as genuine, but Karen had never relied on such frailties before and she wasn't about to start now. When the class ended, they met up with Hershel, Karen leading the way again with surefootedness.

"So, did you have enough room on your canvas to paint all-that-woman?" Karen smirked while elbowing her way in front of Jessica to stand closest to Hershel.

"Boy, how do you deal with her, Jessica?" Hershel asked, as he packed up his belongings.
"I do the best I can," Jessica grinned, tilting her head to eye his finished painting.

Why that traitor. "I can hear y'all, you know," Karen said, arching her upper lip. She visualized cranking up her middle finger nice and slow to Jessica, the way one reels in a big catch with a fishing pole.

"I love your painting," Jessica said, ignoring Karen's remark and stepping to Hershel's opposite side for a closer look.

"Thanks."

"Well?" Hershel stated, bobbing his head at Karen.

Karen's eyes did a quick zigzag. "Well, what?"

"Jessica thinks my work is awesome. What do you think?"

Grunt.

As they exited the building, Hershel suggested eating at Mario's restaurant. Karen didn't give any lip.

When they arrived at the restaurant, Jessica thanked him and flashed a straight set of pearly whites.

"Ditto," Karen mumbled for her 'thanks'. She appreciated Hershel's gesture, but more than that, she felt off balance, mentally kicking her own behind for inviting a man-stealer. This was why she didn't have many female friends. And the two she had, had been questionable . . . as females, that is. Karen wanted to lash out and call Jessica a trollop, ugly, stupid, anything to release the rage bubbling behind her tight jaws. But the words didn't stand a chance against her beauty and kindheartedness. That too, made Karen want to smack her hard across her perky cheek. Nobody could be that happy. Nobody.

She thought about her own beauty, or lack thereof, in comparison to Jessica's flawless presence and size 38-C cups. But Karen, with hips the same width of her waist, knew she wasn't glamorous and that she wasn't dainty or lady-like. She couldn't even figure out a way to soften to Hershel. It seemed ridiculous after all these years. But she had to start somewhere. She had to make him understand that at this point, she was ready to have someone special in her life. She needed this. And that someone had to be him because he knew her inside and out.

After the bald-headed waiter seated them and rattled off the specials for the day, Hershel left for a moment, allowing them to decide on their order. Karen's eyes became mere slits. She gritted her teeth and grabbed Jessica's menu from the top and yanked it down.

"What do you think you doin'?" Karen asked.

"W-well, I'm trying to decide what to order."

"I ain't talking 'bout no dang order. You—Hershel . . . you like him or somethin'?" Karen snapped.

"Yeah, he's cool people. I can see why you two have been friends for so long. He's a gem." Jessica released an offhanded smile and batted her eyes before picking up the menu.

Karen had her lips fixed to order Jessica to keep her grubby hands off her soon-to-be man. But Hershel returned, which shrank her comment to a mere, "Uh-huh. Whatever. You need to chill out."

Karen ordered her usual whenever Hershel was generous enough to take her to this spot. She certainly would never spend money on herself outside of going to McDonald's.

When the waiter returned, he looked directly at Jessica. "Everyone ready to order?"

"Yes, *we* are." Karen closed her menu with a smack. "For me, I'll have the Mariata soup, with extra parmesan cheese, and my main meal, the Broiled Whitefish . . . twelve ounce, that's it."

"Anything to drink, ma'am?" the waiter asked still smiling at Jessica.

"Ice tea." Karen said, feeling salt added to her wounds. While it wasn't Jessica's fault that she looked the way she did, still, to Karen, she became every irritant one could possibly think of; the itch in the center of your back; the tiny pebble in your shoe, and the gnat that flies near your eyes.

Hershel made it his business to ask Jessica, every five-minutes it seemed to Karen, how her meal tasted.

"Dang, boy, you gon' drive somebody crazy," Karen blurted out, although she wasn't quite as irritated because at this point, digging her fork into the tender fish satisfied her more.

Hershel stared at Karen and kicked her leg lightly under the table. "By the way, ladies, I have another surprise for you all. I got tickets for us to see a comedy show." He held up the tickets for effect.

"How you know we didn't have plans?" Karen said flippantly. She had a drink in her hand, stirring the straw with her pinky finger extended out.

"I'd love to go, Hershel," Jessica added. "You are so sweet." She clapped once.

Hershel smiled. Karen looked like an aggravated store clerk forced to listen to a whiny customer.
"Okay, then. I guess I'm in, too. Thanks, Hersh. You the man," Karen said.
"So, Hershel, how long have you been painting?" Jessica asked.
"Aw, man, ever since elementary school." He said it as if it amazed him. Then he added, "Hope I didn't offend you ladies, 'man' is just a figure of speech."

Jessica shook her head in haste, letting on that she understood.

"I enjoy abstract best because of all the colors I can use, but I also like capturing human faces and their emotion . . . it's all in the eyes, you know. If everything goes well, my paintings will be featured at a small gallery in Royal Oak this summer. And, you've gotta check out the Jazz Festival because I will be showcasing my art."

It was more than Karen could take. She felt as though she'd faded into the background. Or perhaps she had become like the orange colored glass candleholder on the table, an ornament, serving no real purpose. So she did the next best thing to gain control. "Hershel," Karen blurted out after pulling the poem from her handbag and handing it to him. "Here. This is for you . . . I wrote it myself."

Hershel wiped at the corner of his mouth with his first finger and took the paper. "Cool, Thanks."

That was it. They'd gone back to ignoring her like she had evaporated or something. Karen observed Jessica's pupils widen as she hung onto Hershel's every word. She leaned into his conversation with her arms open. She was into him, big time. Karen bulked her eyes and rolled them when Jessica told Hershel he was different than anyone she'd ever known, and wasn't a bookish bore who snubbed his nose at the world because he'd been promised a position at Steinberg & Turner upon graduation. She laughed and elaborated on the guy she was referring to.

His name was Rodney Baker and his parents were both attorneys. She went on to explain how Rodney acted as though God had wrapped him with a bow for the universe to behold. "The simplest conversation became draining," she said, slanting her head. But Karen perked up with delight when Jessica said he dogged her out at one of his Kappa parties. "It was the final straw," as

Jessica put it because her 'friend's' chest poked out like a puffer fish, while he strutted two feet in front of her, not even bothering to introduce her as his girlfriend. While it surprised Karen that any man could reject or mistreat Jessica because of her attractiveness, it gave her colossal pleasure in knowing her coworker had been jilted.

Dim lighting and round tables made the club cozy. The walls were covered with memorabilia from years of entertainment. People laughed hard at the comedian who occasionally indulged in spewing light insults to members of the audience. At first, Karen tried hard to remain stoic-looking, still pretending Hershel had forced her hand at something she didn't want to do. But, she'd laughed so hard and so long her stomach began to knot. She slapped at, punched and shoved Hershel's right arm until he threatened to move his seat to the left of Jessica, away from her.

Karen felt great being able to let loose. Still, she had her work cut out. There was no way she planned to let some bright eyed, beautiful and intelligent woman like Jessica, stand in the way of her winning over Hershel; no matter how long it would take, even if it meant doing something drastic.

Chapter 12

That evening, Val felt as if everything in the house had been sleeping. The noises that came from the refrigerator's fan and the heating unit were in an unusual time-out. Complete silence. She couldn't sleep though.

Ever since last Monday's botched date with Brady, her mind was plagued by anguish, along with piercing abdominal pains. It felt like a twisted towel being rung out. She'd replayed her behavior after he'd touched her. It had happened so fast she couldn't control her impulse. There wasn't a rock big enough that could hide her shame. Although she had acted out of character accepting a date with Brady, his gentlemanly qualities lingered and caused her to feel woozy with pleasure, which made her a troll because of how she'd acted. She experienced desire and agony, all rolled into one emotional glob.

When she heard Karen pass by her room, she rushed to put on her pink robe and slippers and emerged from the bedroom into the hallway.

"Oh, girl, you scared me." Karen placed a hand on her chest.

"Sorry," Val said, staring at Karen under the dim lighting from a wall sconce.

"I can't believe you're still up and—wait. You checkin' on me, ain't you?" Karen asked.

"No . . ."

Karen leaned back as if she were pushed.

"Okay, yes," Val admitted. Plus, she couldn't remember the last time she'd slept through the night, even prior to her date-demolition.

"Well, instead of being all up in my grits, why don't you tell me what's been going on with you."

Val blinked, questioning whether she heard what she thought she had heard. She adjusted her robe with the contemplation of opening up to Karen. "I had a date."

"Get out."

"Yeah, I did."

"How? When?"

"What do you mean 'how'?"

"I mean what hap—ya' know what I mean."

Val forced a grin as Karen shoved her back into her room and they both landed on the edge of the bed as the covers heaped against their backsides.

"It was this past Monday," Val blurted out. "And . . . it was spontaneous, really. I met Brady at the Water Department. That's where he works. One thing led to another and he asked me out." Val folded her hands in her lap and looked away from Karen's shock-stricken face.

"You? He asked *you* out on a date?" Karen's eyebrows lifted as she brought an equally dumbfounded hand to her cheek.

"Yes," Val replied, fiddling with the broken ring on her finger.

"What were you wearing?"

Val knew full well what Karen was getting at: her bland wardrobe. "I have to admit I took your advice and bought a nice blouse." She stood and dragged her feet across the carpet as she opened the closet door, pulling out the blouse. "See." She presented a fake 'cheese' smile and shook the blouse on the hanger before replacing it.

"Not bad."

"Anyway, we went out to eat and drove around. You know . . . took in a few sights around the city. I had a great time. He's a really, really nice guy." Val shut the closet door then stood with her hips pressed into the adjacent dresser.

"Well. I can't believe it. Mm. Go ahead, Val. Next you'll be telling me you gettin' married."

Val responded with a pained chuckle. It was a thought that crossed her mind about as often as finding a fifty-dollar bill on the ground.

Karen shrugged her shoulders and said, "Well, I sorta had a good time. Hershel treated me and Jessica out . . ."

Val looked confused.

"Oh. You don't know her," Karen said, as if reading her mind. "She's somebody I work with. And Hershel was practically trippin' over his doggone tongue because of her. I think I hate her. Not somebody I want to hang with, though 'cause she's kinda uppity."

"Hate?"

"Well, I can't stand her a whole bunch." Karen corrected.

Val shot her a disapproving look as she sauntered back to the bed and rested next to Karen. This time she leaned back on her pillow with her legs bent to the side.

"I got my ends clipped on my hair," Val interjected, hoping to deter Karen from the verbal bashing.

"Wow, get out. You went all out for this dude, didn't you? I thought your hair didn't look as jacked up," Karen said.

Then it happened. Almost in one seamless breath, Karen led into her next question.

"Say, Val, I was thinking: what ever happened to Frank? I came across some old pictures and saw him in one of them."

The question hit her the way one stops breathing when they nearly miss a car that ran a stop sign. The inquiry hung in the air until Val forced the corners of her mouth to turn upward.

"Frank?" Val cleared her throat. "Wow. I don't know, Karen. He just dropped out of sight. I have no idea what happened to him?"

"Wasn't he and Mama supposed to get married or somethin'?"

"I . . . uh, don't, know. She didn't talk about him much."

"Well, why not? That's dumb. I can tell from all the pictures he was around for years."

"For God's sake, what did I just say? What the hell is wrong with you, Karen?" Val's teeth were clenched so tight her jaws shook and the veins in her neck popped. She wanted to scream or throw something.

He'd been gone for years; yet, Frank managed to torment her in his absence. He did that often. Val's mind trailed off to the time she'd been playing with her paper dolls and he'd come into her room rubbing her back and breathing on her neck. She scampered from the room saying, "I hafta use the bathroom."

Later that day, Frank insisted that she accompany him to the store.

"Mama, I don't want to go," she'd pleaded.

"Oh, girl, just go. You ain't got nothing better to do."

Every facet of Val's body cried out to her mother to change her mind. Eyebrows that gathered up, folded hands clasped in a prayer, rounded shoulders, her tears, which fell in big droplets, did nothing to dissuade Mama. In fact, she encouraged Val to go with Frank time and again. Mama felt the closer Frank got to her kid, the more stable their relationship would become.

Mama didn't seem to notice Val's disinterest in treats like hot fudge brownies after dinner, or the fact she went off to her room or the attic every time Frank was near.

That finger snapped again, and Val came to herself then blurted out, "Keekee. I have no idea what happened to Frank. That's somethin' you'd have to ask Mama." Even though her voice had calmed, her hands were still in the air.

Karen's mouth hanging open made Val lower her arms and reach out for her. But Karen already waved her off and flounced out of the room.

"Keekee. I'm sorry. I didn't mean that," Val called after her.

Karen rushed back in with her hands on both hips. "You know what yo' problem is?"

Val's eyes moistened. She blamed herself for Karen's reaction. How could anyone love her?

"You always been jealous of me and Mama's relationship. You couldn't stand the fact she loved me best. Get over it."

Val stood like a statue. Karen's statement couldn't have been more false. Karen didn't understand. She wasn't even around—wasn't born to know how things were. Val tried desperately to shield her from any rumors about Frank. She and Mama did. If relatives started talking about him at cookouts or after a wedding, Val and Mama would shush them. How did Karen come across the pictures in the first place? Supposedly, they were all burned. It wasn't fair: Val had been taunted and abused by Frank growing up as a young girl. Now that he was gone, he still managed to torment her miles away, and years later. She thought about the habitual way she'd tried to protect Karen, but realized the only person she guarded was herself. However, she'd made up in her mind, she was going to take an early vacation and start job hunting, and get away from the house, the state, and everything that reminded her of Frank. She looked about her nightstand for the lighter she used to light incense. She smoothed out her robe, and exhaled, then set out to find all remaining pictures of Frank.

Chapter 13

Prior to going to work, Karen almost broke all her nails moving Mama's old, heavy dresser back and forth. Its resting place had been in the basement before she was born. But, the mysterious letter did not show up in the musty drawers, nor did it appear in the clothes shoot that the dresser covered. She sucked her teeth and vowed to find the letter Mama spoke of in hush-hush tones to her best, and now deceased friend, Pearl Patterson. Karen figured Val didn't know anything about the letter because she never mentioned it. Looking about the cobwebbed basement, she sat in a dilapidated lawn chair and daydreamed.

She hadn't meant to eavesdrop on Mama. Months before her death, she had heard Mama so-called whispering, which was loud enough to penetrate the outer walls of her room. Karen had raced to the bathroom and grabbed a glass jar from the bottom cabinet with bags of hair rollers and holding spray, and placed it outside Mama's bedroom. Her face twisted as she strained to hear.

Her ear pressed against the jar, and the jar against the chipped, blue paint next to the bedroom door. She'd overheard her name mentioned a few times and something about something being a "long time coming," according to Mama's muttering. That's it. Karen had no idea what that meant. Mama started spilling her guts when Val came up the stairs. Before she reached the top step, Karen made a lizard face, skidded into her room, and sat on the floor picking her toenails like she'd been there all the while. But what was Mama concealing? Was it money? Maybe Mama had stashed some money aside for her and didn't want Val getting wind of it, Karen guessed, but didn't think that was the case. Not really.

Aware of the present time, Karen left the basement and headed to her room to get ready for work. An entire week had passed before she uttered "Hello," to Val. Prior to that, she'd been walking around eyeballing her like she was burnt bacon. Especially when Val had the gall to stick her head through the bathroom door while she blew out her hair, and said all pitiful like, "I'm sorry."

Karen winced at Val's presence and low tone, which failed to rise above the dryer's noise and blast of hot air.

"I said I'm sorry," Val repeated, cupping a hand to her mouth.

Oh, you're sorry all right, Karen thought.

She knew crazy and Val, no doubt, was bona fide. That apology came the day after the blowup incident. But Karen milked Val's guilt for all she could. Out of the deal she'd gotten money to gas up her car, a packed lunch with chicken salad, and brownies. Karen sweet-talked her into doing her laundry as well.

That same week, she had to work at a different facility because of staffing issues. She had endured smelly diapers with diarrhea and had been thrown up on twice. She'd been slapped, pushed and punched on the knees by stubborn patients. As if that weren't bad enough, she'd slipped and fallen from a patch of water in the hall corridors. Karen caught a couple of patients from the sitting lounge snickering after the incident. *I thought old people was supposed to be caring, not trifling.*

As challenging as some of Karen's patients were at her original location, she'd much rather deal with five-Mr. Hamiltons than work at the center they had sent her to. Although, Ms. Blout was still a trip all by herself, Karen concluded.

By the time she'd gone into work, she felt upbeat enough to let Jessica sit near her without puking. It was mostly out of curiosity because she wanted to know if her suspicions were correct.

"And how're you doing?" Jessica inquired as she joined Karen in the cafeteria, helping herself to a chair.

"Okay." *This heifa' has to know I can't stand her*, Karen thought to herself as she ate the last of her brownie squares.

"Did you miss us?"

"Not much."

Jessica tapped her manicured fingers near Karen's arm. "You're such a kidder. Welcome back."

"I ain't kidding."

"Well, we certainly missed you around here. And Ms. Blout missed you."

"Yeah, I bet," Karen replied, polishing her teeth with her tongue.

"Ms. Blout had her neck craned toward the door every time she heard footsteps. You know she wants you to read to her."

"Come again?" Karen asked, elevating both eyebrows.

"Yes, indeed. She'd gathered books from our library on African American History and had them placed strategically on her bed."

"Why? I ain't gon' read to that crazy ol' woman."

"Well, that's what I said . . . not the crazy part," Jessica grinned, "but I asked her why she wanted you specifically to read to her."

Karen rolled her eyes and faced the window. She knew Jessica prolonged her response so she could turn to face her.

"Want to know what she said?"

"Not really."

Jessica laughed. "She said, 'Reading books works wonders on many levels,' and that she intended to get you to speak more concisely and enunciate your words clearly."

Karen turned her head in one sweeping motion. She narrowed her eyes at Jessica and tooted up the corners of her mouth. Now that was a dig. Karen knew she couldn't trust Jessica. *Always battin' those eyes like you so innocent. Please.*

"W-what are you thinking, Keekee?" Jessica asked.

"What I'm thinking rhymes with the word witch."

Jessica did a little bounce in her seat and looked around at the clock on the far wall. "Oh, another thing . . ."

Karen inhaled and exhaled with equal force.

". . . you know Ms. Blout often embellishes stories of knowing famous people."

Karen jerked her neck. "No, I didn't know that. So?"

"Well," Jessica leaned in, "the poor woman probably confused her years of teaching history with events from her own life. Last year, she'd told the staff she used to have lunch with Lena Horne. Before that, it was tea with John Johnson . . . you know, the owner of Ebony magazine. Thought I'd give you a heads-up."

Karen didn't care about that. She wanted to know one thing and wasted no time leaping at the point. "You and Hershel been talking?"

"Um . . ." Jessica blushed.

"Just answer the question."

"As a matter of fact, yes, we have. Look, you made it clear he was . . ."

Karen stood and slammed her palms against the table, gaining the attention from others nearby. "Well, let me make somethin' else clear: stay away from Hershel."

Jessica stood as well. "Or what?"

Oh no she di-ent, Karen thought. Back in the day she would have yanked out a plug of hair and beat the snot out of her. But she couldn't now. The job was getting better and she took pride in it, in spite of Margaret's claims. No, no, she planned to stay on point, and not Jessica or anybody else was going to make her get sidetracked.

"Just stay away, I'm not playing with you."

Karen kept her head low when she saw Margaret coming toward her down the narrow hallway. She headed for Ms. Blout's room and did a quick pivot before she had to go by her. Karen had her eyes turned to the ceiling right before she'd swiveled her body and spied a stack of books on top of her bed, as Jessica had said. When Ms. Blout came out of the bathroom, her mouth formed a perfect "o."

"Didn't mean to startle you," Karen said, holding her hand up when she saw Ms. Blout's surprised expression.

Ms. Blout allowed her eyes to trail up at Karen's hair; after which, she simply replied, "Oh," and sat in her chair.

"Where do you want me to place your books? I hafta put fresh linens on your bed."

"Actually, I was hoping you'd be able to read to me. You do know how to read, don't you?"

"Of course I can read, old woman. Can you?"

"Certainly," Ms. Blout responded, swaying back in the chair. "Yet, I never quite mastered the art of archery."

Oh, so she got jokes. Karen pressed her lips tight. She snatched up the stack of books and banged them on her nightstand. She didn't care about any backlash from Ms. Blout. She expected some resistance. And after dealing with Jessica, she welcomed it. Karen just wanted to get the old woman's room cleaned, serve her lunch, and get far away as possible. She supposed she still had kinks to work out with handling difficult patients like Ms. Blout. Not having to deal with her for a few days was like getting a slice of heaven. But now, being in the same room with the old bat was like having her big toe stuck in a drain.

Ms. Blout said nothing, rather sulked in the corner staring over at the window, as Karen worked in silence. She shaded Ms. Blout's moping demeanor from her mind. *Hell will freeze over fifteen times before I read to her. Please.* But her fatal mistake was looking up into the old woman's face. Her eyes were like small peas with folds and creases surrounding them; there were tiny lines that had three and four other lines branching out from it. Her upper back protruded out. And she gripped her cane like it was her only friend.

"Ms. Blout." Karen thrusted her name out as she leaned into her left hip.

"Yes, dear?"

"Why you over there in the corner looking like somebody stole your bag of candy? Name one reason why I should read to you? You ain't been nothing but mean to me since I met you. And now you want me to do something extra nice for you?"

Ms. Blout looked down at her lap in a manner that Karen hadn't witnessed before.

"Okay, Ms. Blout. I'm gon' read to you after my shift. But you betta start being nicer to me."

Right before Karen left the room, Ms. Blout's mouth turned pleasant. Karen already had her mind on tending to her next patient who, by now, should have been done with the physical therapist. She also checked the activity board to see when the pianist was expected to do a recital later in the day. Karen's luck dried up when she ran into Margaret again.

Chapter 14

Heaths, lilacs, apple blossoms, and petunias were in full bloom showing off their brilliant colors. The trees were now filled in with leaves, and allergies made Val quite miserable. She wiped at her sore nose and concluded that her condition escalated due to walking outside to the detached garage. After work, Val parked on the street so Karen wouldn't have to move her car out of the way since the garage had everything in it except available space. The junky items dated back to their childhood. Old doll heads, paper dolls, tricycles, inflatable beach balls that were now flattened; all competed for major territory. Paint cans pushed up against broken sidewalk chalk and a red wagon with a missing handle bogarted a rusted tool box. Val promised herself before the year ended, she'd clean it out.

    She rummaged for remaining photos of Frank and managed to find two. She pulled out a lighter and lit the edges of the photos then stared deep into the flames, reminding herself to breathe as each picture became engulfed. She laughed and hugged herself, satisfied that Frank had indeed been destroyed.

Sliced onions, tomatoes and carrots were tossed into the large boiling pot. Val made all the ingredients for homemade soup without giving it much thought. Her mind drifted. *Nothing worse,* was what Karen said once complaining of cramps due to the onset of her period. Val had already stopped having periods because of a hysterectomy. Grapefruit sized fibroids were the reason for the surgery. For Val, it rendered relief from the horrible reminder each month that she was a young woman, as Frank often told her, and that she could have babies. He'd often told her that, too.

    She had to cup her hands between her legs, hoping, pleading even, against his fingers digging under her panties. He would flick his thick tongue around her inner thighs and vaginal area. Her cries were never heard by Mama even though her room was right next door. When Val mustered up the nerve to hint that Frank made her feel "funny" and "uncomfortable," Mama yelled and threw objects at the wall and at her, calling her a bold-faced liar. The outburst had sickened Val to the point her nose began to bleed. It took years for Mama to apologize. Even then, it was through a letter which Val kept in a box on the top shelf of her closet. Well, Val guessed Mama said she'd been sorry, because to this day, the letter had remained unopened.

    This was an extraordinary phase in her life: she'd gotten her period, won essay contests three times in a row, and had been chosen for a position on the Armstrong Middle School paper. She had wanted to be the world's next big author like Alice Walker. She wanted to affect people's lives with her words. Val's dreams of becoming a writer had withered when Frank started going through her papers. "You write anything 'bout me?" He'd ask, snickering. She hadn't. In fact, she'd lost interest in writing altogether, storing all her literary ideas into a folder and burying them deep in her closet. She didn't want Frank mocking anything else she held sacred.

Val stared into the boiling pot, lost in the memory. She snapped to the present, expecting Karen to be there, saying something like, "Whatju gonna' do, jump in?" But she hadn't made it home from work yet.

She hoped that Karen found a way to excuse her repugnant behavior. She'd felt like a madwoman days earlier. But the outburst prompted her to contact Linda and share her plans to visit and job hunt during her stay. It was settled.

Chapter 15

Karen didn't move away from the board fast enough. It was a shame because her shift was almost over. Now she had to hear Margaret's raggedy mouth. She twisted her upper body and faced the dragon.

"Excuse me. Did you make sure Mrs. Anthony had her juice?"

"Oh, yes, I did," Karen answered, swallowing hard into Margaret's stone face.

"Well, you didn't remember it two weeks ago. How would you like to have food with nothing to drink with it?"

Really? "Margaret, I've always given her juice with her lunch . . . and water."

"You gave her orange juice and she prefers apple."

"The cafeteria was short on juices for diabetic condition . . . Margaret, it was an honest choi . . ."

"Uh-uh. No excuses. I don't accept excuses, only results. Got it?" Margaret walked away with her thighs rubbing together with each step. Karen didn't get a chance to respond, not that she could have come up with a sufficient explanation. Why was Margaret so mean? Was it because of the mishap the first day she'd started working? It felt as though Margaret wanted to do her in.

Karen's shoulders slumped. She wanted to snatch the poor quality wig Margaret favored, right off her fat head. No matter what choice she made involving her patients, small or big, Margaret found fault with it. Karen didn't want to do anything but go home and play her music or talk with Hershel. Forget her promise to Ms. Blout. The energy had been zapped out of her. This was it. She'd call Hershel and tell him flat out she was interested in him.

Chapter 16

By 10 o'clock Tuesday morning, Val had washed and dried most of the laundry and began packing as she went along. In the middle of her chores, she spied Karen's lazy shuffle as she crossed the floor to the den in one Dora and one purple fuzzy slipper. She still had on her night clothes. Val scratched her dry scalp and scowled as she watched Karen plop on the sofa and remove the paper wrapping from a pack of Marlboro cigarettes.

"When did you pick up that filthy habit?"

Karen struck the strip on the carton of matches, studied the yellow flames for a second and inhaled once the cigarette was lit. She coughed hard and took a couple more drags before plonking her feet on the coffee table like she didn't hear a word, wiggling her foot every time she took a puff.

Finally she said, "I figured I needed a new hobby."

"I see," Val replied. She reentered the kitchen then quickstepped to the living room then back to the kitchen.

Karen tilted her head and yelled out, "Dang, Val, what the heck you doing? You flying around this house like you gon' miss a train or something."

Val peeped into the den from the kitchen's doorway. "I've been up since five o'clock this morning, washing, ironing. Got things to do ya' know."

"Did you cook breakfast?"

"Nooo . . ."

"Why ain't you cooked breakfast?"

She exhaled. "Oh, Keekee, you aren't helpless. Like I said, I have things to do."

"And eating ain't one of 'em?" Karen rounded her mouth and blew out smoke.

Val fanned a hand in front of her face. "I suppose I could fry up some bacon, maybe make an omelet."

Karen dragged out a giggle. "That's mo' betta."

"Do you work today?" Val asked, interrupting her own schedule to pull raw meat strips from its packaging.

"Nope, I do tomorrow though. Unfortunately, Dragon Margaret will be there. I can't wait till her behind goes on vacation."

Val wiped her hands on a dampened paper towel. "Speaking of vacation, I'm headed to Phoenix, Arizona—job interview coming up."

Karen slammed her feet to the floor. "What? When? Why would you go to Arizona for a job interview? That's dumb, Val." Karen strode into the kitchen and grabbed a chair, holding her cigarette and cup in the same hand.

"I'm leaving Friday and returning in a few days. My friend Linda lives there and . . . well, I can visit her as well. I need to get away. I'm stressed and . . ."

"So, where does that leave me if you get a job in Arizona?" Karen bucked her eyes, refusing to blink until Val responded.

Val softened her look. "I hadn't thought that through, but maybe it's time you get out on your own. I can't handle the bills and . . ."

Karen banged her hand on the table. "That's just great, if you can't handle the bills, what makes you think I can? You make more money than me, Val. You jump up at the last minute and tell me this crap," Karen yelled. "You know you are wrong. I would never do something like that to you."

"Keekee, now wait a minute. You didn't let me finish."

"I don't need to let you finish." Karen rose and stood by her chair. "You always doing something stupid. By the way . . . you know you look like a fool keeping a doggone broken ring on your finger. What grown woman does that? And another thing, I think you are the most selfish person I've ever known."

By the time Karen got her last word out, Val started pounding the worn out laminate countertop, fed up with her attitude. "Stop it, stop it, stop it!" She walked over to Karen, pointing and holding her finger like a weapon. "I've had enough of you."

Val knew she'd caught her by surprise when Karen's face dropped a half a centimeter. She even released her entire cigarette into the cup and backed up into the grease splattered wall.

"Get your finger outta my face. You *are* crazy." Karen's words were elevated. "No wonder you can't get a man—don't wanna be bothered with your wacked out behind." Karen stormed out of the kitchen and through the den and headed upstairs to her room.

Val assumed she'd changed clothes because shortly after, the front door opened then slammed. She could hear Karen's car engine roar as she drove off.

Val dug her fist into her chest and collapsed in the kitchen chair. The toxic words were cutting and felt as though Karen's angry hand gripped her heart, and squeezed with hateful persistence. Val grimaced at her low blow about the ring. Why couldn't Karen comprehend that she'd felt overwhelmed? She was the one who was selfish. But maybe she had a right to be upset, Val thought. After all, she'd held back their true financial state, among other matters she vowed to tell no one; the secret she planned to take to her grave. But Karen's wellbeing was always at the forefront for Val, even if her actions were contradictory. She only wanted to protect her. Right then, Val sniffed hard and looked over at the sizzling skillet and blackened meat. She sat immobile; thinking . . . perhaps, after her trip, she and Karen could talk . . . and set up some ground rules before somebody gets hurt.

Chapter 17

Karen lost her desire for another cigarette and swore she heard her heart thumping over the whiny springs in her bed, which supported her nervous rise and fall. Now her jaws were blown out as Val had never yelled at her like that. Even when she'd taken a pair of scissors and cut small slits at the bottom of Val's favorite dress, she didn't react as harshly. And that wasn't too many years ago.

Still vivid, she remembered the impact of Val's hurt. "I don't believe you. Why would you do this to my dress?" Karen recalled grinning like the devil himself, not caring one bit that Val's eyes watered up. She brought forth the most hateful thing she could produce: her words. "I told you I was gonna' get you back for not letting me borrow ten dollars." To Karen's surprise, Mama even stepped-in, wagging her accusatory finger and shaking her head. That's how Karen gauged when she'd gone too far. Whenever Mama took up for Val, she'd messed up big time.

In fact, this should've been her cue to sit back and analyze why Val blew up. But she had her own issues. She'd run up against a brick wall, standing at odds, it seemed, with the world. She couldn't think without feeling anger.

Karen had no idea where she was driving as a light drizzle began. She knew that she had to leave the house and get away from Val. What nerve. It was so typical of her sister to flip-the-script on things at the last minute. She didn't know if Val was coming or already came and went. The crazy things she'd come up with left Karen baffled. Trying to find a job in another state was dumb. Just because Mama was gone didn't mean they had to leave the house and all its memories. She rubbed at her rumbling stomach. She never did get her breakfast.

Karen leaned her head halfway out of her car window and rolled her eyes at the McDonald's drive-thru speaker. "I said large fries and a shake, not small fries and apple pie." Her forceful words were high-pitched. *Dang. How stupid can you be?* When she drove around to the window, the young girl handed over the drink and food with one hand while covering her ear with the other. Karen didn't care. She twisted her face at the girl and sucked air through her teeth. Without hesitation, she snatched her meal and zoomed off. Now was the time to call Hershel, she thought. Minutes later, she punched in his number and threw all caution to the stinking wind.

"Hey, Hersh-Hersh. What's up?"

"You know, taking it slow, keeping up with the flow."

Karen relaxed her shoulders. She shoved a fry in her mouth. "Hey, guess what, I found a restaurant in Farmington Hills that plays live Latin music. Man, they sound a lot like Santana. Maybe we can check 'em out sometime."

"Yeah, sure. Maybe."

Karen pulled the phone from her ear and glared at it. He sounded funny.

She put the phone back to her ear and said, "There's something I been meaning to ask you."

"I don't mean to interrupt, Keekee, but I have somebody on the other line."

"Who? You ain't never put nobody before me, Hershel." Karen got off the road and pulled into a CVS parking lot, cutting the car's engine off. "Who you talking to?"

"Keekee, you're making me feel bad and I haven't done anything wrong."

"Who?" Her knees felt weak as blood raced through her veins.

"Jessica. I'm talking with Jessica, okay. I'll call you back when I'm off."

"Don't bother," Karen snapped. "I ain't an afterthought, boy." She pressed the end button to her mobile phone. Her chest rose and fell beneath her clothing. This couldn't be happening. If only she'd told Jessica she couldn't go with her to the workshop. If only she had shared her true feelings with Hershel sooner.

She watched the cars on the Southfield Road drive by. The tires made a tearing sound as the rain started to hit the pavement. She'd lost her appetite, mystified as to why Hershel would abandon their friendship at such a crucial time in her life, and with Jessica of all people. Tiptoeing away quietly didn't suit her. She had to find a way to get Hershel's attention, no matter the cost.

Chapter 18

Mid-May in Detroit usually delivered decent weather. Women didn't have to fret over expensive hairdos flopping, though Val didn't have the luxury of getting her hair done anyway. She'd barely scraped enough money together for the trip. It wasn't without sacrifice. A much needed oil change would have to endure for another two weeks.

Friday hadn't come fast enough and now Val sat in her cubicle, irritated, while her eyes wandered to the large wall clock. She could all but hear it going tick, tock, tick, tock, as Dr. Sharma ran down the history and diagnosis of his patient. To Val, he did this in the most annoying fashion. Even though he spoke at a snail's pace, it seemed his words came out like pebbles propelled by a slingshot. Based on prior dealings, Val knew him to be a dear man; however, his thick Indian accent presented challenges for her.

"The patient, a 56-year-old gentleman, has right carpal tunnel syndrome. Now . . ." he said, stopping sharp to cough consecutively into the receiver.

One side of Val's mouth lifted in the direction of her squinted eye.

He continued after clearing his throat. "I reviewed with the patient, various treatment options, both operative and non-operative. After careful consideration of the benefits, as well as risks . . ."

Val rubbed her forehead as she struggled to document what Dr. Sharma relayed to her. "Excuse me, Dr. Sharma, are you speaking on the claimant's wrists or . . ."

"Risks, risks," he said, sounding agitated.

Val supposed they were both ready to leave for the day.

"Sorry. Please continue."

"Yes, yes." He cleared his throat. "Post the patient's IV sedation, a sterile block of the palmar region of his right hand was performed with no incident. A padded tourniquet was then placed on the upper arm which was then sterilely prepped and draped with Chlora Prep solution . . ."

Val managed to type as fast as the words came through her headset.

". . . In conclusion," Dr. Sharma said, "The median nerve revealed some evidence of hyperemia. The patient tolerated the procedure well and was transported to the recovery area in stable condition."

It was close to seven o'clock in the evening. The time quick-stepped two hours beyond her work schedule. She didn't want to wind up late for her trip, so she hurriedly completed entering the information from the doctor onto the Lotus Notes system. She included the ICD-9 codes and documented the claimant's medical history; checked his status screens for consistencies and paid him for disability benefits.

She had been so busy with work, that the fallout with Karen hadn't crossed her mind until now. For days, neither of them spoke to the other, even when Linda called and Karen picked up the phone. Karen scribbled the detail on a piece of paper and shoved it under the bathroom door while Val sat on the toilet. Karen still angered her and calling didn't make sense if it led to another blowup. By the time Val sped away in her car, traffic had smoothed out. The red lights changed to green before she needed to touch her brakes. Her spirits were filled with hope and happiness as she hummed a made-up melody. Even the two cell phone calls from creditors threatening to wreck her already ruined credit didn't put out her fire of feeling alive. The last time she felt this happy lasted only a day, but nonetheless, she enjoyed her time with Brady.

On many occasions she wanted to pick up the phone and say, "Look, I was tripping. Can you forgive me? Can we start over?" Val simply couldn't face the rejection. He probably would in turn, throw a few choice words her way and tell her to jump off a cliff. He'd been one of the nicest men she'd probably met, ever. She fantasized about having someone like him as her husband, a thought she had entertained as of late.

The drive normally took her twenty minutes, but Val made it home and in her front door in thirteen. The house appeared undisturbed. She entered the den and placed her hand on top of the TV. Then she checked upstairs for Karen. She stopped by the edge of her dresser, hesitant upon entering sacred territory. Val looked about the items on her dresser. Placed haphazardly were a pack of cigarettes, gum, pictures of Mama and even Hershel when he'd posed for his high school graduation.

It didn't make sense, reminiscing when she should have been rushing like a crazy woman. Val released a heavy sigh before leaving the room. She felt bad departing in such a sterile manner. In her mind's eye, she could hear Karen saying, "Val is out-cold," by the time she gets home. She embraced this long awaited trip without once second-guessing its importance.

Moment of Certainty, page 107

Chapter 19

By Friday morning, Karen heard Val leave for work. She didn't bother to say, "I'll see you when I get back from my trip." Karen rubbed the back of her sore neck as she got out of bed. She felt let down, but more so, surprised at Val's funky attitude. She thought for sure Val would have caved and begged for forgiveness regarding her poor behavior.

Stretching a sluggish arm to the ceiling, Karen yawned then scratched her left butt cheek. While in the bathroom, she began to snicker at her reflection in the mirror. *Mirrors don't lie.* She looked like death made an early stop. Sleep lines had welted her cheek like someone took a leather strap to it. Her laughter died out when she washed her face with water and used Val's special moisturizing lotion out of spite.

Perhaps Val's departure for a few days would be in her best interest. She could snoop around in peace for Mama's letter without explanation. That was the last thing Karen wanted Val nosing about. Right before she decided to blow dry her hair, she thought about two new places in the attic that she overlooked weeks prior. She'd explore those spots, plus the hall closet with the vacuum cleaner when she returned from work. The letter had to turn up sooner or later.

Karen practically started talking before she'd fully entered Ms. Blout's room. "I'm sorry, Ms. Blout. I ain't gon' be able to read to you tonight . . ." What she wanted more than anything was to go home, cut on the TV and call Hershel. She needed to share her feelings and let him know she appreciated him. And of course, gossip about Val's foolishness. Ms. Blout sat on her bed with a book in her lap and her cane extended out, tapping the center of the corner chair.

"Sit. I'm ready."

Karen's shoulders rounded. All week, she'd managed to avoid reading to the old woman. Now she felt stuck. "Oh, Ms. Blout. I don't know what I'm going to do with you." Karen let loose a weary smile. "Okay so what am I reading first?" she asked, making her way to the corner chair.

"History, dear. Let's start with this one." Ms. Blout raised the large book off her lap and handed it to her. Karen had to stand from the chair because Ms. Blout's reach came up short. She flipped through the pages in silence, still wishing she'd backed out.

"I didn't say look at the pictures. You're supposed to start reading."

Karen's eyes bucked. "Ms. Blout. What did I say? Be nice or I'm leavin'."

She eyed the old woman who nodded in two quick successions then stroked her cane as if it were responsible for the rude comment.

Karen sighed then adjusted her backside in the comfortable chair and began reading. "It was believed that George Washington Carver was born in 1864 in Diamond, Missouri to parents who were slaves." Karen groaned, thinking that the old woman was buggin' for wanting her to read a history book.

"Stuck on a word?" Ms. Blout asked.

"Noooo." Karen allowed the word to hang in the air. "This is boring. Don't you have some Terry McMillan or somethin'?"

"Continue, please." Ms. Blout sat looking out the window.

Karen continued on, squirming now and then as she read. ". . . he went on to obtain a master's degree in science. In 1896, in the state of Alabama, he headed the Department of Agriculture at Tuskegee Institute."

After nearly an hour, Karen closed the book. A slight curiosity swayed her to glance over the cover and the back of the book. "Well, I'm done." She peered over at Ms. Blout who stared out the window as though her thoughts extended beyond the words read to her. "Ms. Blout, did you hear me?"

"Yes, I did."

Karen would never admit it, but she had found the book rather interesting. She placed it gently on the desk before speaking. "Ms. Blout. I'm gon' leave now. I gotta get home."

Ms. Blout, whose pea-shaped eyes glistened, turned to look into Karen's face. "What is your family like?"

"Excuse me?"

"Tell me about your mother, father, and siblings."

"Well . . . my mom recently died. I don't know who my father is. It's just me and my sister left." Karen didn't expect the question.

"What is her name?"

"My sister? Val. She's the oldest."

Ms. Blout tilted her head ever so slightly, looking beyond her shoulders, and settling into a contemplation Karen couldn't figure out. She felt like she'd been placed under a microscope.

"Is this sister close to you?"

"Hah. Well, she tries to be. We don't get along much, though."

"Your sister, Val, does she not show love toward you?"

Karen now fidgeted. She was quite uncomfortable talking about her family. Sure she could run Val's name through the mud with Hershel. But hearing Ms. Blout ask the question about Val, well, now she came up empty. Val wasn't mean. And she did love her, this Karen knew for sure. If she tried to explain it to Ms. Blout, she wouldn't understand. To avoid answering the question, Karen stood and announced her departure again.

"Ms. Blout, take care. I'll see you tomorrow."

The old woman grabbed at her own trembling hand. "Did I ever tell you about the time I met Isabella Baumfree? Well, you'd know her as Sojourner Truth. I was a young girl, of course, but she was so kind to me. My mother was a member of the Methodist Episcopal Zion Church, where she spoke often."

Karen blinked hard and fast. "Wow. That's cool that you knew important historical figures." She also remembered what Jessica told her.

"Yes, dear. But, of course she ended up leaving the church. We missed her terribly. Church members would bring baked breads and crackers, berries and lemon drops and we'd eat after service. She had a way with words," Ms. Blout said, rocking a bit and gazing into space. "She'd get the congregation all riled up with applause; the men nearly jumping from their seats in agreement. Her powerful words would carry from the pulpit to the entrance door. She brought everyone to tears. Oh, but, she moved away. You know she moved here in Michigan." Ms. Blout nodded and shifted her gaze to the floor.

"Oh, yeah," Karen responded.

"She lives in Battle Creek," Ms. Blout said, lifting her brows with the revelation.

"Oh. You mean lived?" Karen corrected. "I'm sure she's dead by now. Right?"

"I'm not sure. Let me think . . ."

Karen watched the woman rub her chin. Her shoulders relaxed as she smirked in private at the old woman. "Okay, for real, this time. I'm gon' have to leave. I'll see you tomorrow, okay?"

Ms. Blout looked away and focused her attention toward the window. Karen stared at the window as well, realizing everything looked pitch black.

Karen said goodbye and waved to Ms. Blout as she exited the room. It came through like the onset of a squeaking door opening. Ever so faintly, Karen heard Ms. Blout say, "I'm sorry to hear about your mother."

Karen turned her head, surprised. Perhaps all the memories calmed her patient down. *Ol' Ms. Blout*, she thought. The old woman acted almost human. Karen tossed her keys up in the air and caught them as she left Golden Walk Nursing Home. She felt lucky and anticipated calling Hershel once she got home.

Chapter 20

High eighties temperatures awestruck Val when she stepped off the plane at the Phoenix Sky Harbor International Airport. But when she arrived at Linda's one-story, Spanish style home, it took her breath away with its clean lines, attractive furnishings and wooden floors with plush area rugs. When Linda showed Val where she'd sleep, she gasped with delight at the king size bed with elegant floor lamps on each side. Val shook her head and laughed.

"What's so funny?" Linda asked.

She allowed her luggage to land on the floor with a thud. "Nothing. I feel like royalty."

"Aww, thanks. Only the best for you my dear friend. I must apologize for not having side tables. You may have to use the dresser drawers."

Val allowed her lips to propel as she blew out air. "Please. I'm fine. You have done all right for yourself," she stated, looking around the decorated walls. "Yes, indeed."

Val watched her friend release a sheepish grin then exited the room after she said, "Call me if you need anything. I'll be in the kitchen making late night smoothies."

Val nodded and lifted a perky thumb in the air. Linda was still the gracious, classy person she'd remembered years ago, sharing her school lunches. It came from parents who'd stressed good manners, even if her mom practiced spreading herself around with every David, Dick and Daniel, as Linda had put it during one of their chats.

She began lifting her luggage onto the bed, unpacking and feeling grateful for the opportunity to carry out her plans. As it turned out, she'd landed two job interviews for the coming week; one on Monday morning and the following job Tuesday afternoon. Val placed her items in the empty dresser drawers in a delicate manner. When she hung her suits in the closet and arranged her shoes, she zipped up her baggage and placed them inside the closet in a corner.

As she'd stated, Linda stood at the kitchen counter, chipper and licking her fingers, after making smoothies and homemade cookies.

Val held onto her paper outline in order to prepare for her interview. She placed that same hand on her hip as her eyes glistened watching her friend's jubilation. *Linda always looked comfortable in her skin*, Val thought, concluding that she didn't possess such confidence. In fact, she'd wished she could get out of her skin, let alone be comfortable in it. Her uneasiness started in elementary school. She became a target for teasing, mumbling and stumbling about when teachers called on her for answers. She was a bumbling fool; Mama had said so. Even though she projected a low self-esteem, it didn't seem to dissuade Linda one bit. She befriended her before the end of third period.

"Everything's ready," Linda chimed. "Here, get that door for me," she gestured with her head and elbow while carrying a large tray.

Val snapped back and responded. "Sure you got it?" meaning the items on the tray.

"Oh, yeah. I can balance anything . . . comes from my waitressing days."

Val held open the door to the patio and allowed Linda to walk through then place the tray on the table.

Val grabbed one of three empty chairs and scooted to the table opposite Linda. "I can't believe you were a waitress."

"Yup. I didn't mind. It helped during those lean college years. What about you?" Linda filled two glasses with a straw in each.

"Me? You're referring to waitressing or college?"

"College," she chuckled. "Where'd you go?"

"Unfortunately I didn't."

"It's okay," Linda's hand sprang up in a light wave. "You still did fine for yourself."

"Perhaps. I don't feel that way with all that's going on. But I'm hoping by coming out here everything will turn around. I'll start my new job, visit you for lunch once a week, hangout from time to time."

Linda grinned. "I'd love that. I can't wait. It'll happen."

Val lifted her face to the night air and clung to Linda's words. She breathed out knowing she had done the right thing. New doors were going to open for her . . . and Karen. Come Monday morning, she knew she would ace her interview.

Chapter 21

Karen fumbled with her door key, cursing the night and the broken porch light for her blunder. She flounced inside the house, dropping her belongings at the door and headed straight for the answering machine in the kitchen. She anticipated an apology from Val, admitting to feeling bad about their argument and her hopes that they'd be able to talk soon. Karen pressed the *play messages* button and connected one hand to her hip. After the voice recordings, *'there are no more messages,'* Karen swore at the walls, snatched up and slammed down the salt shaker in anger.

    She stormed upstairs and flung herself on the bed, facing the cracked ceiling. She replayed her actions against Val's, determining that mirrors were hard to face when the image staring back at you looked marred. But Val was more at fault. How could she react reasonably dealing with a lunatic? If Mama had witnessed the incident, she would have set Val straight. There was no doubt about it: Mama had been her anchor in many ways. Karen used her as a gauge and thought about what she would do in many situations, which in good conscience, didn't serve her all that well.

She sat up and glanced at the time on her cell phone, took one deep breath then dialed Hershel before she lost her nerve. When he answered, she cleared her throat.

"Hey, Hersh-Hersh. What's up?"

"Hey, nothing much. Getting up this wine I spilled on the carpet."

"Oh, that's good, I'm doing all right myself." Karen felt nervous. She heard Hershel's phone go in and out as if he held it between his chin and shoulder.

"Why can't you use speaker phone?"

"That would be helpful, but look. Let me call you back later tonight or tomorrow, okay?"

No he's not starting this crap again, Karen thought. A knot formed in her throat. She blurted out the words she'd longed to tell him for some time. "Look, Hershel. I been thinking we should . . . could . . . you know . . . take our relationship to the next level."

Silence.

Karen held her breath, waiting for Hershel to speak. But it didn't come fast enough and she exhaled in an anxious pant. "Say something, please."

"I-I don't know what to say. I'm going to have to talk to you later about that."

"Why can't we talk now?"

"Because now is not a good time."

She closed her eyes tight. The gesture, to her, felt like a prayer. But she shook her head and opened her eyes. "Hershel, don't . . . please don't do this to me after I poured my heart out to you. Don't you tell me Jessica is over there drinking wine with you." Karen's voice squealed.

"Keekee . . . what can I say. I'll call you . . . we'll talk for sure, okay?"

The lump that crept into her throat expanded, but she wasn't about to let Hershel know he had gotten the best of her. She couldn't give Jessica the satisfaction because she knew the tramp was sitting there listening to every word, happy as all get-out. She calmed her breathing and said as cool as she could, "Okay, Hershel. You do that. Talk to you later."

Karen tossed her phone on the bed and thought about Hershel drinking wine and talking close with Jessica. It ripped at her insides. She could feel the warmth rise up from her chest and out her head. And she could visualize him looking into Jessica's beautiful light eyes and being drawn into them. Had they kissed yet? Karen wondered. The thought of them sitting on his couch tonguing each other to high heaven made her queasy. Or were they on his couch? Before Karen knew it, she'd raced downstairs, grabbed her keys, a light jacket and headed out the door.

Karen crouched down in her car, careful to park a few houses away from Hershel's, which had been left to him by his strappingly handsome *pretend* aunt and mother, when they had moved to Alabama. She stared as if the home revealed all that she sought to uncover, her head bobbing and weaving all the while. She had to know where Hershel and Jessica were in the house. She had to know if they'd been kissy-kissy, or if they'd already done the nasty.

It wasn't as if Hershel hadn't shared his sexscapades with her in the past. She laughed when he had done so. Up till now, he'd always placed her first, even if she called or came by unannounced. They all knew where they stood, as did Karen, in Hershel's life because he made it known. And that allowed her to feel as important as any glamour girl.

When a downstairs light disappeared, she shifted upright, eyes wide and alert. She waited to see where a new light would appear. She blinked. And she waited. Her heart thumbed with the realization that Hershel and Jessica had more than a blasé thing going. Karen slipped from her parked vehicle and with a gentle push, closed the car door. She executed an awkward skip-run up the walkway to Hershel's house, the concrete crackling beneath her shoes. She peeked around into the darkness to see if anyone spotted her before she reached the corner of Hershel's place. Standing still, she looked up at the second level light that came on, which was Hershel's bedroom. She rubbed at her eyes as if they had deceived her. Without pause, she mentally constructed a way to get a closer look.

    Karen examined the steps on the backside of the house that lead to the patio porch. She knew she could climb up onto the lowered roof by way of the awning because she was small in stature. Now it served her well. And that's exactly what she did. With a firm grip, Karen latched onto the aluminum downspout that extended from the gutter. She crunched up her knees and clamped the downspout with her feet. Pulling herself up again, she repeated the process, elated her plan worked. Karen made out shadows through the lighted window. Sheer curtains prevented complete visibility though. Until now, she felt like a true ninja. She looked around again when the wind tossed the leaves of an oak tree in the back yard.

    Karen remembered that old tree and at ten, Hershel thirteen, she had beaten him climbing it. Nonetheless, in order to see what Hershel and Jessica were doing, she needed to get closer. She almost scaled to the level of the second story window. She knew if she leaned far left and grabbed the stone ledge underneath the window, she could make out everything.

    Karen grunted, stretching her left arm and upper torso and wiggling her fingers to touch the tip of the ledge. She mustered up every ounce of strength she had, straining to the point her underarm muscles pulled. All of a sudden, the unthinkable happened when the downspout broke and started bending away from the side of the house. Karen hollered out, frantic. She was forced to clench the fractured pipe as she landed hard on the ground. She felt dazed and shifted her weight on her hands and knees. Leaves gathered in her hair when her head grazed a nearby bush. She spit gravel grains from her mouth and had dirt patches over her face. Without warning, a bright light shown on her.

Still on her knees, Karen sat back with a hand shielding her squinting eyes. Was it Hershel coming to her rescue? When she heard the authoritative voice yell out, "Put your hands in the air," she knew all too well, the police had been called. *Nosy neighbors*, she thought, obeying the officer. All she could think about was losing her job and having to call Val to bail her out of jail. Neighbors in silhouette, to Karen, gathered on the darkened path behind the light. The officer approached, along with Hershel.

"You mind telling me what you're doing out here?"

Karen stood and lowered her arms. She felt ashamed. What could she say? So she lied. Her pleading eyes looked out toward Hershel. When the officer turned off his flashlight, she saw shock smeared across Hershel's face.

"Officer, I was coming from up there," she pointed.

The officer glanced up at the window then back at Karen.

"You were coming out of the window?" asked the officer.

"I-I didn't wanna go out the door, you know . . ."

"No, I don't know. Why don't you try explaining it to me," the officer snapped, pulling up his pants by the belt buckle.

"I, um, well . . ."

"It's my fault officer," Hershel spoke up. "I was with her and I didn't want my girlfriend to know. She'd come over unexpectedly." He stared at Karen when he spoke.

"Is this how it happened?" the officer asked Karen.

She pressed in her lips and nodded. "Uh-huh, yup."

"If he's not pressing any charges, I suppose I'll let you go with a warning . . . this time. Got it?"

"Yes, officer," Karen said. She happened to glance up and saw Jessica staring out the window through the sheer curtain. Neither one of them smiled. Karen knew she would hear it from Hershel and deserved whatever he dished out. When the policeman left, the neighbors bolted as well. Right after, Karen returned her gaze to Hershel.

"Oh, thank you, thank you, Hershel." She folded her hands near her face.

"You have lost your ever loving mind, you know that?"

Ooh, dang, his voice sounded deep. "I'm sorry."

"You're damned right you're sorry. You owe me big time."

Karen's neck shrank into her collar. "Well, I betta' go."

"Like I said, we'll talk. We definitely need to clear the air."

"Yeah, whatever," Karen said, sauntering away.

"Hey." Hershel ran after her and grabbed her arm. "I'm not mad, just surprised you would do something like this."

"That makes two of us."

In an effort to take her mind off Hershel and making a fool of herself, Karen spent the entire weekend searching for the letter. After checking the hall closet and in the attic, she came up empty and irritated. She also decided to work on the computer since Val still hadn't called. Karen checked emails and clicked on sites about rock bands.

She found herself reflecting on what Ms. Blout said and pulled up information on Sojourner Truth. She combed through websites on other historical legends. During her years at elementary, junior high and high school, she either skipped or slept in the history classes, so all this felt new. And to Karen's amazement, she found it somewhat intriguing. At night, she couldn't escape her thoughts and Mama's words, "Girl, you too old to be acting like that."

Karen felt more confused than ever, questioning her path and the steps she took to arrive at the unknown. She tried hard to change her ways and look where it got her; kicked to the curb and alone. Acting mature had to have been overrated as far as she was concerned. She concluded that she may have been knocked down, literally, but she wasn't knocked out. And she wasn't going to hand Hershel over to Jessica on a platter. She may not have been certain about her future, but she knew Hershel had to be part of it.

However, Monday afternoon had Karen's insides pirouetting when she heard Margaret had taken a week of vacation. With Val and Margaret out of her hair, she felt as if she'd won the lottery.

Margaret claimed she needed to visit a sick relative in Chicago, but it was rumored among the workers that she was in hot pursuit of a younger man named Chico who she'd met on a dating site. Margaret even started wearing a longer-length wig made from human hair and had her eyebrows waxed right before she'd left. While Karen rejoiced over her boss' temporary absence, every chance she got, she gave Jessica the stink-eye to let her know she wasn't about to push her out the picture with regard to Hershel.

Chapter 22

Aside from having sweaty palms, Val felt confident in front of a panel of three the morning of her interview. She sat at an elongated, oversized table in the center of a conference room, an overhead projector positioned at the far end. She wore a white, silk camisole under a light-weight, dark blue suit with a pencil skirt that came to her knees. Her black pumps, with three-inch high heels, were also a safe bet. She told herself to *look welcoming* as she made eye-contact with everyone in the room.

"How are you, Miss Williams?" asked the hiring manager, Mr. Cade.

Val sat with her back erect and released a controlled smile, "I'm well, thank you."

"Good. Let's get started then." Mr. Cade glanced at the individual to his left and right. "Also joining us is Mr. Sanchez and Miss Waters."

Val had been advised that she would interview with a team, which didn't bother her, aside from the fact Miss Waters had yet to look her in the eyes.

"You've already been briefed about the position of Claims Manager, right?"

"Yes," Val answered. But the simple response made her head swivel toward Miss Waters who'd made a sound. A belch, to be exact. She looked away sharp, and faced Mr. Cade. No one else in the room seemed to notice. She didn't want to draw attention to herself by coming off as someone easily distracted.

"Tell us about your claims experience," Mr. Cade said.

Val opened her mouth to speak but hesitated when Miss Waters released a chain of blistering coughs, which sounded like a surround-sound system. Ignoring the woman, Val continued. "I-I currently handle accounts from four states. I am responsible for the claimant's disability benefits and any required adjustments according to their holiday pay schedules and guidelines. Of course this is done with each state's regulations in mind."

There it was again. The belch. But this time Val couldn't tell if the gulp was really a cough or a cover-up for her passing gas, because she smelled something foul. Yet, Miss Waters, unashamed and unapologetic, wore a tinge of mockery across her face. Her smirk was uneven at both corners, with one end tilting upward, and the other pointing downward.

"How do you handle tough decisions?" Mr. Sanchez asked.

"We have nurses and doctors right in the department to confer with." *'Confer.' That's a good word*, Val thought. "After which, it's my decision as to how I choose to move forward." Val smiled. And so did Mr. Sanchez as he continued writing on a notepad.

With each question from Mr. Cade and Mr. Sanchez, Val gave herself mental high-fives. She felt she'd passed with flying colors until Miss Waters spoke. The woman's gaze appeared lethargic, which took forever to reach Val's face. Still, she didn't look her in the eyes; it was more at her chin.

"So, why should we hire you?"

Again, Val smiled, but waited a second for the woman to cough, hiccup, fart, or whatever else she'd been doing. When Miss Waters blinked hard, Val spoke up. "Because I'm familiar with the systems and I understand the contracts. I have been awarded bonuses for innovative departmental ideas, which resulted in cuts by means of the company's savings expenses. In addition to my years of experience, I have also trained new employees and I pride myself being the go-to person for advice with the other workers as well as management and . . ."

Miss Waters cut her off with another round of rattling coughs then proceeded with her next question. "What type of background did you come from?"

The question confused Val. She placed a sweaty hand under her chin. Was this a trick question? Should she answer or state its inappropriateness? At this point, Val didn't like the crude woman who had a pronounced lisp and double chin, but in no way would she let on her true feelings. "Well, while I know that my background has nothing to do with this position, everyone in my family, in one way or another, has taught me the importance of working hard."

Miss Waters jotted down notes and looked at Mr. Cade unsmilingly. "Nothing else for me," she said.

Val lowered her hand and wiped away an imaginary particle from the table. With nervous tolerance, she watched them mutter amongst themselves when Miss Waters blurted out, "Oh, one more question," she said, looking down at her notes. "What animal would you compare yourself to and why?"

Val was stumped. And for the life of her, couldn't think of an animal to tie into her work performance. She crossed and uncrossed her legs underneath the table. "Eh . . . well . . ." Before she could come up with a viable answer, Miss Waters held up her hand in a stop position.

"That's quite all right." She placed the top on her pen and stood.

"Thank you for your time, Miss Williams," Mr. Cade said. "We'll be in touch to let you know our decision."

Val nodded and extended her hand. She gave him a firm handshake and did the same for Mr. Sanchez. Miss Waters had already presented her backside to Val and left the room without so much as a nod.

Now she wasn't so sure of herself based on the questions Miss Waters hurled at her. She kept thinking about the woman's stern look, which also contributed to her uneasiness. Val's entire ride down the elevator was consumed with second-guesses and replaying answers she wished she'd given. *Who knows*, she told herself when she reached the revolving doors; *I may still get the job. In any case, tomorrow's another day with a new opportunity.*

Chapter 23

The following workday, Karen tried to make a sharp right before Jessica punched her time clock. She glanced at her long enough to notice a lift to her gait, which had Hershel's stamp all over it. Jessica's hair, loosely twisted up in a hair clip, joined in with her jovial demeanor as it bounced with her every step.

"Hey, Keekee," Jessica called out, joining Karen.

This time Karen dodged her usual plastered fake smile. Nor did she pull off her stink-eye stare. She'd been preoccupied with the fact Val hadn't called and here it was, Tuesday. Facing forward, she addressed Jessica in a low, disinclined tone. "Hey."

"So, I see Ms. Blout got you to look at the books finally."

"Yeah. I'm reading to her."

Karen twisted her neck when she saw Jessica keeping pace with her. She noticed her jaws ballooning out.

"What's so funny?"

"She has you wrapped around her finger."

"How so?" Karen asked.

"Ms. Blout has read just about every book that's come through this place. She just wants the company."

"Oh."

Karen tried to look busy as she walked, but Jessica ignored the body language. And that, Karen felt, was on purpose. It was a matter of time before she brought up the obvious.

"Guess who I talked to last night?"

"The President."

Jessica giggled. "No, guess again."

"Dracula."

"Oh, now you're being silly. I talked to Hersh-Hersh."

Karen stopped in her tracks. She had her teeth clenched tight. She eased her shoulder against the wall of the corridor, right before the room where the vending machines were, and tried to look composed. "So, now you're calling Hershel, 'Hersh- Hersh'?"

"I know, right? Just like you."

Karen detested the inflection in her voice.

"Say, I never got the chance to ask you about last Friday when you came by Hershel's that night."

Whoop, there it was. Karen wanted to smack the sneaky she-devil across the face. "What about it?"

"Is everything okay? Are you all right is what I mean?"

Oh, she's good. Heifa' please, Karen thought. *I'm not letting you know anything so you can have one-up on me.*

"I'm great. Don't worry about me. Just watch your back."

"Is that a threat?" Jessica unleashed a terse smile.

"Nope, just lookin' out for a sister-girl."

Karen trotted away leaving Jessica looking wounded. At least she'd hoped that was the case.

Still bothered by her encounter with Jessica, Karen grabbed one of her patients by the handles of his wheelchair and whisked him away so fast he shuddered, gripping the armrests all the while. She knew she'd acted childish, but it was too late to come back as a rational-thinking adult. She felt she needed to play this out because she had resented Jessica before she took her best friend away. Now Karen begrudged her more than ever.

When she came to Mr. Hamilton's room, her rattled nerves subsided.
    "Why so gloomy, Missy?" Mr. Hamilton asked as Karen helped him out of the wheelchair and into the bathroom.
    "Oh, nothing. I'm just mad today, nothing against you. You ain't done nothing to me."
    "Boyfriend problems?"
    "No. Oh, God no." Karen rushed the words out like a slingshot releasing a pebble.
    "Well," Mr. Hamilton cleared his throat as he leaned over the face bowl. "If that young man doesn't appreciate how beautiful you are, then screw him," he said, raising an arm. "You are the one who should be chased. Don't ever feel you have to do the chasing."
    Karen never thought of it that way. It was good advice, actually, which perked her right up. And from all people, Mr. Hamilton.
    "Thanks, Mr. Hamilton." She patted his shoulder and he didn't even take it further.
    When Karen's shift ended, she made one last stop before she left the building. Something she'd forgotten to tell Ms. Blout. She knocked on her door a couple of times before entering.
    "Ms. Blout," Karen leaned halfway into the room and saw the old woman sitting on the bed, rubbing her arm. "I wanted to tell you I looked up some stuff about Sojourner Truth."
    "Oh. What did you find out, dear?" Ms. Blout inquired, looking earnest. "And come in; stop hanging out

in the doorway." She motioned to Karen with her cane's handle.

"Sorry," she said and moved toward the middle of the room. "But anyway, I learned that Frederick Douglass and Harriet Tubman were members of that church . . ."

"AME Zion."

"Yeah, that one. Anyway she died, though, in 1883, something like that. And like you said, she moved to Battle Creek, Michigan before her death." Karen beamed with pride, her arms folded in front of her. She felt pleased to let Ms. Blout know she looked up the information. Seeing light flicker in the old woman's eyes made it all worth it.

"Well, good."

Karen sat on the bed beside Ms. Blout. "I learned something else, too. You weren't even born when Sojourner Truth was alive." She used her peripheral vision to spy the old woman's facial expression. "So how did you see her?"

Ms. Blout looked to the floor in puzzlement. "Humph. I thought for sure that I had met her. But, of course, it could have strictly been *en passant*, with all of the talk from the elders and my mother."

Karen looked confused. "I ain't sure what you mean, Ms. Blout?" Karen asked, watching her straight on.

"It's, 'I'm not sure'. I'm almost certain I'd met her in passing. I would hear the elders talk of her often, especially my mother. Perhaps that was it . . ."

In private, Karen questioned whether or not her mother was even around, but decided to leave it alone.

"Well, I'm gon' leave. That's all I wanted to tell you." Karen smiled at the woman and left. She felt empowered again. Hershel had called her during the day, which she ignored. She'd also thought of another spot to search for the letter. This time, she was sure to hit the jackpot.

Chapter 24

Val perspired through her business blouse, and not just from the sun's rays that radiated through the single office window. Nerves kicked in. This time, she interviewed with one person, Mrs. Scott. The woman chatted more than she afforded Val the opportunity to showcase her skills. Still, the nice lady leaned in when Val spoke, and at one point, tapped her shoulder in agreement to her response regarding a work ethics question.

When the interview ended, Val felt certain she had the position. But to be safe, she drove to a few more companies and walked in cold. One, she sweet-talked her way into getting an interview for that coming Friday and another, the following week. All of the positions had recently posted and Val couldn't have felt more positive.

After all the talk of interviews and staying on task, it took Linda a bit of arm-twisting to get her to unwind.

"Okay, you've pounded the pavement with job searches, and you've already landed two additional interviews. Relax, it's going to happen. Now enjoy the sights," Linda asserted, grinning and rubbing her back like a protective parent.

Val turned her head away and blushed, allowing her chest to settle with the release of pinned up tension. Linda was right.

Val shouted playfully, "Okay, okay, I'm relaxed. Honest." She rotated her shoulders and tilted her head left, then right. Both women laughed at the gesture. Val achieved more than what she'd set out to gain. Her interviews, overall, had gone well. A new job was imminent. She allowed herself to absorb the welcoming hot, desert air, more heat than she'd been used to living in Michigan.

Linda graciously treated her to one of her favorite barbeque places, *Town Talk II Barbeque* off North 19th Avenue. For the most part, Val had brought business clothes, which prompted Linda to gift her with a pair of casual sandals and a tank top with white and beige shorts. It moved Val in more ways than Linda would ever know.

When they stepped through the entrance of the *Musical Instrument Museum*, and ventured to each section of the building, Val stood awe-struck by the history behind the drums, string and pipe instruments, and how they were assembled. Bright and shiny instruments, which were accompanied by the printed origins behind them, were encased in earth tone backdrops. The wooden floors on each level seemed to play a role as an extended craftsmanship of the instruments. Shuffling of varying sized feet and occasional clanking of heels were the melody throughout the building, as the public walked through, and observed their surroundings.

While Val never took to playing the violin or anything else, Linda played the piano and the flute. That reality made Val's eyes dance as she relished discovering new details about her friend.

Nonetheless, she felt as though she would erupt with the pressure of her secret. Linda's kindness or assurance couldn't ease Val's pain.

She nudged Linda's shoulder and asked, "Which do you like playing best, the piano or the flute?"

"I think I prefer the piano," Linda giggled, squinting one eye. "I feel transformed somehow, like my fingers touching those black and white keys overtake me with the vibrations coming from them."

"Deep," Val said. She glanced at details below the mannequins dressed as various natives from the Indian Penobscot tribe to the African Afar and Danakil people. She smiled after Linda's response, feeling enlightened by the disclosure. In a way, she could relate the feeling to her writing. Coming up with the right word or phrase gave her such a high. She would oftentimes dream up entire stories of characters. When she was younger, she could complete an entire poem within minutes. Now she felt all the more sad because she'd abandoned the very thing that made her happy in life.

". . . Yoo-hoo, did you hear me?" Linda said, waving her right hand and leaning near her face.

"W-what?"

"Hey, where'd you go, huh? I asked if you wanted to take in a movie after this."

Val shifted her weight to her right leg and tapped a finger to her lips. "Um, not sure. Let's go back to your place."

By now, she knew Linda was well aware of her behavior. Whenever she thought of something sad, she wanted to retreat, hide inside her head and away from crowds. Sometimes Linda coaxed her, others, she left her alone. This time, Linda let her be. It was just as well. She had to stay focused and remind herself why she was there. Val also needed to call Karen. She could no longer hide from that fact.

Chapter 25

Karen sat up in bed with an abrupt awareness of the ringing phone. By the time she had stubbed her big toe on the dresser racing to Val's room to pick up the receiver, she'd gotten a busy signal. With that, she sprinted downstairs to the kitchen and played back the message. It was Val. Karen twisted her face and rolled her eyes as she listened. Val had the nerve to say she would return the beginning of next week. It was already Friday.

"You are a trip." Karen snapped a firm hand to her hip and scowled at the answering machine. She couldn't believe Val didn't once say she was sorry for acting a fool. Any other time she wouldn't shut up. Now she had the nerve to wait another week before calling. Karen could have croaked and Val wouldn't have known.

She rubbed her eyes, coupled with a yawn and thought about the letter. Even though Val pissed her off, she needed to seize this time to search. She remembered when she'd researched Sojourner Truth, there were unusual papers clumped together in the desk drawer; like they were hiding out or something. Maybe Mama had stashed the letter in the drawers? But that didn't make sense because Val could have found it with her nosy butt.

Karen entered the den and sat at the desk. She craned her neck to look among the papers in the stuffed drawer. Some papers had rubber bands while others had pen marks on the envelopes. Way in the back and underneath a pile of bills, she saw an envelope that came from the law office of James Johnson & Roy Steinberg, LLC. *Attorneys? What in the world?* She contemplated opening the envelope, finally convincing herself she had every right to look inside the notice. When she read the contents of the letter, her head began spinning with the word: FORECLOSURE. *So, that's why Val is trying to get another job. She's losing the house and bailing out,* Karen thought, as her eyes scanned the notice again. She refused to call Val—getting into a serious conversation about this matter needed a face-to-face sit down. Karen wasn't going to let her off the hook either. She needed to know everything from A to Z regarding Mama's house and their finances.

Like the ease of an old familiar song, Karen and Ms. Blout had settled into a routine that introduced new (and some familiar) historical figures to her. She stayed after work and read to Ms. Blout. One time, she'd caught the old woman nodding off and leaning so far over the bed Karen thought she'd surely fall flat on her face. Though their relationship still had jagged edges, Ms. Blout held some endearing qualities that began to grow on Karen. Ms. Blout, Karen decided, must have been a hell-raiser when she was young. She didn't have concrete proof, but she'd planned on finding out.

"Okay, Ms. Blout. It's getting late and I ain't, eh ... I'm not able to stay much longer."

The old woman looked at Karen and asked, "What are you planning on doing for the weekend?"

"Well, I'm working, unfortunately. I'll be here with you all. Not that I would have had special plans if I didn't have to work." Karen stretched her arms to the ceiling with a yawn.

"What about your sister?"

"Val?" Karen asked, but it sounded more like amazement. "I don't know, sit around looking crazy, I guess. She's out of town."

"Sounds like you two had a disagreement."

"Well, no comment. Let's just say she's always in my business, trying to tell me what to do, who to see, who not to see, who I should call, talking crazy. Stuff like that."

Karen glanced over at the old woman fanning herself with a napkin. She remained expressionless. She felt compelled to say more, hoping to win Ms. Blout over regarding her views against her sister. "Yeah, I don't know. Maybe she couldn't handle how we grew up."

"How so?" Ms. Blout asked, her napkin now limp.

"I think Val was always jealous because Mama allowed me to get away with more. Val got a lot of whippings when she was a kid, and I never did. I hardly ever got spanked. I got to go out more, Val didn't. Mama pretty much let me do whatever I wanted. But Mama and Val weren't close and I couldn't figure out why." Karen sat back in the chair with her legs stretched out.

"Hmm."

"Hmm what?"

"Just hmm."

Karen watched Ms. Blout bend her head as if in deep thought, like she was trying to recall the ingredients to a favorite recipe. "Oh, now come on, Ms. Blout. Don't leave me hanging."

The old woman turned to look at Karen as if her neck were stiff. "Well, my dear, I simply find it interesting."

"What?"

"Through all of her jealousy and injustice she may have felt from your mother, she still manages to look out for you in a compassionate manner."

Karen lowered her lashes as the words became prickly needles. She remained speechless, uncertain if she should be upset or unguarded to the comment.

"Well, dear, I know you must go. Keep this in mind: the best strategy in life is diligence. I don't know who said that . . ."

To Karen, Ms. Blout was coming down on her in a sly way.

Ms. Blout continued. "However, it's still valid and spot-on for everything one does in life. Somewhere in the middle lies the truth. I have no doubt, that this is nothing short of what you too, can obtain."

"What?"

"Diligence, my dear. Diligence." She raised an arthritic hand.

All Karen could produce was a weak smile that slid to one side of her face. She left in silence then walked out of the building in deep contemplation, only waving goodbye to coworkers.

While driving home, she thought on the meaning of what Ms. Blout said about *diligence* and *truth*. It stumped her. Ms. Blout had struck a nerve when she spoke of Val. Until now, Karen never thought of *why* Val and Mama didn't get along. Come to think of it, Val never said they didn't get along. Karen just sensed it. In spite of Val's relationship with Mama, Val did care for her. Karen cared for Val as well, but she made it difficult, always putting her two cents in about everything. Now things were serious. Where were they going to live if they lost the house? Val didn't ask her if she wanted to go to Arizona. She up and left like she was dubbed boss-lady over her.

That weekend, patients sat in wheelchairs and lawn chairs on the grounds of Golden Walk Nursing Home. The sun's rays cast light through every area of matter that wasn't solid. And the sky was so clear it looked like an open and airy room painted in a pacifying shade of blue. A few patients preferred to remain indoors and Ms. Blout was one of them.

"Come on, Ms. Blout. Trust me, you'll be fine. I'll stay with you. You need to get some fresh air. Let the sun kiss those cheeks of yours." Karen patted her own face.

Ms. Blout stood by the window, gripping her cane. "Oh, I don't know. I'm quite fine in here."

Karen had a feeling the old woman would say that. "Ms. Blout . . . now I'm not gon' take no for an answer. You coming with me . . . I have your lunch and everything."

Karen took Ms. Blout by the arm and when she did, she felt the sharp pain of her cane.

"Ouch," Karen screeched, as she bent down and grabbed at the injured area, rubbing vigorously. "Dang, Ms. Blout, you didn't have to do that."

Ms. Blout leaned over like she'd spilled a cup of water or something, except the water was Karen's throbbing foot. The old woman rounded her mouth. "Oh. That one was purely a mistake."

Karen looked doubtful at her. "Come on, old woman, I ain't taking no for an answer."

"It's *'I'm not taking no for an answer'*." Ms. Blout corrected.

"Whatever. You coming with me."

Karen held out her arm and helped Ms. Blout out of her room, through the exit doors and onto the grounds. She squinted as she slipped her own glasses onto Ms. Blout's pale wrinkled face. She'd insisted on walking out with her trusted and ruthless cane, minus the aid of a wheelchair. The old woman eased down onto one of the benches near a weeping willow tree in the center of the brick, circular walkway. Karen thought about Ms. Blout never having visitors, just as Jessica had said when she'd first started working there. Karen felt a bit sorry for the old woman, seeing her look about while other patients, seemingly, ignored her existence.

A welcomed breeze blew gray strands of hair in the old woman's face as she tried to take a bite of her veggie burger with lettuce and a sliced tomato. With gentle strokes, Karen smoothed the rebel hairs back into place. This was such a milestone; Karen didn't want to leave her side for fear she'd panic and plead to go back inside. Other CNAs mouthed: "How did you do it?" Karen raised her shoulders and grinned.

Karen bent down. "You okay, Ms. Blout?"

"I'd like to go back in. I'm not comfortable being forced against my will to be *en foule*."

"What?" Karen's hand slapped at her thigh. "Ms. Blout, I'm not sure if you just cussed me out or what, but I know you are enjoying yourself 'cause I caught you smiling a couple of times. A bit of sun will do you good." Karen placed a hand on Ms. Blout's unflinching shoulder. The old woman turned away like a spoiled child unable to get her way.

"Look, I ain't . . ."

Ms. Blout's head pivoted toward Karen's mouth.

"Eh. . . I mean, I'm not gon' . . . I'm not going to be long. I need to check on the other patients. You'll be fine. I'll be back in a little while." Karen released a kind smile at the old woman before stepping away.

Deep down, Karen knew it pleased Ms. Blout when she tended to her, almost like a granddaughter. A couple of days ago, Ms. Blout opened up and shared a story about a student named Priscilla who had the same cheekiness as Karen. Of course this was many years back, when Ms. Blout taught school. She went on to say Priscilla was a gangly girl, arms and legs looking ill-fitted for her body. "I'd grown quite fond of the student who came from alcoholic parents," Ms. Blout said shaking her head. "In the beginning, Priscilla fought me every step of the way when it came to lectures and tests, challenging even the historical facts."

Karen's interest peaked to the point that she'd asked what happened to the student.

"She'd gotten into college on a two-year music scholarship. Even in that class she defied the professor. It became rooted in her bones, settling in the folds of connecting joints; defensiveness was her survival kit," Ms. Blout said. Karen knew all about that.

Ms. Blout had also mentioned that Priscilla refused to shrink down to size when others teased her about her appearance or her parents; she'd follow up with a clever come-back line to shoot down the sting. "It's hard to relish in a joke when the intended target is laughing right with you," added Ms. Blout. She said in the end, her spirit was cut short one rainy night when TV reporters announced: Freshman killed on campus grounds by a hit-and-run driver. The old woman said she'd blamed herself because Priscilla had left her classroom late after gathering statistical data that coincided with the Civil Rights Movement.

Karen knew full well it wasn't Ms. Blout's fault, though. She took pride in helping the girl from what she could tell. You would have thought it was Ms. Blout's child lying in that casket the way she carried on, pulling out several clean embroidered hankies to blow her nose and wipe at her moistened red eyes. But she'd never gotten close to any other student or young person since then, so the old woman said. Karen could tell Ms. Blout was passionate about teaching, Black history in particular, yet, according to her, students felt she was "a complete mass of ice," the way she put it because they opted to take a less desired subject, purposefully avoiding her class, and the punishment being in its attendance. Ms. Blout said that being liked simply wasn't on her job description. Karen learned something that day: she and Ms. Blout had guarded hearts.

At a glance, Karen watched Ms. Blout head back inside. *What does she think she's doing?* She felt disappointed and quick-stepped to reach the old woman but was stopped by Jessica, who appeared anxious, biting her bottom lip.

"We need to talk." Jessica grabbed her arm and pulled her to the side near the stand with the lemonade dispenser and donuts.

"What now, Jessica? Can't you see I'm busy?"

Jessica pouted. "How long are you going to play these games? It wasn't my intention to come between you and Hershel. I didn't want to damage our friendship either." The bright sun reddened Jessica's cheeks.

Karen didn't want to release the tension between them. "We ain't friends, we are coworkers. There's a difference."

Jessica's smile faded. "Right you are." She turned and walked away.

Karen felt mean for hurting her feelings. But what about her own feelings? Didn't they count for something? Jessica was no saint either. Karen plodded the rest of the way as she directed her attention toward finding out what spooked Ms. Blout.

She exhaled before entering the old woman's stuffy room. As usual, she stood by the window looking out at the world opposed to being part of it.

"You know you could have enjoyed the view much better actually being outside. Why you have to come back in, huh?" Karen looked perplexed.

Ms. Blout turned to look at her long enough to say, "Leave me be. I'm perfectly fine where I am." Her face tightened.

Karen plopped down on Ms. Blout's bed, looking solemnly at the floor. She had her own issues now and Jessica and Hershel were at the top of the list.

"Ms. Blout, why don't you like to be around people?" Karen questioned, twisting her torso to look at the old woman.

The straight-forward inquiry made Ms. Blout turn to face Karen again. "I'm an old woman; I am quite set in my ways. I don't like to be around a lot of commotion, is all."

Karen was well aware that patients with dementia didn't always feel comfortable with crowds. Yet, a different motivation seemed apparent with Ms. Blout. And what happened next surprised her. It was the equivalency to biting into a double chocolate, triple scooped ice cream cone. Ms. Blout sat next to Karen and placed a shaky, vein-riddled hand on her knee. This she'd never done. Both women looked straight ahead.

"You might as well pluck out your eyes because they aren't doing you any good," Ms. Blout said, breaking the silence.

"W-what are you talking about?" Karen asked, turning her head toward the old woman.

"You have eyes, but you don't see. You don't see your sister. You don't see the strength you have within and how great you can be. And you don't see a potentially good friend reaching out to you." Ms. Blout said, looking at Karen.

Karen searched for the words to counter back. "Who are you talking about?"

"Why Jessica, dear. You've allowed the green-eyed monster to stand in the way of a friendship that has the possibility of lasting a life time."

Karen shook her head. "Naw, you are wrong about that."

"There is nothing wrong with my eyes, hearing or insight." Ms. Blout snorted.

The mixed bag of observations left Karen wondering if she should cling to the words or shove them right back at the old woman. She'd never complimented her before. What strength?

"Ms. Blout, what did you mean about 'my strength'?"

"You don't know?"

Karen held her hands in her lap. "No, I don't. Why won't you tell me?"

Ms. Blout eased herself to the edge of her bed and pushed off. She took a few steps toward the chair and lowered herself carefully into the familiar cushion. She concerned herself with adjusting her cane against the wall, then, fiddled with the doily on one of the arms of the chair and slowly poured herself a glass of water from a pitcher that rested on the nightstand.

I'm gon' puke if she messes with one more thing. Karen sucked in air. "Ms. Blout, now I know you ain't stalling . . ."

"This was back," Ms. Blout shot in, and then took a sip of water to quench her thirst. "Toni Morrison was her name . . ."

"Oh, no, I ain't . . . eh, I'm not feeling up to hearing another history lesson." Karen brushed her thighs.

"Everything's a history lesson. Your life is a history lesson."

Karen tilted her head in surrender.

"Talk about a talented woman," Ms. Blout continued, placing her hand over her heart. "She wrote books, plays, won awards, and had setbacks like the rest of us."

"What happened?" Karen asked, muffling a yawn.

"Well, she started out studying English, and then she taught English. She'd even joined a sorority—Alpha Kappa Alpha. But, life always gives a balance of joys and sorrows, the good and the bad. She'd gotten divorced, lost a son, and suffered a house fire that destroyed her written works. She even talked about it, saying it felt like a death."

"Get out." Karen could only imagine how mad she would have been. Once she'd lost a school paper she had worked on for two hours because the computer crashed and she didn't save it. She would have had a stroke working on a book for a year or more then see it go up in smoke. Literally.

"But, life goes on," Ms. Blout added. "She has much to show for her efforts. Pulitzer Prize, Pearl Buck Award, Norman Mailer Prize, you name it, she's been honored for it."

"Wow. That's cool."

"Yes, indeed. You two have a couple of things in common, you know."

Karen eagerly awaited the answer. "Like what?"

"You both were born in the month of February."

"Oh. Okay. That's cool. Do you know when?"

"I believe February—18th. She is Aquarius, like you."

"Ah, shoot, now, Ms. Blout. What do you know about zodiac signs?" Karen stood up, allowing her laughter to circulate.

"I know about astrological signs." Ms. Blout gave a pencil thin smile.

"So, what's the other thing?"

"She's courageous."

Karen stood motionless like one of the crew members on *Star Trek*, waiting to be beamed up to the Starship Enterprise. *Courageous? Her?* What was Ms. Blout looking at? What courage? Did she secretly observe her lift a smelly bedpan without cringing? What? Karen needed to know because to date, she couldn't bring herself to set Margaret straight. She couldn't. She'd promised herself to be different and make something of herself. That meant holding onto a job and trying harder in life, being respectable and all. Even if she didn't know what her next step was going to be.

Moment of Certainty, page 145

      Karen wanted to feel the words, but they didn't belong to her, especially since her best friend dumped her for Jessica. Nevertheless, Karen marveled at the fact Ms. Blout noticed something positive in her, even though the old woman called her a moron when they'd first met. *The ol' bat did have a gentler softer side after all.*

Chapter 26

The night air was thick from the heat of the daytime sun. Val tried to convince Linda to skip purchases of the tickets to the jazz club, but she'd already phoned-in three reservations an hour before they'd turned down West Jefferson Street.

"Sure you want to go? Come on . . . it'll be great," Linda said in a jovial tone.

"Yeah. I'm sure it will be cool," Val lied, confirming it didn't bother her to go out and meet Linda's boyfriend, Daniel. Although she felt pretty in her new cream colored sundress and flat sandals, she wanted to remain in her room and read or think. She had to consider what to tell Karen when she returned to Michigan. Karen deserved to know why she wanted to leave the house, at least in part. In no way could she tell her it had more to do with the nightmarish memories, which were worse than getting a foreclosure notice.

Val sulked in secret and threw her right hand under her chin. Once Linda found a parking spot, she phoned Daniel and sat for a minute with the air conditioner running. Val stared out the passenger's window while her friend answered a text message.

She wondered what Daniel looked like and whether he had the same generous nature as Linda. In a matter of minutes his face appeared. He knocked on the car window of the driver's side with his knuckles. Linda completed her message before both ladies exited the car. Val walked around to where Linda and Daniel were standing, awaiting an introduction.

He didn't look at all how she'd pictured him. Daniel stood the same height as Linda, who wore flats. In Val's opinion, his ever shifting demeanor and facial expression easily categorized him as a geek. However, when she observed him smile, Val knew she disliked him.

"Hey, nice to meet you," he beamed and extended his hand.

Val barely spoke, directing her attention to his likeness of Frank; a grin too broad with teeth fencing in a hidden agenda. Her breathing became heavy as she disregarded Daniel. His arm went up like an usher at the theater, gesturing for the women to start walking.

Everyone stopped alongside the stone wall to the entrance. There were others as well, lined up and waiting to be seated. Val held her clutch close, looking everywhere but at Daniel.

"So, how are you enjoying Phoenix?" Daniel asked, directing the question to Val.

"Good. It's nice." Val's tone sounded like a monotonous hum.

Once inside the club, Linda validated the pre-paid tickets, and they too, were seated. It didn't take long for a cheerful waiter with an earring in his bottom lip to ask if they wanted anything to drink. Daniel ordered a beer; Linda and Val ordered wine.

Daniel plucked Val's nerves because he continued to conjure up reasons to toast.

"To Val getting a job."

Everyone held up their glasses.

"What do you do, Val?" he asked after a long sip of his beer.

"What?" She didn't want to look at him. And why on Earth was he insistent on talking to her? He must've picked up on her distaste toward him?

"Whaaat dooo yooou dooo?" he questioned again, in mocking sign language.

Linda slapped at his shoulder and laughed. "Stop that."

Val gritted her teeth. She wanted to take a swipe at him, too. "Excuse me. I'm going to the ladies' room." She pushed out her chair and lifted. She walked through the darkened club and followed the direction of the neon sign. Once she stepped inside the restroom, she stared at her reflection. She felt drunken fury toward Linda's boyfriend who took it upon himself to tease her at every turn. Who did he think he was? Or was he like that with everyone he met? Perhaps she didn't like him because of his likeness to Frank?

By the time she returned to her seat the second performance, which was a Kenny G tune, had gotten underway. Once she'd settled, Val endured more shoulder-noogies than she bargained for from Daniel. Meanwhile, his limitless sarcasm caused her blood to boil. Every fiber in her body wanted to burst free from his aggravating vibe. But she didn't want to make a scene nor did she want to cause Linda any embarrassment.

"So, Val . . ."

Val's shoulders sagged.

". . . are you dating anyone?"

"Why, you're interested in my personal life?" She couldn't help herself.

"Of course not." He leaned over and kissed Linda's cheek. "I'm just wondering who blows your hair back."

"Don't talk to me the rest of the night, Daniel," Val huffed, squaring her shoulders. She pretended to tune into the saxophonist's number. She blinked nonstop and tried to relax the creases in her forehead. *Get it together, get it together,* she told herself.

"Ooh, booyah," Daniel called out. "I guess you told me, huh?"

"Yes she did," Linda said. "You need to lay off the drinks if you can't behave. Don't run my friend off acting crazy."

Val felt happy for her long-time friend, even if she couldn't tolerate her man. They certainly appeared in love, often touching hands and looking seductively into each other's eyes. As the evening went on, Daniel did simmer down. He'd even complimented Val on how lady-like she carried herself. At first, Val blinked, waiting for the punchline. When it never came, she mumbled "thanks." Daniel balanced his attention and conversation between Linda and Val. Yet, with the protracted discourse between her and Karen, bills, creditors and the threat of losing the house . . . she needed a stiffer drink to help her forget what her real life was all about. That evening, Daniel followed them back to Linda's place. Everyone played board games and had more drinks. Linda insisted Daniel stay put opposed to driving home tipsy. As far as Val was concerned, that's when all hell broke loose.

Chapter 27

The most devious thought crawled into Karen's head: destroy something that belongs to Val. She eased her way through the upstairs hallway as if at any moment, Val would appear shouting, "Gotcha." She stood by the doorframe and looked around before stepping fully into the room. Without further delay, she rummaged through drawers and jewelry boxes then plowed through her sister's closet. Her upper lip curled while sifting through shoes, boots and purses, most of which were probably as old as Karen. She pulled down winter sweaters, tops and scarfs, which she thought were too hideous for a street dog. Papers and folders tumbled down with the garments. *Hmmm, what have we here, love letters? A secret?*

Karen looked through the papers hoping to find something she could hold over Val's head. She came across a letter that read: from Mama to Val, but written in Val's handwriting. Karen's thumb began to inch between the seal, and then she stopped and heaped her body onto the floor, still holding the letter in contemplation. She'd eased her thumb in the corner fold and thought. What did Mama possibly have to say to Val in a letter? Just as she convinced herself to open the envelope, the phone rang.

Startled, Karen jumped up and raced to her room to catch the call. Her phone I.D. showed it was Hershel.

"Hello?" she asked for effect.

"Hey. Is this a bad time?"

"Nah. I was about to get ready for work."

"How was your weekend?" Hershel asked.

"Too short. And yours?"

"Busy. I had a lot of painting to do. You know . . . preparing for my art show."

Silence.

"Did you want to talk tonight?"

"Sure, why not."

"Tonight, then . . . your place?"

"Yup, why not."

Karen overheard Hershel chuckle. She knew her drab mood amused him. Besides that, their conversation would be about her behavior and not about them getting together. Still, Karen looked forward to seeing him once her shift ended. She rushed and got ready for work as though it hurried the day. By the time she'd gotten on the road, she realized she'd left Val's room in a mess with clothes and papers thrown about.

Karen grinned with approval every time she witnessed a smile form on the old woman's lips.

"That's enough reading for tonight, Ms. Blout. Don't think I don't know what you're doing."

The old woman lifted from her chair and sat next to Karen on the edge of the bed. "Whatever do you mean?" The old woman put a shaky, loose hand to her chest.

"Don't play, you know what you been up to. And thanks, I appreciate it. The reading is helping."

Karen now loved reading to Ms. Blout and enjoyed learning about her roots.

"Ms. Blout, I hope I'm not being too personal, but, tell me something about you."

"What do you want to know?"

"Anything . . . everything."

"Okay, then. If you think it's fair to ask me questions when you've refused to answer mine."

Karen knew she meant Val. She had been carping about Val so much, she felt ill, especially since the last blow up. It left her insides twisted. And so did Hershel, but in no way was she about to open up on that topic. "I think me and Val just don't get along, Ms. Blout. I can't see outside myself to fix it either. I don't know. It's all so confusing."

Ms. Blout fanned herself with a menu and rested the other hand on Karen's shoulder. Karen's eyes darted toward the thoughtful act. She hadn't realized she needed it until that moment when she reminded herself to breathe. She couldn't remember the last time someone made such a penetrating gesture, burrowing through her tough exterior.

"You must continue to try," Ms. Blout stated in a meddlesome manner. "Your journey depends on it. When I was young, people used to call me white-girl. Even those who knew I was African American. By looks alone, I'd been sized up to be a snob." Ms. Blout leaned her shoulder into Karen's. "Well, I was the biggest snob, but not for the reasons they assumed. I loved education, books. The more I learned about people and the world, the more valued I felt. I was important no matter what others thought of me. Including my brother Matthew, who'd grown increasingly jealous of me over the years. His pigmentation resembled dark chocolate, while I resembled what most blacks wanted to be in my day: accepted."

Karen slipped her fingers over the piece of paper and took over fanning Ms. Blout.

The old woman continued, "We'd both buried the guilt and shame over what happened to our mother. She'd been raped by a white man. The man went unpunished and my mother dealt with the ignominy as best she could. While I benefitted from my fair skin, still, I was the product of my mother's molestation."

Karen shook her head in disgust. Before she knew it, she sat Indian-style on Ms. Blout's bed, facing her, and hanging on the edge of her words. Up until this point, Karen hadn't seen her quite so animated.

"One time as kids, a distant cousin came to visit," Ms. Blout said. "I can't recall his name because he died from drinking not long after. Well, that brother of mine couldn't stand being played with second, or handed candy after I'd had first pick. He couldn't shake the bitterness that swelled up in his heart. At me. Every instance that placed me first, in his eyes, it had been because of my skin color. He seemed to ignore the fact that because I was a girl, I got to choose candy first."

Karen blurted out, "Are you sure they never treated you better than your brother?"

"Dear, yes, indeed. I received special treatment. I also got picked on as a child and beat up. There were times Matt watched and didn't lift a hand. Even the time a distant neighbor hung me on a wired fence. I dangled there with my panties showing and my dress draped under my arms," Ms. Blout tilted her head back and clasped her hands together. Both women laughed.

"But, of course, I had no power to change who I was any more than Matthew could the color of his skin. For as long as my memory served me, there had been underlying tension between Matthew and me. It existed just beneath the surface, always, seemingly, suspended in the air, on the verge of eruption. I never stopped trying to reason with Matthew and reach out to him. "

"Wow. I don't know if I coulda' chased someone that long?"

"When you love someone, you hang in there with them. If it weren't for Matt, I wouldn't have had help in a number of sticky situations. We all get old, if the Lord is willing, and we all need help now and then."

Karen sat in silence with her chin resting on her palms.

"Is there something on your mind?" Ms. Blout asked.

"I don't understand? He was so mean to you. I would never forgive him for that."

"It's not easy. But, Matt acted out through his own experiences. This was how he saw the world. He eventually matured over the years." Ms. Blout closed her eyes with the thought.

"So . . . what made you want to become a teacher? And history of all subjects?"

"I suppose my initial experience started within my own family. With all the secrets from generations back, I found it quite thrilling. Who married whom, whose husband remarried a sister, a cousin. The cover-ups in the family seemed an endless thread, including my mother's. She led others to believe she was nearly ready to walk down the aisle when her lover suddenly took ill and died, leaving her an unmarried woman with two children. Only those closest to her knew the truth, which in her eyes, felt uglier than the lie."

"Wow. That's a trip."

"Yes, a 'trip' indeed. But, more importantly, my family, with all of its buried skeletons and treasures of secrets, had a rich relationship with prominent past figures. That fascinated me."

Dang, here we go again with the fantasies. Karen heaved a sigh.

Ms. Blout looked up then down, before talking. "It may have been back in 1800s, maybe the mid-1800s or so," she said rocking a little. "My Granny Gertrude worked for Master Andrews along with his wicked wife and their two kids. By the way, I was named after her, which is a name of German origin. That is another long story. Anyway, she worked in the kitchen and often met the acquaintance of the field-hands. One of whom actually survived the Amistad uprising. His name was Djimon Hounsou."

Karen's eyes grew the size of hub caps. Her cheek twitched as laughter bubbled up behind her tightly bolted lips. She may not have known all the facts about the Amistad, but she did know the actor, Djimon Hounsou, because he had a fine body and played in the movie, *Beauty Shop* with Queen Latifah. Poor Ms. Blout: she didn't understand fact from fiction. A single chuckle managed to escape even with Karen's fingers covering her mouth. She touched Ms. Blout's shoulder gently in a gesture that conveyed encouragement. When she did, the old woman stiffened beneath her cotton, floral housedress.

Ms. Blout gazed straight at Karen as if she didn't recognize her. "Dear, if you think it's fair to ask me questions when you've refused to answer mine, okay, then. I'll tell you about my brother Matt and me."

Karen felt immobile. Her smile vanished like a hand print to a cold window. Ms. Blout looked confused. Just like that her mind went haywire, repeating phrases as if she'd never said them.

"Dear, do you think it's fair to ask me questions when you've refused to answer mine?" she restated, yet again.

Karen uncrossed her legs and stood up saying, "Okay, okay, Ms. Blout, let's call it a night."

"It's not fair to ask questions when you've refused to answer mine," Ms. Blout whispered.

Karen gave the woman a sympathetic look as her shoulders slumped. "I think you need to get some rest. Yeah. Rest and I'll see you later on." Karen assisted Ms. Blout with removing her house slippers and helped her get underneath her sheet. Twice, she'd pushed Karen's hand away, irritated by her touch.

Karen would make note of tonight's incident to Dr. Rampart. As she turned out Ms. Blout's light, she wondered if the old woman needed to be taken off Razadyne and put on a different drug.

Once Karen logged her notes and left the nursing home, she drove home deep in thought without the radio blaring; just silence, except for the rattling sound under her car. She tallied up the events of the day, wondering what happened to Ms. Blout's brother. Was he still alive? And if so, why didn't he visit? So many thoughts hurled her way from Ms. Blout, to Val, with everything in between. She nearly ran a stop-sign, but spied a police officer on a side street practically panting with anticipation for some sucker-motorist to break the law. She obediently looked left, right and left again before proceeding to her street. Once she pulled into the driveway she released a weighty sigh. She couldn't wait to see Hershel.

Chapter 28

With few glitches, Val managed to avoid Daniel. Not only did he stay over Friday night after they'd gone to the jazz club, but he ended up hanging around the entire weekend and into the following week. Val wondered if Daniel's deliberate act had been to unsettle her. Nonetheless, she remained in her room most of the time and busied herself with articles from old magazines and TV reruns. Even when Linda asked her to join them for a game of cards or pizza, she declined replying, "Maybe later," as her go-to excuse. At one point, Daniel banged on her bedroom door like he was a law enforcement agent. He yelled out in his usual playful and annoying tone, "Open up woman, come outta' there." Right after, Val heard a pop then Linda's voice cautioning, "Stop it," and that was that. They'd both let her be.

Val lay in bed, comforted by the cool air circulating the room and cocooning her body. Her lazy lids blinked at the white ceiling until she twisted to glance down at the clock next to the floor lamp. Val squinted, disbelieving she had fifteen minutes to get ready for her interview. That meant she needed to brush her teeth, shower, get dressed, comb her hair and have her foot on the gas pedal ready to drive off in order to give herself sufficient time. How did she oversleep? Did she forget to set the alarm? Perhaps she could call and reschedule the interview? But what if that wasn't possible? She didn't want to blow her chance altogether.

  Val spun out of bed and slid each foot into a slipper. She grabbed the necessary toiletries and raced to the bathroom across the hall. Recognizing her urge to pee, she dashed to the toilet which was enclosed by another door within the bathroom. Val couldn't urinate fast enough as she panted while getting ready. She flushed then stepped out of her nightie. But when she opened the door to shower, to her horror, Daniel stood there, eyes bulging at her. She was naked as a store bought turkey. He held a pack of razor blades that Val guessed he retrieved from an opened drawer.

  She went wild, arms flapping and ashy legs kicking. "What are you doing? Get out!" she yelled.

  Daniel laughed as he raised one knee and bent his back against the blows. "Whoa. Look what I stumbled upon," He said, hooting.

  Val crossed each hand under her armpits while crossing her legs. "I want you to leave," She yelled again, hoping to summon Linda.

  "Okay, okay. This was an honest mistake, you know," he said with his hands positioned in surrender, still holding the item. He remained mobile, staring at her crotch.

  "Yeah, I bet. So why are you still in here?" Val's heart palpitated. Was he going to try something? For a second, she thought to retreat back into the water closet. No way would she give him the chance to violate her. She reached for a glass jar on the counter with Q-tips inside and slammed it to the side of his head, shattering glass everywhere. Daniel looked stunned and dropped the razor blades. He wiped dripping blood from his cut ear and looked at her with wide eyes.

"You are nuts."

"Get out!" she bellowed and stomped her foot. She pushed him toward the door until he staggered out. His departure allowed her to slam the door shut. She leaned against the door then slid to the floor. With all the commotion, her hair rollers fell loose from her head and her broken costume ring cracked further with glass pieces shattering onto the counter and basin. She stared at her hand and began to rock, tears streaking her face. For the life of her, she didn't understand why Daniel would do such a thing. She tried to keep the peace, and her distance. Yet, he went out of his way to antagonize her. And where was Linda? And more importantly, how would she break the news about Daniel? Val held herself tight and thought about Brady and how gentlemanlike he had treated her and knew in her heart, Daniel couldn't reach that status if he'd sold his soul.

Chapter 29

Karen put on her cutest workout outfit, a sleeveless orange and purple striped top trimmed in black, made with a blend of polyester and spandex. She placed her hands on her hips and twisted left then right as she admired herself in the full-length mirror. Her form-fitting black pants landed below her waistline and ended above her knees. Her hair was freshly blown out, subtle highlights of brown and auburn popped, especially in the sunlight. Of course Hershel wouldn't be able to notice with the dim lighting throughout the house. And after three coats of Sheer Cherry lip gloss, her lips shimmered.

She didn't have time to clean up the mess she had made in Val's room earlier that day. Seeing Hershel took priority. Besides, she had all the time she needed to clean up. Val wouldn't know a thing. Karen checked her cell phone as well as the house phone. Nothing. She called Hershel and received his voice mail. She figured he had already left the house, but after an hour went by, she became spitting mad, knowing full well Jessica had everything to do with his nonappearance. She didn't understand his insensitivity even if Jessica had been the cause.

Karen decided to go by Hershel's house and tell him off. In any event, he'd be able to see how cute she looked. In a matter of minutes, she had zoomed out of the house, started the engine and sped off. Heading east, she drove down to Orchard Drive until she came to Finmore Street. Karen bit into her bottom lip as her car's speed slowed, mimicking her hesitation. But when she neared Hershel's colonial house, she saw his smoky gray Grand Cherokee coming from the opposite direction and pulling into the driveway. Karen gasped when she spied Hershel exit the vehicle and walk to the passenger's side. It was Jessica. Karen's brown face turned varying shades of red.

"W-What da . . ." She stopped her car four houses from Hershel's. Her knuckles were now white from gripping the steering wheel, and her emotions were flying off like a bottle rocket. She couldn't believe her eyes. Hershel grabbed Jessica's shoulders as if she were too weak to walk on her own. The lump in Karen's throat amplified. She felt the blood rush to her head as she turned off the car's engine, and pulled the keys from the ignition, realizing she'd played out a similar scene days ago. Karen stared down at the largest key she had out of the keys on her key ring, some of which she didn't know what they were for and placed the key tightly between her first and second finger.

An old man in the house she'd parked in front of started peeking between tattered horizontal blinds. He probably thought she was there for him. She knew, without a doubt, she planned to key Hershel's car. Even though nighttime had fallen, Karen feared being spotted and worse, apprehended by the police. Even so, she couldn't stop herself and continued to step from her vehicle. From a near twenty feet distance, her car's knocking noises cried out like a baby bawling after its mother. She looked straight ahead, her jaw gritted so tight she started grinding her teeth. She moved with care up toward Hershel's jeep, although she stalled once she stood next to the vehicle. Her racing thoughts now puttered. She stared at the shiny chrome and checked out her shadowy reflection in the paint. It was his fault, she convinced herself. He should have shown up or called.

    Karen glanced at Hershel's house through narrowed eyes, but widened them as she faced his vehicle. She stood by the back tire of the driver's side, and without another thought, pressed the key into the metallic paint as hard as she could. A razor-thin line extended from the back to the front. Afterwards, she moved around to the passenger's side to complete the process. She walked away like the cool characters did in the movie *Takers*. The scene captured a large explosion going off in the background while Idris Elba and his crew walked toward the camera, never looking back. Well . . . Idris did, but he looked cool when he did it.

From afar, Karen watched Hershel stop cold at the top concrete step of his porch. Jessica, who walked close behind, bumped him. In truth, Karen had sat in her car for three hours into the night, waiting to see if and when Jessica would leave. Karen snickered with mischievous delight, witnessing Hershel's hands spring up to his head. When he began walking like he'd slipped into a trance, she knew he saw his car's conversion, courtesy of a nearby lamppost. He began pointing feebly at his vehicle.

    She imagined what they were saying even though she couldn't hear them. To add to the hysteria, a neighbor's German shepherd started barking while being walked by its owner. The dog sprang at Hershel against the pull of his thin leash. He looked as if he could have torn a chunk of flesh off and spit it out. Hershel, that is . . . biting the dog. He looked about scratching his head while Karen ducked for cover. After they left together, she drove to Palmer Park.

    Late night joggers appeared at peace with the world as they glided with the rhythm of their own bodies, passing expansive sweeps of green grass and elderly maple and oak trees with earned rings of wisdom on them.

Karen sat in her car in the parking lot watching a woman with a ponytail gear up with stretches and knee-bends. She stepped in place on the gravel while clamping her headset over her ears, and then gracefully took off running, her hair swishing left and right.

Karen's eyelids lowered like a kitten fighting to stay awake. But, she was far from sleepy. She regretted her actions and couldn't remove the guilt from her mind, her flesh. The presence of *it* filled the air in her car. Why did she do it? She cared deeply for Hershel, although her actions revealed otherwise; a contradiction, an oxymoron. It was like listening to church music and watching porn. Karen didn't know how to make this right. She'd done some mean things in her life, but this, by far, was the lowest. Her cell phone rang. She allowed her head to fall against the headrest. It was Hershel.

Chapter 30

Val refused to move from the floor with broken glass. She'd slipped back into her nightgown and remained in the same spot until Linda's calming voice came through.

"That you?" Val called out. Confused and afraid, she hated the way she felt.

"Yeah. Who else silly," Linda said, her head pressed against the door.

The joke flew over Val's head as she lifted from the floor and cracked the door open. Linda's one eye came into view. "I think I'm going to pack up today and head back home."

"I heard what happened. Let's talk, okay," Linda said. "Can I come in?"

Emotions swelled in Val's throat. "Sure. Come in."

The startled look on Linda's face exposed her apparent shock; towels and decorative soaps scattered about the counter, in addition to broken glass everywhere. That's how Val took it as she watched her friend tiptoe across the floor. She stood near the shower stall and asked, "Are you okay?"

"Yes, I-I'll be fine," Val replied.

"Don't lie to me. I know you're shaken."

Val cried into her palms. "Why did he do it? Why was he trying to hurt me?" Her mumbled voice quivered.

Linda inched over to her friend and hugged her trembling shoulders tight. "He wasn't trying to hurt you. I don't know why Daniel behaves like a child at times. But that's his way. He really is a good person. And he is truly . . . truly sorry."

Linda pulled back from Val, tilting her head.

Val's sobs subsided. "Yeah, I bet."

"No, really. He said so, over and over before he left to get stitches for his ear."

Val's mouth fell open. She didn't mean to send the man to the hospital. But before she could say so, Linda's hand stopped her.

"It's not as bad as it sounds. And frankly, Daniel had it coming with the way he plays around. Not everyone can handle him." She rubbed Val's shoulder.

"I became afraid is all."

"I know. It's going to work out. I want you to stay, though. Daniel won't come around until you leave. I threatened him if he disobeys."

"What did you say?" Val asked.

"I told him I wouldn't give him any for a month."

Val sniffed hard but a slight giggle arose. She turned and sat on the side of the tub.

Linda laughed, too. She tiptoed over to the counter and snatched up a couple of tissues. Careful with her steps, Linda handed the Kleenex to Val.

"Thanks."

"Sure. Before one of us gets hurt, let me get this up." She opened a bottom cabinet and pulled out a blue, miniature broom and dustpan and began sweeping up the glass. Val stood and tossed her tissue in the trash, after which she retrieved the dustpan from Linda, lifting it at an angle on the floor. When they were done cleaning all the surfaces, they left the bathroom and strode to the kitchen.

Linda prepared them both steak sandwiches with fried potatoes. Val sat at the kitchen table, as Linda cooked, wondering how she would disclose her ongoing plans to leave. It seemed her arrangements faltered. She second guessed the successes of her interviews and her stay with her best friend presented a problem. Although Val had to admit she enjoyed sightseeing highlights of the city. Yet, the fun couldn't stand up against the weight of her guilt. This trip was about finding a job, not pleasure.

Val flared her nostrils with the aroma of fried onions over sizzled meat. Linda slid in the chair across from her and grabbed the salt shaker. She seasoned her fries with light, even jiggles. She repeated the process with the pepper.

Val looked down at her plate and released an eager smile. "Umm, smells good. I can feel the pounds coming on."

"Please. You have a nice figure. You should show it off more."

Val gave an appreciative grin as she shifted her hips and lifted her sandwich. She didn't have an appetite but bit into the meat anyway so Linda wouldn't feel awkward.

"So, how's it going with you and Karen?" Linda asked.

Val took a finger and dabbed at the side of her mouth. "Not good. She doesn't understand why I want to move out of Mama's house and live somewhere else."

"Wow. It's probably a lot for her to take in; dealing with the death of her grandmother, finding out you're her real mother, and now this. That's a punch in the gut for anyone."

Val laid her sandwich down with ease and cocked her head. She knew the subject would come up. Yet, she didn't want to talk about it.

"Uh, oh. What? What's that look for?" Linda asked.

Val's chest rose and fell with the release of a heavy sigh. "Yes and no."

"What does that mean?"

"Yes, it is a lot to take in, but no, she doesn't know that I'm her mother. I just can't bring myself to tell her."

"What? You haven't told her? Why not?"

Val's head snapped to attention when Linda's words climbed with indignation. This had been the first time she'd done that since their union from childhood. Now Val felt defensive and wondered if she could justify her actions.

"Look, I'm not sure if it's a good idea for Karen to know I'm her mother."

"A lie, no matter how painful is never good to keep."

"Well, this is my lie and I'm keeping it, okay?" Val pounded her fist into her opened hand.

Linda swallowed her last bite and said, "Val, dear, I'm not trying to come down on you, but Karen has a right to know the truth."

Val welled up again and her voice shook when she blurted out, "I'm not too keen on bringing up the past, especially when it involves something horrible I'd been involved in."

"Oh no, no. She would understand it wasn't your fault. Anyone in their right mind would. You shouldn't be so hard on yourself, Val. At some point, you need to forgive yourself. Why not start now?" Linda's right elbow rested on the table while her hand supported her chin. This time, she seemed to ignore Val's tears.

Val knew in her heart, she wouldn't tell Karen; nor could she forgive herself. It was the reason she'd stopped praying to God and the basis she no longer pushed Karen to go to church when she herself shunned entering the walls of worship. Val stood, her chair sliding away from the back of her legs. "Look, I better get packing. I suppose I should start heading back home."

Linda sprang up and folded her arms. "I don't believe you. You're punking out."

At first Val shook her head. After a moment, she knew their lips had favored the term many times when they were children. Not 'punking out' meant enduring sissy tests, holding your breath under water and standing up to school bullies.

"I'm not," Val responded.

"I don't believe you nor do you believe yourself. Like the time Tyrone Adams stole everyone's pencils and you witnessed it. When the teacher asked if you knew who the culprit was, you said nothing. Punking out."

Val teetered, wondering how Linda remembered that. "I didn't punk out. I was looking out for him because I thought he was cute."

Both women threw glances at each other before laughter erupted. "You are too much, you know that?" Linda said shaking her head. "So you'll stay?"

"Oooookaay. I'll stay."

"Good. Finish what you set out to do."

"Just let me call Karen and tell her my plans."

"Fair enough."

Val continued on up the hallway through the ranch home and pivoted to her room. She retrieved her cell phone from her purse and sat on the corner of the bed. As the phone rang, she hummed. On the third ring, Karen picked up.

Chapter 31

Karen cleaned the house from top to bottom, even inside the oven and refrigerator. *Humph. This is gonna' shock her socks off,* she thought to herself, eager to see Val's mouth drop open once she checked out the condition of the house upon her arrival home. Deep down, Karen knew the act was her way of saying "sorry" without having to puke up the word. She refused to answer Hershel's call and that, plus the thunder made her melancholy.

When Val called late that night, it took everything in her to avoid going off.

"I'm planning on staying another week," Val said.

To Karen's ears, she practically crooned the words. "You what?"

"I have another job interview lined up, and I'm hoping I can reschedule an appointment I wasn't able to keep."

Her sister's getaway reached the two-weeks mark. She couldn't believe Val would pull a stunt like this.

"Okay, so why you just now springing this on me?"

"I'm telling you now, Keekee."

"Okay, guess I'm gon' starve to death because I already cooked up the last pack of chicken. Ain't no mo' bread either." She scuffed at Val's cool answer for everything.

"There's some money in my black purse behind the floral hatbox in my closet. Take it. Get what you need."

Karen perked up, hopping off the Windex-cleaned kitchen counter.

"There may be about fifteen or twenty dollars."

Karen's mouth dropped as she snapped a hand to her hip. "What am I expected to buy with that . . . a bag of Funyuns . . ." then she caught herself, but wanted to say, ". . . and some Grey Poupon Mustard?" *Be cool, be cool.* She was supposed to make nice. She shook her leg, adding, "Okay, Val, I'll get it. I'll be all right. I hope you don't call yourself already moved there and you ain't telling me." She heard Val chuckle, assuring her that wasn't the case, but, of course, Karen knew better because of the foreclosure notice.

"Yeah, whatever. This is the very reason why we can't come together."

"How so?"

"Cause you keep too many secrets, you big liar."

Karen slammed down the receiver, her frustration getting the best of her. She questioned her sister's plans and the reasoning behind her trying to get a job in Phoenix. She didn't understand her determination to leave Mama's house when all of their childhood memories were in it; growing up with neighborhood kids like Lenny and Peaches; staying out till the streetlights came on; watching Mama run off teens with a flyswatter for trampling her mums; waiting on the ice cream truck to drive by; popping popcorn late at night while watching TV; mastering how to dodge the squeaky floorboards and hiding in the attic.

Why couldn't Val come clean? She deserved to know everything about the bills and their financial situation. At least Karen would've respected her for being honest. She looked off into space, replaying their brief conversation. Without wavering, Karen raced to Val's room to get the money.

She entered the area and opened the closet to pinpoint the black purse. But more than anything, she wanted to know what was inside the letter. Her chest rose and fell with devilish excitement. She lifted the clothing and retrieved the letter from the spot she'd carefully placed it in when she'd cleaned up Val's room earlier. She sprinted back down stairs and into the kitchen to fill a tea kettle with water. While she waited, she searched for glue in the writing desk in the darkened den.

When the kettle whistled out, Karen turned the nob to the stove and held the letter near the rising steam. Loud thunder followed, startling her. *I know, I know, God don't like ugly, but forgive me this one time . . . two times for what I did to Hershel.* With the letter and glue in hand, she climbed the stairs to Val's room, licking her lips all the while. In a snap, she pulled the letter from the envelope and began reading. "I'm writing this letter . . ." it started out, except Mama wrote 'leter,'

". . . to tell you how sorry I am for your pain." Karen thought about the many times Mama didn't understand a word or situation, and instead of asking, she'd make up an alternate meaning. *Oh, Mama, I sure miss you and how you made me laugh.*

Once, when they were at Sam's Club, a store clerk walking toward them pulled down his eyeglasses then placed his hands on his hips. When he passed them, Mama went into a fit. "Why he lookin' at me all crazy like that? Like I'm stealin' something. Humph. Ain't got good sense," she huffed as she sifted through discounted toilet paper. Karen knew that the clerk's gesture was meant for another worker directly behind Mama because it seemed that he'd stocked a shelf wrong. It tickled Karen to no end.

Still grinning, Karen brought her attention back to the note and the next few words snatched at her so hard, she couldn't wrap her mind around what she'd read. She gasped placing one hand to her chest. Her stomach muscles tightened, her smile dissipated. Words began lifting from the page while others faded into a blur. *Wait a minute; Mama was confused*, was Karen's initial thought when she read the words: "You are a good mother to Karen." Then she mentioned, ". . . regret for what Frank had done," that she was weak herself, for not being able to help Val out more and stop Frank from "coming at her."

The letter slipped from Karen's fingers and spiraled to the floor. This had been the very item she'd searched for and didn't even know it; hoping it would add meaning, value, anything, to her life. Having read it now reduced her to nothing. Another round of thunder ushered in heavier down-pours of rain.

Karen's hands covered her nose and mouth. What just happened? Was this some joke? It couldn't be. Jokes are shared for a reaction and this was hidden from her. Karen's knees buckled as she fell to the floor, looking down at the letter. So . . . Mama wasn't her mama? Val was her real mama? No, that couldn't be right because she was only twelve years older. The breath that caught in her throat came rushing out alongside soft choppy cries. Tears that refused to fall for the person she *thought* to be her mama, now came gushing out in unrelenting waves. She cried for Mama, she cried for Val, who was now her mama, and she cried for herself.

Karen sat unmoved for over an hour, rereading the letter, hoping its meaning changed. Perhaps she'd misread the words and all of a sudden, the truth miraculously emerged. But the truth stayed ugly and it made her heart rate accelerate and her mouth water. She raced to the bathroom with stomach muscles contracting and threw up until nothing remained, so she thought. When she reflected on what Frank did to Val . . . it meant . . . he was *her* father. It sickened her all over. He had raped a kid over and over, yet Mama did nothing to stop him.

Karen stuck her head over the toilet as she regurgitated, yet again, the awful reality. Her head began throbbing as tiny veins, which felt as though they would pop any moment, sketched on her temples. She had shortness of breath and felt warm. She wanted to explode. The thought occurred to her to call Val after she'd flushed the toilet and cleaned herself up. But when she picked up the phone, she placed it back just as fast. No, she couldn't talk to Val, not now. With her keys in hand, Karen sprinted out the front door and into the pouring rain.

It was one-thirty in the morning. The rain settled and Karen spent countless minutes trying to make pebbles skip in the Detroit River while standing safely on the embankment at Hart Plaza. But no matter how many times Hershel had shown her the trick, she couldn't master it. After she'd tossed the last rock, she hunched over, staring down, watching the motion of the gentle waves. They seemed to nick at her drifting thoughts, carrying them further outland. She didn't know who she was anymore.

A group of loud, giggling teens strolled by and yelled, "Don't jump! You have too much to live for!"

Karen whipped her head around at the sound of their voices. She freed a snicker, failing to realize how far over the railing she'd leaned. "I ain't, don't worry," she called after their distant yapping. "I won't," she repeated again under her breath, looking out over the dark, glistening water. *I got too much to live for, even if my life is crummy now.* Karen walked away, her small frame rigid, displaying her usual tough exterior persona even though one feather-like push could have toppled her.

She looked over her shoulders as she headed back home in the wee hours of the morning, all the while, thinking back on what Ms. Blout said; she had something special. What, she wasn't quite sure, but if Ms. Blout saw it, she sure-as-sugar was gonna' try and be it. She longed to be fearless. Not like she used to be as a young girl, bad as all get-out, and Mama publically blaming everybody else's kid for destroyed neighborhood mailboxes and whatnots while, on the sly, questioning Karen about telling the truth. The memory jarred her because she still couldn't believe Dottie Williams was not her mama.

When Karen arrived home, she was able to rest her weary body. But only a few hours had passed before Margaret called, requesting that she come into work due to short staffing. Karen wrinkled her nose at the sound of the woman's irksome voice. No apologies or admission of understanding the inconvenience. Karen would rather have stayed home and nursed her sunken spirit.

"Okay, Margaret, I'll be there," she said, exhausted from speaking, and even more drained with the realization Margaret was back from vacation.

"Good. I want you here ASAP. And by the way, I'll need you to work extra hours." She ended the call.

When Karen arrived at work, she discovered Jessica, who'd never taken a day off since her employment, according to one staff member, was among the absentees. Come to find out her mother had died. That explained why Hershel bailed on seeing her and why he probably called her after Jessica left his house late. Upon hearing the news, the light in Karen's widened eyes deadened. It was as though she'd contributed to Jessica's troubles because of their war of words, and what she'd done to Hershel's car. Her head felt light and warm at the same time. Yet, she forced her attention toward work.

Karen tensed when she saw Margaret walk by and glanced over her shoulder when she asked, "Yes, everything's fine." Karen responded in a half-baked tone and rolled her eyes.

Some of the CNAs made fun of Margaret because it seemed she purchased some new features. Her lips were noticeably larger and her face a bit plump. "Too bad her personality couldn't get a cosmetic lift," one girl said. "Not even a million dollars could help her attitude," chimed another. Karen was guilty as well, laughing and high-fiving everyone she agreed with. Frankly, it didn't surprise her to see Margaret lurking about. Margaret hadn't bothered to speak to anyone, and no one bothered to speak to her, let alone ask about her vacation.

Karen and another CNA took their patients outside after lunch. And wouldn't you know it. Karen seated Mr. Hamilton right next to Ms. Blout. *Let him try to make a move on her . . . he'll get a cane stuck up somewhere that ain't gonna' be easy getting out.*

Ms. Blout pulled at the edge of her solid colored skirt whenever a breeze kicked up. Her eyes squinted against the sun's intensity and when she fanned herself with her hand, Mr. Hamilton grabbed a magazine and started cooling her with it. The old woman took a peeved double take then looked off toward the main entrance to watch traffic drive by. Karen drank in the sight with the seniors, eager to escape her own troubles. Every so often, her downward thoughts zoomed in on Val as a young girl with no one to turn to.

Karen gave a weak smile whenever she walked near the elderly pair, eavesdropping on Mr. Hamilton's small talk. It would have been funny if they started a love affair, she supposed. While the idea wasn't entirely unheard of, Karen didn't expect it. She hoped for it, though. The way one hopes the teller mistakenly places an extra one-hundred dollar bill in their withdrawal. It's not likely to occur, but you can still dream.

After she'd walked and wheeled in all her patients, she noticed Ms. Blout seemed light-headed once back in her room.

"Ms. Blout, you feeling okay?" Karen placed her hand on the old woman's back.

"I think I need orange juice, dear."

Karen sprinted from the room toward the cafeteria; however, her attention drew to the main entrance with a

CNA struggling to get a rebellious patient back inside. When Karen saw the security guard come to her aid she resumed with her own task at hand. In an instant, she looked about the cafeteria at coworkers who were congregated in a gossiping huddle, while others ate by themselves. She filled a glass of orange juice then grabbed a pitcher with freshly poured ice-water and headed back to Ms. Blout's room. The main hall now smelled of Pine Sol. Karen turned into Ms. Blout's doorway when she heard that old familiar voice. She forgot to breathe a second or two when Margaret summoned her. Karen quickly placed the items on Ms. Blout's portable tray and grabbed the glass of orange juice and handed it to her. By then, Margaret stood outside the room looking in, her hands folded in front of her.

"I called you," she snarled.

To Karen, she said it with the expectancy of someone who knew the art of intimidation. Margaret didn't wait for a response so much as a reaction. And Karen delivered; enlarged pupils, stammering speech, exaggerated hand gestures.

"I'm waiting," Margaret barked.

Karen grabbed the emptied glass already in Ms. Blout's room and steadied her hand while pouring the ice water. "I-I'll be right there," she said over her shoulder. When she turned back to face Ms. Blout, the flicker in Karen's eyes vanished.

Her eyes no longer had to falsify her mood. The truth spilled all over the floor, exposing Karen's reluctance to rock the boat. She capered out of the room like she'd completed the last step to an exhausting dance number. Passing Mr. Hamilton's room, she veered toward the nurse's station where Margaret stood drumming her fingers on the counter.

"Yes, Margaret." Karen licked her dry lips.

"Around here, we show team work. You wanna tell me how you can see a team member struggling with a patient and you just walk on by—head in the clouds and don't lift a finger to help."

Karen felt her head grow heavy, her breath caught in her throat and her shoulders tensed. Now she wished she would have declined on coming in. On-lookers stopped what they were doing to watch the drama play out. Karen questioned whether Margaret actually saw what happened, or did someone run and tell her their version of events? If Margaret truly saw the whole incident, why didn't she realize she'd kept going only after witnessing the security guard giving assistance to the CNA? And now, she had the nerve to question her integrity to her job and others.

Karen wanted to kick Margaret square in her oversized butt and throw nearby labeled urine samples, in her Botoxed face.

"Margaret, I only kept going because the situation was under control. Stan had already made his . . ."

Margaret cut her off like an enraged motorist. "You don't sit back and let someone else do the work you should be doing. What . . . you expect everyone to do your job? You think you are too good to do your share? If it doesn't fall within the guidelines of your job description, you can't comprehend what your duties are?"

Karen leaned into one hip and perused the room at workers trying to look busy. That's when she lost herself. She had her fist ready to connect with Margaret's silicone lip implants. As she lifted her hand, a rubber tip on the end of a cane crossed in front of her.

It was like the scene from the movie *The Karate Kid*, starring Jaden Smith. In the scene, he squinted and turned his head, thinking his face was about to be pulverized by his tormenters. That's when Jackie Chan's character showed up out of nowhere and saved the boy. Karen's savior came in the form of Ms. Blout. Her tongue practically rolled onto the floor as she stared at the old woman, wondering, waiting to see what her next move would be.

Ms. Blout supported herself, leaning into her cane, then said, "I've watched you bully this child ever since she stepped foot through that door." She pointed her cane toward the main entrance. "Before her, it was Kelly, then Shanika," she continued. "You lay a hand on this girl and I'll go to the Board of Directors and tell them how you've been accepting sweetheart deals with the privileged patients around here."

Margaret excused herself from work and went home with some sort of virus. Karen and everybody else knew the real deal and the staff whooped with delicious hatred as the main entrance door closed behind Margaret's departing and oversized butt. The place buzzed the rest of the evening and the whiff of Pine Sol seemed sweeter upon Margaret's departure. Stories about her lover, Chico, surfaced. According to the rumor-mill, he plastered insults about her on Facebook; including pictures he'd taken of her while she slept. He had bragged about how she gave him money and that she was an old faked-face fool.

When Karen's shift ended, she made her way back to Ms. Blout's room. The old woman had her head buried in a book. Karen, smiling from ear to ear, sifted in some air and got ready to spill out her appreciation.

"Ms. Blout, I can't tell you how much it means to me—you taking on Margaret was cool."

Without so much as lifting an eyebrow, Ms. Blout patted the bedspread and said, "Come. Let me tell you about the man I wanted to marry."

Karen exhaled and scratched the back of her ear. She expected it as much. Ms. Blout didn't seem like the *gushing type*. She knew the gesture well. The old woman wanted to make this a teachable moment. For a brief second, Karen thought of opening up and sharing her unsettling news. But saying the words out loud panicked her. Instead, she obediently sat next to the old woman. Her gratitude already accepted and understood before she opened her mouth. That made Karen more admiring of Ms. Blout, even if her mind was fading fast.

The old woman glanced over at her and gave a gentle pat to her knee. Her thin hand had veins bulging out. "The seventies had been an interesting time," she stated. "Protests of war, Kent State killings; Muhammad Ali refusing to serve his country, and terms like *afrocentricity* carried with it a sense of pride."

Karen nodded, captivated, happy to focus on something other than her own depressing thoughts.

"The students also had their own little sayings," Ms. Blout chuckled at the remembrance. "They'd say, 'take a chill pill 'or 'that's so bogue.'"

Karen's eyebrows rose symmetrically. "Dang, Ms. Blout, you were down."

Ms. Blout smirked, "The kids said that as well."

"What?"

"Dang."

Hearing the word coming from Ms. Blout's mouth sounded hilarious, and somehow, she managed to make "dang" sound like some artifact once used by an African tribe.

"I was never a boxing fan, but my . . . m-mama loved Muhammad Ali. Didn't he have a stroke or something?" Karen's eyebrows now scrunched in.

"He suffers from Parkinson's disease, dear."

"That's too bad."

"Yes it is. However, his life is that of a metaphor, wouldn't you say?"

"How so?"

"He is a fighter." Ms. Blout closed her book and placed it on the nightstand facedown. She looked deep in thought. Karen waited. She suspected Ms. Blout did this deliberately. She didn't have to rush for anyone, not even in her speech.

"Professor John Hope Franklin. Occasionally, we found ourselves in the same circles. I'm sure you know who he is." She said it in a rhetorical manner, opposed to a question.

Karen blinked. She did not.

"Look him up some time on the Internet. He'll impress you. Well now, I'd run into him during NAACP functions, and at seminars and lectures from various universities. He'd even graced us at Lawston University as a guest lecturer on one or two junctures."

Karen refused to feel dumb listening to Ms. Blout, although it wasn't hard to do with all the fancy words, people and places she'd been familiar with. It was nothing like listening to Mama. She'd laugh saying, "Oh, chile, I ain't got time to figure out all those nouns and proverbs and what-not." Well, at least she read the bible, Karen concluded. When Ms. Blout spoke, Karen nodded, often faking understanding, secretly retaining the foreign word in her mental file cabinet to look up later.

Ms. Blout continued, "Well, I simply assumed that since Professor Franklin and his wife were such lovely people, his acquaintance, Sam Rutherford, was cut from the same cloth. Back then, you couldn't have told me otherwise. A man of a distinguished posture and a deep voice set my knees to knocking whenever I heard mention of his name."

No she didn't. You go, Ms. Blout. "Wow, Ms. Blout was in love." Karen slapped at her own knee.

"Indeed." She rolled her eyes like the single measure of a grandfather clock pendulum. "But his heart belonged to another, and another, and another. John tried ever so kindly to tell me. I would stubbornly justify or counter his claims. I made excuses for the times he said he couldn't be with me on holidays or for my birthday because of a sick family member. He didn't bring me around his family nor did he make attempts to be around mine. Meanwhile, there'd been a fine young man by the name of Christopher Rinehart whom I met when I myself attended college. Chris had the most penetrating blue eyes and boyish smile."

"Blue?" Karen turned her face up.

The pendulum shifted again. "He was of the Caucasian persuasion."

Karen interrupted again. "He thought you were white, too?"

"No, he knew I was of African American descent. He'd even run into my mother and me early on as we left a downtown bookstore. He wanted to bring me around his friends and family. I couldn't bear looking into flaming faces time after time. His friends were bad enough. Turning up their noses whenever they saw me or when I spoke. Sometimes they over-talked me and ignored me altogether. Chris never said a word. When I could no longer be silent, I brought it up to him one day."

Karen determined her own ending to Ms. Blout's story; except her version concluded with cussing everybody out and slapping her own butt before storming off. Karen was quite surprised that the young man wanted to date a black woman back then. She wondered what Ms. Blout looked like as a young woman. "So, what'd you do?" She could feel her insides jumping for the revelation, her eyes blinking rapidly.

"I looked him square in the face and told him he'd clearly been obtuse when it came to his friends' treatment of me."

"W-wha . . ."

"I felt he was being obtuse, simple-minded, if you will, as to how his friends treated me, putting them before my feelings."

"He was, wasn't he?"

"I thought so until he stared right back at me then burst out with laughter."

"He was making fun-na you, huh?"

"I didn't know what to think," she said, lifting her hand to her mouth. "But he grabbed me and pulled me close, and said, 'I don't care what they think. In fact, I delight in the idea that they can't stand I'm with a beautiful woman. All I care about is what we have. Everyone else can buzz off; parents, friends, everyone.'"

Karen's smile slid to one side of her face. "Okay, okay, then, what happened next? Don't leave me hangin', Ms. Blout."

Ms. Blout held up her opened hand to Karen, timelines rolling in her head. "Unfortunately, I found myself in a bad way with Mr. Rutherford. I had gotten pregnant and couldn't seem to locate him. I did, however, receive a nasty phone call from one of his women. Through it all, Chris still wanted to marry me."

Karen's eyes widened. She watched the old woman pause and adjust her thin lips like she was chewing nuts. The facial expression accompanied many of the elderly, as pouting belonged to a child. "Ms. Blout, he had mad love for you. Did you love him back? I mean Chris . . . did you?"

"Yes, I did. I didn't realize it until it'd been too late. I pushed him away until he stayed out of sight forever."

Karen sucked at her teeth, shaking her head. The most obvious question hadn't been answered. The baby. What happened? Did she raise it alone? Did it die? Should she dare ask? Karen had a flood of questions. Ms. Blout pressed in her lips and strained a bit while lifting from the bed. She steadied her weight against her cane, allowing it to assist her over to the window. She watched and listened. To what, Karen couldn't figure out.

"Ms. Blout . . ." Karen bit her fingernails then turned toward the woman.

She shifted around soberly, smiling in Karen's direction, but looking at the floor. Karen had an overwhelming urge to get up and hug the woman, but resisted. When she thought it through, Ms. Blout wouldn't have wanted it. She didn't like patronizing gestures. So, she sat, and waited.

"I know what you want to know." Ms. Blout turned back to face the window. "I regret it to this day," she said.

"What?" Karen gulped down her anxiety.

"Destroying my unborn child. All I could think about was the disgrace, my career, and my mother's legacy pressed upon me, even though I hadn't been molested physically, just emotionally." She sighed. "I was a selfish fool."

"No, you thought you were doing the right thing."

"My unborn child has manifested throughout my life; in a child walking with its mother, in a favorite student . . . in you."

It was like a curtain being pulled back. Karen had no idea the woman cared for her like she did. She wanted to pocket the moment, freeze-frame it and store as the antidote for her life. But more than that, she felt grateful Val, through her shame, didn't abort or put her up for adoption.

Chapter 32

Val turned from the opened suitcase that rested on the bed. She began packing up clothes and shoes because extending her stay at Linda's seemed pointless. The interview she had earlier in the day with Mr. Baker, the HR manager, proved challenging. His goofy, fish eyes and stupid grin made him look pervert-like. It didn't take much for her to reach that conclusion. Her responses turned salty. He lectured her, widening his grin as he continued, and asking few questions of her. So, she packed, but stopped when a strange sound came from the hallway.

    Val leaned her ear into the empty space in the room and stepped toward the closed door. With uncertain fingers hooked over her lips, she cracked open the door and stuck her head out. Her shadow towered off the wall as she eased a few feet in the dimly lit hallway. Grunts, moans, plus name praises came from Linda's room. She even heard a couple of 'oh God's' in the mix. Val quickly ducked an invisible ledge and tiptoed back to her room. She closed the door, thinking: *that little sneak.*

    Just yesterday her friend claimed Daniel wasn't allowed over. Linda must've fallen prey to Daniel's despicable charm, if there was such a thing. Val frowned and shuddered at the sounds from their lovemaking, which surprised her. When she'd last sat with Linda, she lay relaxed on the sofa watching a documentary on farming. Soon after, she had drifted off to sleep. Now she was howling to the moon. Val's eyes crisscrossed as she continued to eavesdrop, though brief. She pretended Brady's body covered hers, loving her fully. She never had that. Love from a man. She shook off the thought and like that, switched gears. She had to. Frank's scent and sweaty body thrusting wildly down on her plagued her mind, even though she knew that wasn't making love.

     Val decided to call Karen and let her know she would be home the following day around noon. She wandered over toward the window, farthest from the door and thought about the awaiting situation back home. She knew she wanted to get the bills and mortgage under control. In addition, she knew she wanted to get a fresh start by selling the house. Most of all, she wanted a better—more loving relationship with Karen. She missed her.

Chapter 33

Karen sat on Hershel's porch that evening after work. She didn't ring the doorbell. In fact, his SUV wasn't in the driveway, which led her to believe he wasn't home. On her shift, she'd been able to postpone her emotions. Now they smacked her in the face. And wouldn't you know it; it began raining again. Sporadic thunder and lightning decided to join in. Karen withdrew her neck into her collar, her blown dry hair now shriveled into wet coils. Somehow the earthly wash allowed her to purge when the raindrops turned into a downpour. Karen's drenched clothes stuck to her cold body. She'd drawn within, unable to shut off her brain. Each layered thought divulged a new revelation, which now revealed her poor treatment of Val and how she'd habitually called her every demeaning name she could think of: stupid, crazy, hobo, asinine, weird, psycho, fool, nut. The list went on and on.

    The thought of her own childish behavior sickened her. It became clear why Val came off as a pest. She was just being a mom, looking out for the interest of her only child. *But who'd looked out for her when Frank came into her room at night, forcing himself on her? Who protected her?* Karen replayed the disgusting visual over and over.

Without a doubt, the truth should have been disclosed. Yet, not a word slipped from Mama or Val's lips. Were they going to carry this to their graves? *Mama did.* Karen lifted her wet face to the nebulous sky, a gesture daring lightning to strike her.

Without warning, Hershel's door opened. But, it had become secondary, playing out with little importance in comparison to the drama of her life. Even if she wanted to look around, she'd become too numb to do so.

"Keekee?" The recognizable voice called out to her. "Oh my God, why didn't you ring the bell or knock?"

Karen couldn't speak. She sat rocking and shivering in the pouring rain, her shoulders hunched over her gathered knees.

"Come on inside," Hershel called out to her.

Karen held her back to him, teeth clattering, shaking her head in response. Then the door closed. She didn't deserve to go inside and feel safe and warm, she told herself. Not after the way she'd treated Val. Certainly not after what she'd done to Hershel's car and not after her ugly handling of Jessica. Not only did she feel confused as to *who* she was, now, riddled with guilt, she didn't even *like* who she was. There were too many bitter emotions coming at her. Processing it all felt daunting.

She heard the front door open again and saw with her peripheral vision, Hershel standing beside her, shielding her with a large, black umbrella. She figured he'd do something like that.

"What the hell, Keekee, come inside," he stated a second time. "Didn't you hear me calling you?"

Karen shook her head. Then, to her surprise, the word, "No," tumbled out. For some reason, the sound of her voice seemed unfamiliar. But it indeed belonged to her, even though she'd been forever changed.

"Please . . . I'm not leaving you out here like this," Hershel uttered.

Karen looked away, now sobbing, still locked in her own thoughts. How did she become so small and weak? It made her feel rotten.

She heard Hershel but didn't look his way.

A passing motorist in a rusted truck, with headlights far too bright, rolled down his window and called out, "E'ry thang all right?" He quickly tucked his head in and squinted. Both Hershel and Karen looked dumbfounded at the other, as if they were asked a question pertaining to quantum physics.

"No, no, man, we're fine," Hershel yelled, waving his arm. "Thanks anyway." They watched the truck drive off.

"See how ridiculous we look. Come inside, Keekee. Please."

"No."

"Why? What happened?"

"Nothing."

"Come on." He extended his hand.

Karen ignored the offer. She wiped her damp face and said, "I heard Jessica's mom died?"

"Yeah. It happened the night I was supposed to come by your place."

"I'm sorry Hershel . . . for everything."

"See, that's why we need to go inside and talk. We never got the chance, right?"

Deep down, Karen wanted to talk. But what would she say? She felt too ashamed to speak of what she'd learned. Nor did she want the conversation to sway toward her wall-climbing, vehicle-scratching irrational acts. Twenty-four years old and acting a flat out fool. *The talk* would only point to her inadequacies. Now she knew how Ms. Blout and her mother felt. *The cloak of shame.*

Karen looked away in humiliation; away from Hershel's caring face. She felt another flood coming.

"It's okay," he told her, barely above a whisper. "Hey, hey," Hershel said, sounding concerned. He reached for Karen's trembling shoulder but retracted when she cringed. She didn't know why she did it; pretty much everything she did didn't make sense. Why did she come by Hershel's house and not want to talk? Not want him to reach out to her or touch her? That's what she longed for more than anything, to be held.

When she stood, her clothing stuck to her backside. It didn't matter. She headed for her car without a word, Hershel following close. She knew she had to get away. Once inside her car, she turned the key and . . . nothing. She pumped the gas pedal then turned the key again, and still, nothing. If Karen wanted to be dramatic and put on a one-woman show, this would have been the time, she thought. Minus the subsiding rain, she could have lifted her head toward the sky with outreached arms for affect. They did it in *The Shawshank Redemption, The Notebook* and *Cool Hand Luke*. Karen could have won an Oscar if she so chose to. Once again, Fenmore Street had claimed her relic-of-a-car. She was certain it wouldn't be the last.

It came as no surprise that Hershel, looming over her like a black god, demanded he would drive her home in his vehicle, even though her protest came off as illogical, whirling hands, a bit of neck rolling. In the end, she slapped her arms against her drenched sides, feebly obeying.

"I didn't think you were home 'cause I didn't see your car."

Hershel gave her a direct look. "Yeah well, someone decided to scratch it up. So now I keep it in the garage."

Karen looked straight ahead. She also knew Hershel would find a way to repair her car and give her money toward alternate transportation. After he raised the garage door and unlocked his car doors, Karen slid inside. When Hershel repeated the process, he got into the car, leaned in and said, "This is my AAA card. In the meantime, use it for your rental. Here," he said, reaching in his pocket and pulling out a wad of money. This should help out a bit."

She always said Hershel should have been her brother. She wanted him as her lover, but that opportunity had passed. Perhaps she had been too blind and dumb to see a good man right in front of her, like men were falling out of the sky and flocking after her. Karen gave Hershel a thoughtful look and took the money.

"Thanks."

She didn't say anything to Hershel, but she planned to attend the funeral. Hopefully Jessica would see that she was trying to make amends.

Chapter 34

Val became repulsed by the once pleasant, chatty woman sitting next to her on the plane. Jane Flanagan was her name. After ten minutes, the woman began picking flaky skin from her feet and placing the pieces of dead flesh into her mouth. The woman took her nails and scraped the skin then allowed her teeth to clear the crust from her fingernails. Frown lines framed Val's face as she wiggled her tongue then gulped behind the sickening execution. Grateful for a window seat, she kept her head facing the baggage cart and watched the men load each piece of luggage as if they were tossing trash. When the woman's elbow bumped her, Val turned with a scowl. She shifted, tucking her arm in her lap.

Earlier, and seemingly normal, the woman spoke of her thriving business in real estate. She bought duplexes and leased them out. She too, lived in Detroit, Michigan. Although her properties were in the Dearborn area; blacks didn't normally live in the known racist zone. Still, the woman handed over her business card and went on jabbering about her two cats and husband of forty years.

Val needed a distraction so she pulled out her mobile phone and texted Karen, something she seldom did.

"I should be there by the time you get off. See U Soon, LOL."

Val leaned back and mentally rehearsed what she would say to Karen when she saw her. She had to step into her fears; confront the unknown. Not just with Karen either, but with life. She had no choice but to speak up and do something about what was happening around her. She had to take control.

A stewardess walked past pushing a cart with bottled water and cups. Now was as good as any, Val thought.

"Oh, Miss, I'd like to move to another seat."

Chapter 35

It stunned her, watching Hershel sob at the funeral. He and Jessica were seated in the front pew of the church, while Karen sat back five additional rows. Her eyes fixed on Hershel as he held Jessica about the shoulders, crying just as much as she did, if not more. She shook with nervousness as she watched, not with anger or hatred, but with a sad longing. Jessica dabbed at Hershel's eyes and in turn, with the tip of his thumb, he wiped away her tears. Surprisingly, Karen felt moved by the gestures.

The high cathedral domed church seemed to echo the weeping of grievers who filled its pews. Their gloom inflated Karen's own depressed mood, leaving little room for other feelings. Yet, she appreciated the hour off from work. It was hump-day; the day Val would return home. This day stood to be life-changing.

Wearing black, along with other mourners, Karen observed Jessica's demeanor, her bravery. Whether the persona was true or not, Karen took it to heart and drew from Jessica's strength as she wanted to offer her grieving coworker her condolences. One thing was for certain: she knew how Jessica felt. One by one, family and friends of the deceased stood and spoke candidly about her impact on their lives. Now and again, Karen glanced around the room at the sullen faces, admiring how elegant everyone looked. A different crowd, for sure, than what showed to her mother's funeral. No one wore red suits or alligator shoes or miniskirts up to their hoohas. Karen's eyes watered a tad when a gentleman, who looked a little like Mr. Hamilton, except shorter, sang the Lord's prayer. The beautiful words held her hand.

At the end of the service, mourners walked around one last time to view the body. The sentiment continued as quiet smiling faces ambled carefully on the burgundy colored carpet, moving as if they didn't want to wake the dead from a peaceful slumber. Karen stayed put until everyone had been directed out of the church. Once outside, she squeezed through the congregated crowd as they hugged one another. She headed toward Jessica and Hershel, determined to say "sorry" to Jessica. Hershel saw her first, although he whipped his head around as he helped Jessica into the black limousine parked in front of the church. Karen stood next to Hershel then cleared her throat. She leaned in.

"Jessica . . . I want to say how . . ."

"You. What are you doing here?" Jessica's face, wrung with disdain, was now like an impenetrable mask.

"I'm sorry about your mom."

"Get away from me, stalker!"

Hershel's hand popped up, a warning to back off. But Jessica's brash words already knocked her back. Karen's blown-out hair accentuated her shock. On top of that, her ankle turned as her heel dug into the crack between the side walk. She hopped away from the car with a now broken heel, fluttering her eyes at spectators. She felt embarrassed. But more than anything, she wanted Jessica to know this was truce. She had to figure out a way to make up, not only to Jessica, but to Hershel and Val, too.

Chapter 36

Right away, the revolving flashing lights startled her. Val knew with much trepidation, she stood to lose far more than paying for a simple traffic ticket from the Detroit police. Her mind raced. Her eyes welled up. She slapped at the steering wheel as she veered over to a nearby parking lot on the side of a mom and pop store with graffiti decorating the wall. Her headlights caught a cluster of insects near a creeping juniper shrub.

Val shook her head with disgust. First Miss Stinky Feet, then it took an hour to retrieve her luggage, now this. She already knew the problem. No insurance. For a split second, she thought about charming the officer. But her expired deodorant, bedhead and bland clothing gave her pause. He probably would have written two tickets. When she saw the policeman in her rear-view mirror, she rolled down the window, allowing a gush of nighttime air to sweep in.

"Do you know why I stopped you, ma'am?"

"Y-yes, I do," Val said, her eyes watching his every move.

"I ran your plates. I see that you don't have insurance."

"Yes, I was planning to take care of it this week."

"I can't let you drive without insurance. It's against the law. I'm going to have to tow your car."

"Officer, please, I just came back from a trip to Phoenix. All I want to do is get home to see my family."

"You should have taken some of that money and paid for insurance. Step out of the vehicle."

Not only did Val lack funds to get the car insurance, she didn't have the money for a tow or a cab in order to get home. Her account, now close to depletion, seemed her only ally. It was meant for the electric bill and food. She pulled all of her personal items from inside the car; her CDs, sunglasses, car registration. When she stepped outside, her head felt heavy. She popped the trunk and retrieved her four-piece luggage set. Hopelessness again, invaded her thoughts. No doubt, she was back to reality.

Chapter 37

Karen headed into work after she'd left the funeral. She slipped into the restroom with metal-framed mirrors, brown paper towels and green hand soap, and changed into her uniform. At the last minute, she spied a text from Val. It made her shake her head and smile because "LOL" at the end of a text didn't mean you were cool. By the time her shift ends, Val would be at home.

    Her stomach knotted thinking about the likely answers to her numerous questions. She wanted to know about the horrible secret Val had been harboring; how did she feel . . . was she scared . . . why didn't anyone help. She needed to understand the circumstances involving the house.

    Admittedly, Karen's finances weren't the best. She didn't have to pay much of anything except her car insurance and cell phone. By the second week of her pay-period, she had five bucks to spare after treating herself to fast food. The thought made her suck her teeth. Nothing seemed to be going right. Everything felt like one muddled mess lodged in her throat.

    When she punched in her time card, one of the CNA's grabbed her shoulder and uttered, "Be prepared to give a statement. There are men investigating what's been going on around here with Margaret and all. From what I've heard, she'd been cheating the Medicaid and Medicare programs out of thousands of dollars." Then, she cupped her hand to Karen's ear and whispered, "By the way, she's been fired."

"Get out." Karen stood there at the time clock grinning like a hyena. The light in her eyes flickered. The news almost made her feel better about her present situation.

Sure enough, she'd been summoned into Margaret's office, or what used to be Margaret's office, and advised to take a seat by a powerful looking man. Karen eased into the chair and folded her warm hands in her lap. She swallowed so forceful, she swore it was audible.

The black man in a white shirt and black tie sat behind the desk. The seat next to her was empty for a minute, then a white man with eyes like Clint Eastwood, and a chin like Jay Leno, came and sat beside her. He too, wore a shirt and tie, except his tie was plaid.

"I'm Mr. Cowan, and the gentleman beside you is Mr. Murray." She looked over at the man who simply nodded and blinked his "Hello."

An overkill of *Dunhill* cologne filled the office. Karen was nervous and now had a slight headache with pain thumping at her temples. She swiped at her nose then rubbed shaky fingers over a set of knuckles. Through moistened lips, she responded to their questions with, "Yes," and "No," and "Not that I know of."

A couple of times, Mr. Cowan probed, then stared blankly long after her reply before he resumed writing. She stared right back and became aware her neck jerked because her answers were truthful. She wanted to tell the men how funky Margaret had treated her but decided against it. She'd already been fired and that was good enough for Karen. The office shrunk with each question.

And her muscles tensed observing the investigators' unsmiling faces.

Mr. Murray, on occasion, shifted his eyes toward her, but mostly stared at the floor or at the corner of the desk as if he had something to be ashamed of. Mr. Cowan only looked at her when he asked a question, then his head dipped down to his report. With the exception of his pen scratching against the paper, the air stood dead. When the interview ended, Mr. Cowan thanked her for cooperating; Mr. Murray nodded and blinked "Goodbye."

Karen exited the office, taking a deep breath. The interrogation had somehow latched onto her revolving mood. Not even the news of Margaret could keep her frame of mind boosted. Even though the ex-head nurse's forced departure meant her life at Golden Walk would be a lot easier. To think nearly three months earlier, she hated Ms. Blout, or so she thought. Now she cherished the woman because their talks felt real. Although, and with elevated nervousness, she needed to talk to Ms. Blout about Val, which included the letter and the two of them losing the house.

Heading down the main corridor, Karen decided to tell Ms. Blout everything. How she felt growing up without a dad, then finding out his true identity and what he'd done to Val. She wanted to tell her all about Val being her real mother. Karen had two other patients to tend to. And throughout her entire shift, everyone stayed on their Ps and Qs, as if they too, were being investigated, Karen observed. When she reached Mr. Hamilton's room, he wasn't there; he'd decided to go to the second floor lounge area where the upright piano was.

After she'd cleaned his room and replaced his toiletries, she went to check on him and say "Hello." When she rounded the corner, her eyes widened. *Oh, my Lord.* There was Mr. Hamilton and Ms. Blout sitting together, talking and smiling at one another. Mr. Hamilton wore a cool green short-sleeved shirt with white shorts and sandals. Ms. Blout looked charming in her mint green dress and matching tie-belt. As usual, her short hair was done, this time in medium curls. She even wore soft peach lipstick.

Had Mr. Hamilton made a move on Ms. Blout? Had he worked his charm on her to woo-her-in? "Well I'll be," Karen said under her breath as she approached them. This had been the knife that sliced through the meat of her miserable day. "Well, well, didn't think I'd find you two here." Karen almost sang the words as she grinned at each of them.

They both looked up with smiles.

"Is this young gentleman behaving himself?" Karen joked.

"Why yes. We've been enjoying each other's company all afternoon," Ms. Blout said.

"Well . . . okay then. Don't let me disturb you. I'm just gon' keep it movin'."

Karen departed from the lounge wondering: did Mr. Hamilton know that Ms. Blout was black? And would he have talked to her had they met, say fifty or sixty years earlier? Karen chuckled with the thought as she checked her wrist for the time, but realized she'd forgotten her watch. She turned the corner to take the elevator. It was just as well, she thought, not having the opportunity to talk in private with Ms. Blout. Maybe it was a sign; perhaps some things should be kept private.

Chapter 38

Val turned halfway to see if the cab driver hung around. He did. She lifted her chin at him then turned away to face the front door of her house. The porch light was still broken and a strange car sat parked in the driveway. She took a deep breath, her luggage snug by her feet. Already, her mind raced with a weighty, mental checklist. After she unpacked, she and Karen would chat. She'd promised Linda a call once she made it home safely. And she needed to find a way to get her car back and pay the insurance. On top of that, she now had to take time off from work to appear in court regarding the ticket she'd been given. Her thoughts alone overwhelmed her.

    She turned the key and pushed open the door. At first glance, the house appeared neat and clean. She smelled the lingering scent of candles. Val's face softened.

    "Hello?" she called out, leaning back outside to gather her remaining suitcases. She closed the door and allowed her eyes to wander up near the stairs then placed her luggage on the floor. She relaxed her shoulders at the sight of Karen standing in the hallway off the den. In her eyes, she'd aged ten years in two weeks. After all, she had held down everything in her absence.

"Oh. Hey. I'm home," Val said. Her tone was pleasant but her smile weakened when she checked out Karen's stone-cold manner.

Karen jutted out her left hip. "What the hell happened to you?" she shouted.

Val's eyebrows sprang up. She didn't expect that reaction. The fact that Karen looked her up and down like she wanted to stomp her throat didn't help either. Besides her sharp tongue, Val thought she looked as though she was on the verge of tears. Her mouth went dry. *Stay calm.* They'd already fought prior to her trip. She didn't want to return with the same burdensome drama.

Val released a stunned look, irritation getting the best of her. "Keekee, I just stepped foot in the door. Is this how you treat me? I had a series of issues that delayed my getting home. Is there something else going on with you that I should know about?"

"No. Is something going on with you? Why didn't you call? An honest person would have called. Anything could have happened."

Now Val found herself mimicking Karen's same gawk. "Excuse me, but my phone battery died. So, my not giving you a blow-by-blow account of my trip isn't something I thought would bend you out of shape. You normally wouldn't think twice about this. Look . . . I had a rough trip. My luggage was delayed, this cop decided to ticket me for no insurance, and aside from having my car towed; I had to pay for a cab ride." Val heaved a sigh. "And did you basically call me a liar?"

"Humph. Take it how you wanna," Karen barked, now picking at her nails and tapping her toe to the floor.

Val extended her arms to Karen. She tilted her head in surrender. "Can I at least have a hug? Is this how we're going to greet one another?"

"No."

"No, this isn't how we're going to greet one another, or no, I can't have a hug?"

"No, you can't have a hug."
Val's mouth dropped when Karen about-faced and headed back into the den. Somehow it became her fault, a self-proclaimed affliction she donned more times than she could count.

Chapter 39

Karen twisted her mouth to one side of her face, a feeble attempt to stop her tears. She picked at the frayed, dingy material on the armrest of the chair she plopped down on, feeling like a bottle of Coke after being shaken. She didn't know what had come over her. She'd been glad to see Val. Anxious, but excited all the same. It was the reason she'd raced through two red lights to get home from work.

She had changed into a pair of cutoff blue jean shorts and a red tank top. Then she made sure everything was spotless, wiping down the bathroom basins and toilets, also running a damp mop over the tiled floors. Lit Airwick candles were placed throughout the house.

Now this. Her body tensed and her head felt hot with anger. But why did she lash out at Val like that? Was it because she'd come home a couple of hours late? Or was it the fact she hung onto her words? Were they more lies or the truth? The truth of her life shamed her because she'd come into the world worse than a bastard child.

She wiped at her streaked face. When she opened her inflamed eyes, there was Val, standing in the doorway.

Her bitter tears broke free again. "I'm sorry. I really am."

Val came closer. Karen stood and met her half way.

Her arms flapped once by her sides. "I could sure use that hug you offered."

"Of course, of course," Val said, stroking her back once they'd connected.

It felt warm and intoxicating, Karen thought. She was actually hugging her mother, the woman who had brought her into the world. She could hardly believe it.

"I missed you," Karen said. The words came out weak but were no less heartfelt. Tiny beads of perspiration formed above her lip. She didn't know how to act. She had treated Val horribly and it sickened her to think about it.

"Whoa. So what happened?" Val tossed her to and fro like a penguin walking.

Karen figured it was her way of easing the vibe in the air; even so, she withdrew from the embrace. "We're losing the house?" Her voice cracked. She couldn't bring herself to ask about the letter; not yet. She needed a camouflage; something to hide behind, guarding her from the newly found revelation. Where could she disappear?

"Come on. We can go upstairs," Val said in a sobering tone.

Karen headed for the front door, finding an escape route from her emotions and the truth she ached to hear. "Let me grab one 'na yo' bags. That's the least I can do." She bent down to lift the luggage. What she wanted to do was inhale Val and waddle in her warmth; to ingest her with love and ask for forgiveness for all the mean and nasty things she'd done to her.

"Oh, you don't have to do that, Keekee."

"I got it now," Karen said, grunting against the weight of the bag.

"Okay, if you insist."

"I do."

"Was everything okay while I was gone?"

"No."

"What happened?"

"The usual crap; no food, no money, you know."

"I'm sorry about that."

"No problem."

Karen knew Val was trailing behind her as she climbed the steps. She had so many questions and no clue how to begin the conversation. Even her thoughts made her feel like Porky Pig. *Badeeba, deeba, deeb.* That's the way she sounded when Mama was alive, trying to ask permission to go over to Canada with friends. "Chile, you betta' spit it out, I ain't got all day." Karen eventually mustered up the nerve to say a half-truth, telling half the reason why she wanted to go, giving half the facts. Then Mama would reply flat out, "No." *What? Well, dang, whatever happened to everything's gon' be all right?*

"It smells good in here," Val said.

"What?" Karen wasn't sure why she pretended not to hear her.

"The candles. They smell good."

"Oh, yeah." Karen flicked on Val's light switch and tossed the heavy luggage onto the bed. She also went over in her mind whether she'd put everything back in its original place.

"Thanks."

"No problem," Karen said, easing out the door.

"Don't you want to hear about my trip?"

"Oh, yeah, sure."

Val laughed. "You don't sound too convincing."

"Sure, sure. Tell me all about it." Karen re-entered the room and flopped on the bed next to the baggage and fanned her fingers a couple of times at Val.

"Well, first of all . . ."

Karen leaned back on her elbows and smiled, nodding now and again as Val talked about Phoenix, her interviews, the places she and Linda had gone, meeting Linda's boyfriend, the long talks, laughing and relaxing. Karen was pleased. Val getting away and trying to find a different job was something important, this Karen now knew. But she wanted to explode again. She'd yet to share with anyone the news that shook her world. She couldn't think clearly, nor sleep soundly. Even food made her sick to taste. It was all so confusing and jumbled.

". . .okay, okay. I've talked your head off going on and on and on. How were things for you?" Val pushed in a drawer with her hip. She'd unpacked all of her belongings.

Karen blinked, too choked for words. She lifted off her elbows and swung her legs, almost like a child.

"What's wrong?"

"Can I ask you something?" Karen's heart pounded when Val approached her.

"What is it?"

She stared into Val's eyes. They were indeed beautiful. And they saw her. They'd seen her all along. Karen coughed, then, swallowed. "Why . . ."

"Yes, go on."

"Why . . ." Karen's words staggered.

Val sat next to her and touched her shoulder. "Yes?"

"Why didn't you tell me we were losing the house?"

Val let out an exhausted sigh, which drew out Karen's own tangled up worries.

"I know it hasn't been easy for you, but, I think things will get better," Val said. "I'm trying to work things out so that we won't lose the house. And you have every right to be upset with me. I should have kept you in the loop all along. I was trying to protect you. I know it has been hard on you, dealing with Mama's death and all. I didn't want to add to your problems."

Dang. She told the lie for so long, she said it without thinking twice. "Val."

"Yes?"

"Is there anything else you want to tell me?"

"No, nothing that I can think of. Just . . . well," she chuckled. "Be patient with me."

"You sure there's nothing else?"

"I'm sure. I'd like for us to not fight so much. All we have is each other. Let's try to get along better. Okay?"

Karen bowed her head, staring at her now motionless feet. She looked up at Val and said, "Yeah, you're right. I agree." Karen left out of Val's room, too chicken to further the conversation for the truth.

She remembered chatting with Ms. Blout about her brother Matt. She admitted she'd gotten treated better than her brother. Truth-be-told, Karen knew she'd gotten away with murder several times over compared to Val's occasional missteps. Mama was brutal toward Val. Karen did feel sorry for her, but at the time, and before she knew better, it was more fun snickering and teasing her when she'd gotten beatings and placed on punishment.

Ms. Blout always said, (while holding onto that ol' cane) "When you love someone, you hang in there with them." Val had done that with her. It also occurred to her that she now had a chance to prove to her *real* mother she could make something of her life. Her *real* mother would be able to know that she loved her, too. Karen knew that when the time was right, she would tell Val what she found out.

That's when the idea hit her like a ton of bricks. Because of the letter, she was going to find Frank.

Chapter 40

That Monday morning, and the first of June, Val caught hell as soon as she opened the front door. She had just yelled out to Karen "I'm gone to work" and punched twice at the stubborn screen door. Her eyes sprang up at a man sitting inside a blue rusted pick-up truck snapping pictures of her house. His dark glasses made him look underhanded.

With indignation, Val adjusted the shoulder strap to her purse and stood there with her lips tight before figuring out what was going on. She wanted to speak to him, but he'd driven off. Her narrowed eyes scanned the block to see if anyone else saw what occurred. The foreclosure folks hadn't forgotten about her after all. She hoped for it because it bought her more time to get financially stable.

She thought about going back inside to let Karen know what had happened, yet, at the last minute, she decided not to, but second-guessed the decision. *Am I being deceptive?* Val figured she'd bring it to Karen's attention that evening.

It was a shame too, she felt, because all weekend, they'd gotten along with no arguments. They'd even taken in a movie at GM's Renaissance Center, nicknamed 'Ren Cen'. Afterwards, they had wandered around Greektown, passing an array of tightly fitted stores, including a beads arts and crafts shop, and a costume joint before settling on fudge squares at a local pastry shop. The hustle of the crowds walking in the streets and on the sidewalks, plus the street artists wooing in patrons to paint their portrait, delighted her further because Karen accompanied her. Val took it all in, and not once did Karen complain. It was as though she'd been reborn.

Chapter 41

Something new was in order. Karen's hair had grown out a bit, so instead of her usual blown-out look, she decided to curl it. The new style gave her a softer appearance, the way a whiter smile catches one off guard in the most pleasant way. For the first time in a long while, Karen felt more than cute. She felt pretty, which prompted her to walk more ladylike as she flipped her narrow hips left then right down the long hallway at work, plowing through the fresh scent of Pine Sol. The other CNAs smiled and nodded with approval as they glanced up from their patients.

What she didn't expect was to see Jessica at the nurse's station. The cadence of her walk faltered and before she knew it, a sobering, "Hello," broke from her lips. Jessica never looked up from her clipboard even though Karen stopped dead in front of her. She didn't have the courage to say more; however, it stunned her to see Jessica at work in the first place—so soon. Why would she do such a fool thing? Karen reflected on the difficulty she had working at the nursing home a month after Mama's death. No way could she have pulled off what Jessica did, returning within days of her mother's funeral.

Karen figured she could say as much to Jessica, that she was impressed with how soon she came to work. She'd even heard through the rumor mill that Jessica had been adopted. Hershel never told her that. But, then again, he was a vault when it came to spilling someone's business. Jessica, according to gossip, was found in a dumpster and adopted at three months of age. The news made her more interesting and Karen's ears perked up with hopes of learning more from the head tattletale. Karen squared her shoulders and mustered up the nerve she thought she lacked.

"I can't believe you came to work. I could never do that."

Jessica stared at her hard then answered a ringing phone, still holding her gaze. When she ended the call, she tilted her head at Karen. "What are you trying to say?"

"I just meant that you're strong for being able to come into work so soon after your mother's passing. I'm sorry 'cause I had the same thing happen to me when I started work. It ain't easy."

"So what? Is that supposed to make us friends again? Does that mean we have some instant bond?" Jessica rounded the counter and left without waiting for Karen's response.

Karen knotted her lips but knew she had that coming. She'd been nasty to Jessica from day one and certainly couldn't expect her to drop everything and play nice. The rest of the day, Karen made sure she stayed out of Jessica's way and focused on her own patients.

"Everything all right there, Mr. Hamilton?" Karen asked, placing a hand on his shoulder, ready to assist further if necessary.

He looked up from his bushy eyebrows then wiped his mouth with a handkerchief. "Oh, yes, yes. I'll be okay. Just choked on my own saliva is all."

Ewww. Karen extended a glass of water to him. His hand shook as he reached for it. He coughed more and insisted he needed help using the bathroom. Karen took the glass from him and helped him off the corner of the bed. He reached for her waist and allowed his arthritic hand to rest at the top of her butt.

"Mr. Hamilton, I'm warning you . . . I'm gon' pop you one good one if you continue," she said, placing the glass on his tray.

In Karen's eyes, his innocent stare did nothing to ease what he'd done. He was predictable, too. She could just imagine the scoundrel he must have been in his heyday. He probably seduced all sorts of women from the young and dumb to the old and lonely. In her mind's eye, Karen saw him smooth-talking women out of their paychecks to buy him clothes, fine jewelry, even expensive trips. Aged bimbos were probably kept warm many nights by him. Now, he was old himself with few visitors to check on him. Karen had to ask. Mr. Hamilton came back looking thankful he was able to relieve himself. He sat back in the same spot, even though Karen had since freshened-up his linen.

"Mr. Hamilton, don't you have family living here? I mean in Detroit?"

He brought a hand up to the side of his face as if to say, *'Hmmm, that's a good question.'* Instead he sighed. "Oh yes, yes, I do." His raspy voice practically hummed. "My sister, Martha. She lives in Clarkston."

"Does she ever come to visit you?"

He laughed. "Oh, I doubt she'll ever come. She doesn't want to have anything to do with the likes of me. I burned that bridge a long time ago." He started coughing again.

"You okay?"

When he shook his head, Karen rushed to pat his back, even though she knew better. There was no funny business this time.

By the time Karen made her way to Ms. Blout's room, she was in her usual spot by the window.

"Hey, Ms. Blout, how are you?"

Karen placed her hand over her mouth and chuckled when the old woman turned around sharp and came close to dropping her cane. Again, she stared at Karen's head as if a sparrow had performed a rendition of the Riverdance on her scalp.

"Good Lord, you look like a completely different person. You are truly a pretty girl."

Karen's laughter simmered. She looked sheepishly and said, "Oh, thanks," patting one of her curls.

Ms. Blout stepped closer, squinting like she was examining a crack in a vase or something. Yet, Karen felt her words were truthful and longed for them. Ms. Blout had no reason to lie. Even when her stories were fabricated, they were straightforward in her mind. And what an interesting mind she had, Karen concluded. She even caught a sliver of a smile from the old woman. And now, here she was, this wise woman with years of experience and stories to tell, stood before her, in her personal space, touching her hand lightly to steady herself and observe her new hairdo.

Chapter 42

On her lunch hour, Val migrated to the cafeteria then moved to the compact lounge with an oversized, blue sectional in the center of the room. She sat at a booth along the wall nearest the entryway. She wanted privacy. Normally, her car would have served that purpose. But she didn't have her car. That was another matter she had to check on.

She noticed Bridget Goodall grinning like a fool and coming in her direction. The woman had bottled orange juice in one hand and a tuna salad in the other. Bridget, tall in stature, had a pear-shaped face and physique to match. Val shuffled papers to look busy in hopes of deterring her coworker from coming over. Everyone in the claims' department knew she and Bridget didn't get along.

In the past, Val had trusted her former lunch buddy, unaware that the woman ran back to her supervisor, spilling Val's personal affairs; not that the information deemed earth-shattering. Still, it was her private business and certainly not to be shared with her supervisor. Val also knew, on more than one occasion, her coworker had gone to their manager. Bridget found every opportunity to berate her work.

This happened when Val's name came up as a contender for a team lead position. And because Bridget was tight with her supervisor, and the supervisor didn't care for Val, she'd been discredited at every turn. And honestly, after Mama's death, her concentration wasn't worth diddlysquat.

Right before Bridget flopped her rear end down and dwarfed the chair, Val contacted the bank and asked for a bit of leeway on the house. She held the phone in disgust while the woman on the other end of the line took twenty minutes to read through her case. Meanwhile, Bridget sat across from her mouthing something and quacking with her hands. Then she began chomping on her salad and fake-reading from a leftover *Detroit Free Press* newspaper.

The backstabber made Val's neck hairs perk up with reactional loathing. When the woman on the phone returned, Val switched the phone to her opposite ear, cupping her hand over her mouth and responding in code as best she could to get her point across, yet not give Bridget any ammunition.

When the call ended, Bridget smacked her southern lips and took a sip from her drink. She slurped hard through the straw. Her broad smile meant she was up to something. What, Val could only wonder.

"How was yo' vacation, Missy?" She shifted her hips. "We sho' missed you around here, ya' know."

"Eh, it was fine. I mostly took care of business. But overall, I had a good time."

Val shuffled her papers again, thinking she needed to check on her car. But watching Bridget move around like she needed a fix gave her pause. It was the very reason she didn't trust many women. They seemed to have a hidden agenda most of the time. Val didn't trust men, she didn't trust women—quite a burden to carry around.

"I'm glad you had a good time. So, other than that . . . what's been going on?"

Val rubbed the back of her neck and said, "Nothing, Bridget, just surprised you're over here, is all."

"Uh-huh. Well, you know. I wanted to check on you. Make sure everythang's all right and all." She lifted and squeezed between the table and chair, grabbing the newspaper as she departed. "Well, see you upstairs, then."

She smiled as though Val had congratulated her. "See ya."

When Val returned to her cubicle, she spotted the main entrance security guard and her supervisor standing in her workspace. Bridget stood nearby as well. Even though all eyes were on her, Val still didn't get it. For a split second, she thought someone got sick and needed assistance. Wrong.

"Val, I need to see you in my office," her supervisor barked, then marched ahead.

"Sure," Val said, tensing her shoulders against the angry words. She looked around at the curious, sad eyes of others in the area.

She couldn't figure out what was going on until she saw two large empty boxes sitting on her desk and then she knew. Her head started spinning as she shadowed her boss into the claustrophobic office. They were letting her go.

The company that she'd devoted ten years to and many overtime hours of her life to now decided they didn't need her.

"I don't understand," Val said, almost pleading in tone. "My audit scores are good and you've never complained about my work."

"Well, your scores have slipped over the last three months. We cannot promote someone with a track record like that."

Val's mouth fell open. *Promote? They were getting rid of her.* "They dropped to ninety seven percent. That's still a great audit."

"Not if other workers did ninety eight percent or better. Besides, this is not the time to slip in your performance when the company is at a pivotal point with its staffing."

Val shook her head. "Please, I need this job." Her hands were clasped in her lap. "I just have a lot going on. I can bring my audit scores up. You know that I care about my job. I do what is asked of me with no questions."

"I'm afraid it's too late. Here, sign these forms." Her supervisor's lips twisted into a scowl on one side and a smile on the other.

Val couldn't believe it. How cold. But she refused to cry or act a fool at the expense of losing her dignity, so she suppressed the urge. She glanced out of the rectangular glass insert and saw Bridget cheesing from ear to ear. Val turned back to face her supervisor, after which she scribbled her name then allowed the pen to roll across the paper as she walked out of the office with her head held high.

The security guard followed her back to her desk, and she packed up her belongings amid the stares from coworkers. Once Val had loaded up her personal effects, she threw a look at the security guard and he carried the extra box for her. As she walked through the department toward the elevators, colleagues tapped her on the shoulder and wished her well. Val smiled, though she kept her head facing forward.

When she made her way to the lobby, she pointed to the floor where she wanted her items placed. The guard nodded, plopped the boxes down at her feet, and strolled off without a word. She wished she had her car. Pulling creased papers from her purse, she called a cab. From there, she would get her vehicle. And after that, she would be completely broke.

Chapter 43

In an awkward display, Karen stared at Hershel and he glared right back. It had been a tacit game of chicken—power between two wills. But the standoff ended when one of *Denny's* finest, a short older woman, with a pencil tucked behind both ears and a wad of gum in her jaw, came to take their order.

"How you fine folks doin'?"

"Good, good," Hershel spoke up, his forehead creased, one shoulder tilted as he relaxed on the cushioned bench.

"Can I take your order?"

"A burger and fries for me with lemonade."

"And you?" the waitress asked, looking at Karen and popping her gum by mistake.

"The same for me except I want sweet tea."

"All righty, then. Be back in a jiffy with yo' order."

Karen didn't know where to place her eyes or her fidgeting feet. It was time to talk.

When she had gotten off work that night, Hershel had been there waiting for her in the well-lit parking lot. He had the rental car she'd been driving returned, and hers repaired, as he'd promised.

"Oh, man," Karen said, and took a deep breath. She patted her chest when Hershel delivered the news about her car. "I just wanna say thanks sooooo much Hersh. I'm —that day when I came over—you've . . ."

She knew that he knew she was struggling.

After fifteen minutes, their food and drinks arrived, circulating the space with the smell of beef and onions. She stared at her plate with a complete loss of appetite. When she glanced up at Hershel, his thumb bent like a hitch hikers, except it flicked the tabletop near the napkin dispenser.

"What's wrong?" she asked him.

"I don't see any Ketchup," he said, his hands now on both sides of his plate.

Karen twisted her head to the table behind her. "There's some over there," she replied, pointing. She watched as Hershel retrieved the condiment and returned to the table. He peeked around at other faces before he looked directly at her; she sat across from him sipping her drink and wondering what he thought of her while her insides squirmed. Did she stand a chance? Of course not. She had known that at the funeral. He tended to Jessica like any concerned lover would have.

"Something's wrong with your food?" Hershel asked, pounding his palm against the bottom of the bottle.

Karen's eyes zigzagged. "W-what?"

"You haven't touched your food. Why order it if it's not what you want?"

"It's fine. I want it."

"Okay, I'll start," he said, replacing his bun over his burger then double-pinching the tip of his nose. "What happened the other day?"

"I can't talk about it. At least not right now," she said in a flat tone.

"Because we're here?" Hershel questioned in a low voice, hunching his back a bit.

She shrugged. "No. I'm not ready yet, period."

"Why not? We've talked about everything under the sun. You're not getting shy on me are you?"

"It's not that. It's just hard to talk about."

"Why did you come by my house then if you didn't want to talk?"

Karen took in a quick breath and tucked a piece of hair behind her ear. "I don't know why I did. Honest." She turned away.

She sensed he knew she wasn't putting on by the curve of his mouth.

Hershel avoided pressing her on that subject, but moved to the next topic. "Did you scratch my vehicle?" His words fell out in a jarring tone.

"Hershel, I know you've been a good friend to me. And I know I give you grief . . ."

"Just answer the question. Why are you dancing around?" In a gentle manner, he grasped her wrist before she crunched her fry. "Tell me. I'm not going to be mad."

She pulled her hand away and slid the fry into her mouth.

"Okay, so that's how it is." Hershel sat back, pushing away from his plate. "I came here with the intention of us communicating with each other. Don't you have anything to say?"

"No."

"Why not?"

"I-I just don't . . ."

"You just don't what?"

"I can't get into it now."

"I'm not going to let you off that easy, Karen."

"Okay." Her arms rose. "Yes, yes, Yeeees. I did it. I didn't mean to, though. I know that sounds crazy but . . . *I became crazy.*" The outburst quieted the chatty voices around them. Karen wished she could have peeled their stares from her body.

Hershel became still and her emotions mushroomed with each moment of silence. She couldn't tell if he looked at her with pity or if he was pissed off.

"Why?" he lowered his voice, now leaning close to the center of the table.

"I don't know."

"Yes, you do."

She watched him a second while clearing food away from her back molar with her tongue. "How can you tell me what I know and don't know?"

"Because you do, that's how."

Karen twisted her lips as if to protect an aching tooth. "I was jealous, okay."

"Jealous?"

"Boy, you heard me, don't act like you didn't."

"Do tell," he said, rubbing his chin.

"I wasn't used to sharing my time with yo' big head, that's all." Karen smiled at the waitress as she refilled her drink and left. "When Jessica came into the picture, I felt you didn't have time for me. Seeing you and Jessica together and all, and seeing you two getting closer by the day . . . it tore me up inside."

"You women are something else. Jessica's jealous of you, you're jealous of her, on and on and on."

"Don't flatter yourself."

"Oh, I'm beyond that. You scale the side of my house like . . . Spiderwoman, and . . . in fact, I don't know if I'll be able to fit my head through the door when we leave." Hershel sat back again, with his hands folded behind his head.

Karen rolled her eyes, but grinned just the same.

"You must have forgotten when we were younger, I asked you to be my girlfriend, remember?"

"No . . . well, yeah. But we were kids. That don't count."

"I kissed you during spin-the-bottle and you nearly threw up in both of our mouths. Remember that? Or does that not count either? The truth is; you want me now because Jessica likes me and you know it."

She chewed another small fry then said, "That's not true."

"What? It is and you know it, Keekee."

"It was *Twister*, not spin-the-bottle."

"Whatever. You didn't like me like that. So, admit it."

"Admit what?"

"That the only reason you now want to talk to me is because Jessica is in my life."

Karen swung her leg under the table a few times before responding. "I'm talking to you now."

"Look, stop playing these silly games. Come on, now."

Karen cleared her throat and added, "I am being honest. Jessica had nothing to do with it. I decided . . . or thought up the idea before you two hooked up. Guess I was wrong."

Karen demanded so much from Hershel. But, he always came through for her, as he had with her car situation. He'd been a brother, friend, pretend father. She supposed it wasn't fair to expect him to wear so many hats.

Karen sat muzzled while Hershel drove her home. Exposing her true feelings drained her. When they arrived in front of her house she gasped when they drove up behind her parked car.

Her voice chirped, "Oh, thank you, thank you, thank you." Without hesitation, she threw firm arms around his neck and kissed his cheek with all the vigor and longing she wished she could have given his lips. He had her car sitting in front of her house, cleaned, repaired, and painted.

"Humph. Now you want to make nice." He pushed her away playfully, grinning.

"I don't have the money right . . ."

"Stop. Don't insult me. I told you I'd pay for the car repairs."

"Car repairs, not a dang-gone paint job."

"It was a cheap deal."

"Still."

"I just want you safe. If I could afford it, I'd get you another car. But, I ain't made my millions yet as an artist. Henh, henh." A loose hand connected under his nose.

Karen's shoulders slumped as she gave Hershel a tender stare. "Thanks."

She plowed through the darkness, stopped, glanced at her car, and shook her head with a smile tossed back at Hershel. He waved for her to come back and she obliged, leaning into his car window. He gave her a serious stare and said, "I want you to know I don't take our friendship lightly. You are important in my life. You always have been and you always will be."

"Thanks."

"You're welcome," he said louder than necessary as he threw the car in drive. Right before she opened the front door, she turned around again and waved. He drove off. He loved her. And he got her. This she knew for certain, if nothing else.

Chapter 44

Sucked in by a vortex of bitterness, Val found herself at the Woodlawn Cemetery. She drove up as far as permitted before she sure-footed over to Mama's grave staring, motionless and blank-faced as she stood amid the ocean of the dead with rows of tombs to her left and right, front and back. Her chest heaved in and out while her eyes grew black. Next, and without reservation, she hawked up and spit on her mother's tombstone. "I hate you, you hear me." Her words poured out evenly, like flowing lava. "I hate you! Why? Why weren't you ever there for me? Why did you detest me so much? I had . . . no one." Val fell to the ground, her knees landing on the crisp blades of grass, her nose runny. Now what was she going to do? Where would she and Karen live? How would they eat? Several thoughts zoomed by her at once with zero solutions penetrating through to her psyche. She placed total blame on Mama for all her flops and misfortunes in life, which no doubt, would have been reversed had her mother been more supportive. Val clutched herself and rocked back and forth until a nearby streetlight, like a watchful eye, shown down on her.

Chapter 45

As far as Karen was concerned, the summer had already gotten underway. Downtown held its Festival of the Arts annual event and Hart Plaza had loads of weekend entertainment. Right around the corner was the Fourth of July. At this point, she still didn't know what she wanted to major in, although she did have a college picked out. Wayne State University, which had been around since the 1800s, had an outstanding health program. She yawned when she read that because being a CNA was hard enough. Majoring in their nursing program or any other healthcare curriculum, would be agonizing.

Karen now had eleven patients, half of whom wore out the call light as though they were game show contestants. And although they were demanding, mean, and needy, they kept her on her toes.

She also read more, making one visit to the library each week. Overall, she wanted to be better, to speak well, express herself more eloquently in addition to understanding the history of her people and country. If someone would have told her a few months ago, that she would enjoy writing papers for fun, she would have laughed them out the room.

When Val entered the room with a quiet reverence to what she was doing, that was how Karen knew she'd made strides with improving her life.

"Sure you don't mind running errands with me?" Val asked, holding her purse and the keys to her recouped car.

"Nope."

"I know this isn't exactly the ideal way to enjoy your Thursday and your day off."

"It's okay. It's the least I can do."

Karen spied the stunned look on Val's face. Her parted lips said it all.

"Keekee?"

"Yeah, what's up?" Karen asked, still leaning into the computer screen.

"Stop typing for a minute. I need to talk to you."

"Oh, sure, I was just sending a "thank you" letter to Wayne State University."

"Why're you doing that?" Val asked, bending over her shoulder.

"I'm scheduled to meet with a student counselor. I said that I was interested in attending the college. I didn't put down how sucky my high school grades were, though." Karen threw her head back and giggled. "I'll worry about that later." She clicked "save" and pushed away from the computer with what she'd accomplished.

"That's great, Keekee," Val said, standing straight again.

Karen watched Val rub her throat as if it ached. She had rows of lines creasing her forehead, and her shoulders appeared weighted with stacks of barbells. "What's wrong? You look like somebody died."

"There is a serious problem I need to talk to you about," Val said, her eyes moist. "I don't know how else to tell you except to come right out and say . . ."

Karen felt she'd been a bit insensitive and when she touched Val's hand, it had a duel meaning for being sorry and stupid, all rolled into one. "What is it?"

"I lost my job," Val said, shifting the weight of her stance.

Karen's heartbeat quickened. Her throat knotted. She then managed to say, "Oh, no. How did that happen?"

"They just let me go without so much as a warning."

"You'll be okay, you're smart, and you know your stuff. You can get another job."

Val's voice quivered. "It's only a matter of time before we lose the house. We'll have to move, you know. I don't even have a plan. Not yet, at least."

Karen studied Val's face, which had intensified. Her rigid body looked like it had been mummified in an invisible cloth from her neck down to her feet. In any case, she'd shouldered all the problems solo. Karen imagined she knew just how rotten Val felt. She leaned to the right, causing the chair to squeak, and said, "Sorry."

"For what? You didn't do it." Val swiped at her tinted cheek.

"No, but I tell ya who I do blame . . . Mama."

Val moved her head forward as if she hadn't heard Karen correctly. "What do you mean?"

"You know doggone well Mama didn't handle her business. She didn't do what she was supposed to do and I'm mad. Yeah, I said it. Sometimes she makes me sick when I think about her."

Karen twirled her neck to look up at Val as she closed down her programs. She knew the scenario had changed and that she should've told Val right then and there what she'd come to know. In fact, she'd spent many late nights thinking about the word "mother," repeating it in her mind to the point it had little impact on her, like saying shoe, building, or pencil. But other times, when she stood in the truth of its meaning, it brought her to her knees.

Val's mouth fell open. "Keekee."

"Don't Keekee me. You know I'm telling the truth. She-didn't-handle-her-business! And she didn't do right by you, Val. I see that now."

"Don't say that."

"It's the truth. Why can't you face it? Accept the fact Mama was weak, that she didn't treat you fairly, and she sure as hell didn't show you the support that . . ."

"Enough. Don't, just don't." Val held up her hand and shook her head.

Karen knew her words had stung. Val eased down on the edge of the desk.

"I'm proud of you . . . glad you're sticking with this," Val said.

"Yeah, but I still need to look for a part time job to help out with the bills and all."

"Unh-unh. Nooo. You have enough on your plate. Absolutely not," she said, walking out of the room. That blew Karen's mind because people didn't give you a pass, you had to prove you deserve one. Here Val had lost her job, yet she had faith in her. There was no way she would let her down.

In the past, Val would have come off as annoying. Now, Karen welcomed the attention. Before she'd researched college majors, she'd been up since 7:30 in the morning, reading up on the life of Oprah Winfrey, her childhood and how she started out hosting a show in 1984. She wanted to be more positive like the icon and focus on things that mattered. And this newly found attitude seeped over into how she dealt with Val.

During their drive, while passing a number of corner stores with liquor licenses, their conversation slid into a light-hearted debate over the worst way to die.

"I say a fire is the worst."

"You don't think being shot is bad?" Karen asked.

"Nope. Fire and drowning. Those are the worst. Oh, and falling."

"I still say being shot up is pretty bad." Karen felt angry enough to shoot Frank between his beady eyes for what he'd done to Val. But with her newly discovered outlook on life and all, she figured confronting him and cussing him out would be good enough. She also contemplated whether she should ask Val the big question but every time she glanced over at the side of her face, the timing seemed off.

Sad to say, she knew that Val wasn't quite right in the head, and felt bad for the times she said, "Don't stand near me; I don't wanna catch your case of crazy." In addition to uncovering Val mumbling to herself, she rocked a lot and did some weird creepy finger-jiggy. Karen associated it with watching a live horror flick. Yet, she had to bring it up. And she had to face an embarrassing truth: Val truly did have mental issues.

The first stop was the Water Department. Val gathered papers and made sure her check book was in her purse. As they headed up the wide walkway toward the entrance, she forced out a nervous breath.

"Oh, boy. I sure hope I don't run into . . ."

"Who?"

"You know . . . Brady." Val batted her eyes.

"Oh, yeah, right. Why? Is that a problem?"

"Let's just say I'm the last person he wants to see," Val stated, straightening out her clothing.

"You two haven't talked?" Karen asked, holding open the door for Val.

"Not since the date. It didn't end that well, to be honest, Keekee."

On that note, Karen left it alone. But it didn't stop her from wondering. In her mind, she'd already come to the conclusion Val jacked it up, not on purpose, though. Once inside, she took a seat in the lobby area, while Val got a number to be serviced. Two rows of metal chairs lined the wall, opposite the customer service vicinity. There were lots of people seated as well as standing in line, and they all looked pissed, like they'd been waiting since Lionel Richie first left the Commodores. When Val sat down, she placed her purse on her lap with her hands resting on top.

Karen glanced around at the walls, the workers and the angry customers before she asked Val another question. "Heard anything about the jobs you interviewed for?" she whispered, her hand cupping her mouth.

"Not yet. I've called back on all of them for an update. It'll take time. I'm positive I'll get an offer from at least two," Val said, her chin lifted.

Karen figured things had to work out . . . somehow. After their long talk about the bills, the house and moving, she felt in-the-loop and had no doubts about their luck changing for the better. She even held out for hope that they'd get to keep the house. The cut-off date had already passed and yet, they hadn't received a notice to vacate the property.

Interrupting her thoughts, Val tapped her on her outer thigh when a man, carrying a stack of files, came out of his office and allowed a customer to exit. He followed behind the slew-footed woman until they parted ways. As he walked past the lobby, he took a double peep at Val and grimaced. Both Val and Karen's head followed him until he was out of sight.

"Ooph. What did you do to him, Val?" Karen had her face scrunched as if she'd smelled a pair of stinky feet.

Val raised her shoulders once and looked away.

When Brady walked back past, he looked straight ahead. Karen felt bad for Val and wished she had someone nice in her life. When Karen leaned a little to the left, and away from Val, she could make out what Brady was doing in his office, which was across from where they were seated. His door was ajar while he spoke into the phone. *Braces?* Karen mused, still spying on him. Well, if that isn't cute, she chuckled.

Val looked at her with enlarged eyes, meaning 'what?' and Karen shook her head, meaning 'nothing.' Periodically, Karen would tilt her head a bit to check on Brady. It hit her: if they had made it work, he could have possibly been her dad. *Step dad.* Karen wondered if he would have made a good dad. For all she knew, he could have been a bum or a murderer. Although, looking into Val's unhappy eyes, she sensed otherwise. She saw having a dad as a luxury and not a way of life because she'd never experienced a father. Frank didn't count, not even as a human being.

When she attempted to mentally dehumanize him further, Val whispered back, "I meant to tell you, I like that you're wearing your hair curled. Either way. But I like this way better."

"Thanks," Karen grinned, her eyes lighting up. She patted Val's fingers.

When Val's number was called, she didn't have to see Brady. Instead, she met with a heavy-set man with a thin mustache. After twenty minutes, Val walked out and lowered her tight shoulders.

"How'd it go?"

"I was able to work out a payment plan."

Karen knew Val had paid some money down with her severance pay. The main thing was, they were able to keep the water on.

When they started to leave, Karen looked back at Brady's office and had an idea. They'd exited the building down the wide walkway and made their way through the parking lot. Val rubbed up against her shoulder as they walked side by side.

"Okay, next, the phone company and. . . you hungry?" Val asked, lifting her eyebrows.

"I can eat." Karen opened the car door and slid in on the passenger's side and buckled up. She nearly forgot her plan just that quick when she blurted out, "Oh. I think I forgot something. Wait here. I hafta go back."

Karen darted through the parked cars and headed back inside the building. She went straight for Brady's office, ignoring the mean stares from everyone in the lobby. He still had the door cracked a bit but was no longer on the phone.

Karen's pulse skyrocketed. "Excuse me," she said, after a couple of knocks.

He looked up surprised before his face dropped into a scowl. *I guess I'm guilty by association*, Karen thought. Brady stood and walked toward her, widening the gap in the doorway.

"Can I help you?"

She took a deep breath and said, "Yes, I'd like to talk to you for a minute."

He blinked a few times, looking undecided.

"I promise I'll only take a minute," Karen added.

He opened the door all the way and allowed her to enter and take a seat. Karen felt so tensed it seemed as though her shoulders were up by her ears. Her eyes pivoted around the semi-tidy office, finally settling on the corner of his desk. She stared uneasily at a pencil holder with pens and a pair of scissors inside.

"What can I do for you?" He walked back and repositioned himself behind his desk.

Karen felt a rush of warmth come over her, the bulk of it settling behind her eyes. Did he assume she and Val were together? Just because two people were sitting near each other doesn't mean they were acquainted. But then again, they *did* look alike. "I know this may seem odd, but . . ."

He gazed at her while his elbows rested on the desk. His clasped hands under his chin pushed out his unsmiling lips.

"Eh . . . can we go somewhere? To eat . . . can we go out to eat somewhere? I can't go into details here."

"Excuse me?"

"I need to talk to you about a personal matter."

Karen could tell by the way Brady stiffened that he assumed she and Val knew each other. Plus, she felt as if she were talking in circles because she couldn't get a straight sentence out.

Karen knew this wasn't going well. She sounded crazy even to herself. She squirmed a bit in the chair then blurted out: "I've been going through a lot of changes in my life lately." She spoke the words glancing at her hands, then looked dead into his eyes and said, "I heard the date with my sister Val ended poorly. And I wanted to say, I'm sorry."

"No problem." His lids lowered at that point. When he lifted them it was gradual and agonizing for Karen, as he untethered a piercing stare. "Is that why you came in here?"

Karen fidgeted and struggled to make eye contact. There it was again, the flood, ready to burst through her eyes. She couldn't speak.

He waited.

"No," she finally muttered, her chin dimpling a bit. She searched his face and added, "She could use someone wonderful like you. Won't you reconsider? Give Val another chance?"

Brady shook his head and stood.

"Please," she begged.

"I don't think so." His tone was harsh.

"If you only knew how wonderful of a person she really is . . . people make mistakes."

"I'm going to have to ask you to leave, sorry." Brady opened the door for her.

Karen sniffed and stood, but not before she said, "I wish you could see inside her heart and know everything she's gone through. She deserves someone like you, that is, if you're as nice as you seem to be. Even if it's only as a friend." She sauntered out without another word, never looked back, nor glancing at the glaring faces in the lobby. All she wanted to do was help Val be happy. In the meantime, she would find Frank, tell him off, after which, let Val know Frank had been put in his place and confess that she knew about the letter, that she was her mother. Karen felt the plan could work, even though its execution remained sketchy.

Chapter 46

Val remained hopeful that one or more of her job interviews would pan out, even though three weeks had gone by with no word. She drummed her nails on the kitchen table when the receptionist told her to hold on.

"Um, the position is still open and you are among the serious contenders," the woman said when she returned.

Val perked up with an eager grin. Her fingers froze. "Okay. Can you tell me when a decision will be made?"

"A decision has already been made."

"Wait . . . a decision has been made?" Val asked.

"Yes."

"Look," Val said, hesitating in an attempt to compose herself. "Can I talk with Mr. Cade or Mr. Sanchez?" There was no way she'd ask for Miss Waters. She was a bear to deal with.

"I'm afraid they're both in a meeting."

"What time is the meeting over?" Val scratched her head as she began pacing.

"They are at another location. I can't say for sure."

"Well, can you have one of them call me?"

"I can't make any promises, but I'll try."

Val stopped cold and eyeballed the receiver. *I bet you can't*, she thought before hanging up.

She made follow-up calls to the other companies she had interviewed with.

Another lame excuse came from the HR assistant's mouth. "It's just that right now, they've temporarily put things on hold until the Workmen's Comp department is merged. You do understand, right?" Val needed to hear something fast, like yesterday. Despite the waning results of her interviews, she tried to stay positive.

One thing worked in her favor and that was her relationship with Karen. It meant more to her than air. All the mess with the house, bills, a job, took a back seat to Karen. But a job was necessary to have a decent life, a life that Val knew she couldn't fulfill comfortably at the moment. In fact, she tried to please Karen whenever she could. That was why she'd agreed to head over to Golden Walk Nursing Home to meet one of her favorite patients.

She'd bragged on Ms. Blout so much, Val had to admit she felt a tad jealous when Karen revered the old woman as though she'd never met anyone like her before.

She glanced at the clock on the stove and figured she could resume worrying about her job situation once she returned home. The moment she scooted back and lifted from the wobbly kitchen chair, the phone rang. For a second, she thought it was a response to her job interview. But it was her neighbor, Janice, the neighborhood watchdog.

She knew when folks were coming and going and those who didn't come home at all. Val raked her fingers through her hair. She didn't have time for Janice. For all she knew, the woman wanted to borrow something she didn't have. Besides, Janice talked too much, was too nosy, and too fanatical to deal with at the moment.

Val pulled at her polyester skirt and shook her head, saying, "Uh-uh. Not today." Sure as she'd reached the front door, the phone rang again. *What was going on?*

She raced back to the kitchen and checked the caller I.D and sure enough, another neighbor, right next door. This time, she picked up. Something was going on. It was Old Man Sammy who she'd seen earlier when she got the newspaper from the driveway. He had come back from his dialysis. Three times a week. Poor man. Val pressed in her lips with the thought, although he had been looking like death ran him over five times for the past seven years.

"Hello?"

"V-V-Val? Is th-th-that you?"

"Yes, Old Man Sammy, it's me. Is everything all right? You need something?" She asked but quickly regretted it because his stuttering response could take a while. Her one arm folded under her breast while she tapped her foot on the floor.

"Nooo," he said real slow. "I was eh, g-g-gonna' ask you the same th-th-thing."

"What do you mean?"

"I-i-i-is everything okay over there?"

"Yes, I believe so. Look I have some place I have to be. I can't talk now." Val cleared the line in the middle of the man's sentence. She felt guilty but by the time he was finished talking, a new day would have come around. Nonetheless, she didn't want to be late after giving her word to Karen.

When she got to the front door she almost toppled over with shock. "What in the world?" She slapped her hands to her head. Her car was gone. All she saw were tire tracks where it had been towed away.

"I don't believe this!" she yelled, storming outside with her hands now on her hips and eyes as wide as the space between her opened mouth. She trudged over to the driveway as if what she saw deceived her. She walked up one side of the driveway then down the other. She blinked in quick succession before looking up at Old Man Sammy now standing on his porch looking smug. He took his sweet time and sat on the railing, a butt cheek hanging over both sides.

"I didn't think you'd get too far, not having a car and all. B-b-but if-if-if-en you need a de-de-de-description of the fella, I can g-g-give it to ya'."

Val shook her head. "No, that's okay. Thanks anyway."

"Sure thing." He too looked at the driveway before entering his house. He managed to say that last comment just fine, Val thought, fuming.

She felt as unsteady as a bobble head shaking on the dashboard of a car. She no longer had a job, lost her car, was about to lose the house, and didn't have a clear answer as to when and if she'd start another job. How would she get around to pay bills, buy food, and look for other jobs? Now her head pounded with a relentless fury, with every step she took. She could hardly lift her feet to climb the concrete steps to the porch. When she made it inside, she eased the door closed and thought about the conversation she and Karen had on ways to die. At this point, any one of those means would surely put her out of her misery.

Chapter 47

It still tickled Karen to see Ms. Blout and Mr. Hamilton sitting together, like old friends, in the lounge area. Better yet, an old married couple. Mr. Hamilton had it all planned. As soon as he'd gotten wind of the Rayland High glee club's plans to come and sing, he had gone and told Ms. Blout he wanted to sit next to her during the performance.

"You know, a famous actor once attended the school," he told Karen while touching her shoulder and hoisting himself to a standing position.

"Oh, wow," Karen tried sounding interested as she steadied him.

Here he was; a wrinkled up kid in a candy store. Mr. Hamilton made it his business to walk over to a table with napkins, grab a few, then, shuffled back to Ms. Blout, handing her one as she bit into a sticky pastry. He may have moved in slow motion, but he was up for the job. The gesture made Karen think of Hershel's attentiveness.

Her heart fluttered with hopeless desire because whomever he decided to marry, she figured the woman would have it made. Hershel was an amazing man. It surprised her that she'd taken herself out the picture. She knew her chances had faded.

More people than expected crammed themselves into the lounge to be entertained by the Rayland High School glee club. Karen sat on the far side of Ms. Blout with Mr. Hamilton on her other side, watching the old woman like he was going to catch a crumb if it fell. Karen's eyes peeled away every corner of the room. No Val. It disappointed her in the same way a child reacts to a parent forgetting to attend their daughter's piano recital. She wanted Val to meet Ms. Blout. She sucked her teeth and shrugged it off.

But her dispirited mood shifted once the unified voices of the Rayland students started singing, *Alfie*. Their harmonious notes were so sweet the corners of her mouth lifted. She felt as if the catchy tune had been written for her. The youth sang several well-known songs from movies like *Breakfast at Tiffany's* and *Evita*. A few of the residents stood and applauded. Ms. Blout did not, although she did clap a few times.

Fruit punch and pastries lined the tables against one wall and the glee club members helped themselves. Most of them stayed a bit and chatted with the staff and residents. And everyone appreciated how well-mannered the students were. Karen sat back and observed. When the servers had cleared out and cleaned up the area, she finished out her shift at the nurses' station and decided she was too disappointed to call Val. She handled a few discharges after clocking out then pranced into Ms. Blout's room.

"Knock, knock," she said, sticking her head in the doorway.

"Well, hello, you." Ms. Blout sat in her trusted chair, holding tight to her trusted cane while leafing through pages of a *Time* magazine.

"What are you looking at?" Karen inquired. She sat on the edge of the bed and leaned over toward the old woman.

"Just looking through photography shots by Gordon Parks. Here . . ." she slanted the page so Karen could see. "Quite profound, wouldn't you say?"

Karen nodded as she surveyed the black and white photo of a young mother and three children in a cramped space. "Oh. Yes."

"He was a brilliant man and self-taught. I see the same light in you. You can do and be anything you want, my dear." She lifted her eyes to the ceiling before allowing them to close.

Ms. Blout was so smart, Karen thought. She loved when the old woman made comments like that because it gave her hope.

Karen fidgeted. "So, you enjoyed the kids singing?"

Ms. Blout chuckled then wiped her hand beneath her nose.

"What?"

"You don't look much older."

"Yeah, so I'm told. That's because I'm tiny, though," Karen said.

Ms. Blout nodded at her hips and smiled.

"Oh. I nearly forgot. Here." Karen handed her the paper she'd completed on Oprah Winfrey. She wanted to impress the old woman. "I did some research on her. Thought you'd like to see what I wrote."

The paper shook lightly in Ms. Blout's grasp as she looked it over in silence, only releasing an occasional, "um-humph" for approval.

"Ms. Blout, what do ya think about Mr. Hamilton?" In truth, she wanted to know if he knew she was black. Then, of course, she was dipping in their business.

"He's nice enough, I suppose. Not that that would make me want to go to the prom with him."

Karen rushed her hand up to her mouth. "Get out, Ms. Blout. You do have a sense of humor." Karen bit her nails until Ms. Blout finally handed back her paper.

"Well done. Excellent job, Karen."

"Are you sure?" Karen's eyebrows rose. "I mean if you see errors in it, I'll go back and make corrections. I want to do a good job."

"There were minor errors here and there. Don't concern yourself with them yet. Continue to read with a watchful eye and study your grammar. The errors will dwindle."

Karen lowered her shoulders and smiled at the old woman. "You made me happy."

"Well, you should be proud. I think you'd make a fine writer," Ms. Blout said, swaying in the direction of her tilted cane. "Have you thought about that?"

"Me? Oh, no, not really. I used to write poems when I was in high school. But, the real writer . . ." she stopped, briefly contemplating whether or not to tell Ms. Blout about her revelation concerning Val. She'd intended to do so anyway. ". . . is . . . Val." Maybe not, she thought.

"Oh, my. Well, talent runs in your family because your writing is delightful. You write from the heart. That's what makes your work relatable."

Karen stood and hugged the old woman, then kissed her forehead. "Well, I didn't want to keep you any longer. Is there anything I can get you before I leave?"

"No. Thank you anyway." The old woman looked up at her in a trusting manner.

Karen moved toward the door then stopped. "Ms. Blout," she'd been wondering about this for the longest time.

"Yes, dear."

"Whatever happened to your brother?"

"Oh the poor thing, he's been paralyzed from the neck down for some years."

Karen snatched both hands up to her mouth.

"Seems he'd gotten himself drunk after gambling with friends and drove the wrong way on the road. No one else was hurt, thank God, but he'd totaled his car and altered his life, basically."

"I'm sorry to hear that. I wondered why he didn't come to see you. I know that must make you feel sad and lonely."

Ms. Blout's smile turned upside down. "Yes, perhaps, but I try to focus on the wonderful times we had. When you get to be my age, all you have are memories, you know." Her laugh settled with a slight cough as she glanced at the floor in contemplation.

Karen leaned into the doorway, waiting.

"I've made mistakes in my life. We all have. But, I wished I would have embraced more people instead of shielding myself from them."

"You sound like Mr. Hamilton."

"Oh."

"Ms. Blout . . ."

"Yes?"

"Why did you say I'd make a fine writer, instead of suggesting that I go into nursing or something? I'm curious."

"Because, dear, that's not what I see in you. It doesn't mean that you aren't great at what you do now."

The maintenance crewmen were now on duty and the hum of the floor polisher began. It almost sounded relaxing. Karen was certain Ms. Blout had experienced a lot of disappointments in life. In fact, she knew it; a lost love, a baby, her brother. Karen was only twenty-four and had been given some doozies. Life was tough, she thought. Ms. Blout, without a doubt, would understand what she'd gone through the pass few weeks. Karen waved her hand. Much like an afterthought, she blurted out, "By the way, I'm getting along with Val better." She exited the room and the building, feeling motivated.

Karen decided she would shift her focus on reading and writing more reports. She was on a roll, getting compliments, doing well, looking out for her future. No more hanging out with the wrong crowd and hurting others. But what she planned to do to Frank would be an exception to her new rule.

Chapter 48

Val kneeled down on the floor in her bedroom. She had all of Mama's old prescription bottles set up like a tree-lined neighborhood. Some of the medication dated back more than three years. Crestor, Prevacid, Tylenol, Bystolic, the list went on. Val's baggy, lifeless eyes circled the contents of each bottle. She swiveled and shook each plastic container before placing it back in its spot. She allowed her thoughts to go all the way this time; the place where you make the decision to end it. She wondered how many pills it would take to give her peace, freedom from pain and loneliness. While other women, perhaps, were planning a Friday night out on the town, that evening, she contemplated her death. It taunted her to crossover. Thoughts of Brady couldn't even save her. She was tired. Every time she took two steps forward, she got knocked back ten. But would she go through with it? she wondered as she hugged herself. When she turned her eyes toward the ceiling, she caught Karen standing in front of her bedroom door, her face displaying one big question mark.

"What are you doing?" Karen probed, her arms raised in the air.

"Just looking through Mama's old meds. Sorry I couldn't make it to your job. As you can see, I don't have a car . . ." Val rested on her backside and stretched both legs in front of her. "They repossessed it right when I was about to leave out. Old Man Sammy tried to tell me and so did Janice."

Karen inched into her room. "Val, what were you planning on doing?"

"About my car?"

"No . . . this . . . right here?" Her hand drew a circle in midair.

"I told you, I'm getting rid of Mama's old medications." Val stared at Karen hard, hoping to convince her. She didn't blink either and witnessed Karen's chest cave in a little. But she continued coming closer. She was bullheaded that way. Her slow, deliberate steps made Val uncomfortable because they too had inquiries she didn't want to fulfill. She didn't want to have to explain her behavior or why she felt the way she did.

"Keekee, don't look at me that way. Whatever you have to say, I'm not in the mood to hear it."

Karen snorted and knelt beside her. "Well, you're gonna' hear it. I'm sorry Val that your car was taken but this ain't the answer and you know it."

"W-what . . . you think . . ." Val forced a laugh which resonated from her throat opposed to her knotted belly. "Please, Keekee."

"Naw, don't Keekee me. I know what I see. It's gonna' be all right. Look, I care about you . . . I love you."

Val stared at Karen wide-eyed. She couldn't remember Karen ever saying "I love you," except for that time she gave her money to see Michael Jackson in concert. When she knew that she could attend the show with her friends, she jumped up and down screaming into hands that snapped to her mouth. "Oh, thank you, thank you, thank you, Val. I love you." She grabbed the dollar bills quick, practically skipping out the door. Looking at

Karen's face now she wanted to believe the words. Before she knew it, she began pounding her fists into her thighs, screaming, "I can't take it anymore, I can't take it!" Heat had risen to her head and settled in the sockets of her eyes as tears rolled down her face and slid into her mouth.

She hadn't realized how animated she was until Karen restrained her hands.

"It's okay. It's okay," Karen told her like she was the parent.

Val felt like a helpless child. And she didn't care.

Chapter 49

Karen drew in a quick breath as she hurried back into Val's room with her ice water. She wasn't thinking clearly though because she should've taken Mama's old medication from her before she left her alone; no telling what Val was up there doing. It pained her to see her real mother that way, withdrawn and broken. And there was nothing she could do to take away Val's anguish. She wished she could place her pain into her own heart. But, Val had to find her own way to cope. When she reentered the room, Val was rocking. Karen thought some of the medication bottles were missing. She glared at the containers then at Val, who by now, sat at the head of her bed with her knees pulled up to her chest.

"I need to know what happened to the rest of the meds, Val."

She didn't answer right away. She leaned back then pushed forward. "Nothing. I haven't touched anything."

Karen didn't believe her. Val avoided looking into her eyes. She sat there, toying with that old broken ring. Karen told herself she wouldn't bring up the letter until she found Frank, but this seemed like a good time to get everything out in the open. She gulped in air and despite the fact that her tongue felt like sandpaper, she spoke up after she placed the glass on the nightstand, which already had a bunch of existing water rings.

"Val, I have to tell you something. I know the secret you've been keeping . . ." she started, as she sat by Val's feet.

Before she could complete her sentence Val began yelling, allowing her knees to fall out to her side in a frog position.

"No, no, no! No more secrets, okay! Okay! I don't want to hear it!"

Karen's head began to swim. The muscles in her shoulders on down to her back knotted. She had never seen Val like this. She looked like a crazy woman who was on the verge of a breakdown. She was sweating, her eyes were bulging and her hair looked wild. Well . . . Val's hair normally looked like that. Still, she appeared scary.

"Oh, Val. You need help. I'm sorry for upsetting you but you need to talk to someone and stop holding all this pain and anger you been carrying around for so long."

"I don't want to take any more trips. I shouldn't have done it. Couldn't afford it."

Karen drew in a long breath and thought about continuing the conversation, but Val wasn't even in her right mind to understand what was going on. "Look, I'm going to throw out Mama's stuff. It's no good. We'll talk later."

Val stared off into space as if Mama had died all over again.

That Saturday morning, before Old Man Sammy got up to water his petunias, which were planted in the front of his house, Karen thought Val looked a lot better around the eyes. Though she looked kinda haggard-like, her spirits were improved. She drove Val around to do her errands and buy groceries. Karen loaded up more grapes and oranges in the cart because she'd planned on paying for most of the items, plus the cheese cake Val implied she wished she could purchase but couldn't afford, neither could her hips. Karen told her she was delusional. Of course she was trying to say Val was a nice size in a roundabout way, but just the same, felt she shouldn't have said it the way she did.

"Mm, I didn't expect you to pay for these items. Save your money for when we need it, okay?" Val grabbed the extra carton of grapes and the cheese cake from Karen's hands and placed the items back.

Karen wanted Val to relax, stop acting bullheaded, as she watched everything go back onto the shelf. "You don't think we need it now?" Karen asked, talking to the back of Val's head as she walked away, drawing her attention to a head of lettuce.

"Nope."

"Val, I'm buying. I can help out a little. Honest, I don't mind."

Karen didn't want to bring up the fact that last night, she'd wailed to the moon that she couldn't deal with the pressure. Confounded, Karen stared at her and huffed harder for exaggeration. Val ignored her and continued weighing the head of lettuce in her hand like she didn't have a care.

"Val, you been saying I need to do my part for the longest. Well . . ." Karen stretched out her hands as if she held an invisible package. "Now I want to. You don't have to do this on your own. We're . . . a team."

Val continued on to the freezer section and grabbed two bags of breaded okra. Karen's shoulders shook with a swift breeze of chilled air when the door closed.

"Save it for the time we need it, Keekee. I appreciate you trying to help out, though."

After that, they left and ended up turning onto Joy Road and buying apples, corn-on-the-cob and turnip greens from Joe Randazzo's Fruit and Vegetable Market. Once at home, Karen decided to tackle the junk that had plagued the garage for more than a decade even though she ignored Val's gentle pleas for her to leave the mess. For years, Val claimed she would clean out the garage. Karen could understand why she sidestepped the challenge with so many ugly memories lurking at every inch of the chaos. Karen ignored her. Every so often, she would stop sweeping or moving dusty boxes, elated over some toy or item she'd found, reminiscent of her childhood.

    She also stumbled on an old picture of Frank and Val stuffed inside a faded forty-five with Aretha Franklin on the cover. He was sitting on a park bench and holding her on his lap. Mama probably took the picture, Karen assumed. Right then, her insides churned. Poor Val. She didn't have anyone to turn to. Mama ignored and punished her time and time again. Frank abused her sexually, and her own father never showed one ounce of concern for her.

    Karen stared at the snapshot for a long time. It convinced her to carry out her plan; that and the fact Frank's eyes were gouged out with a red ballpoint pen.

    All weekend, she worked on her papers, and on the sly, googled information regarding Frank. She pulled out a yellow notepad from the side junk drawer of the desk and wrote down four locations as to where Frank may be living. Three places were in Detroit, the other, Ypsilanti. Karen gasped when she took a chance and typed his name in Facebook. She wasn't certain, but it looked like it could have been him with his semi-up-to-date photo. Karen knew full well though, how people perpetrated. It didn't matter. She would find him if it was the last thing she did.

Chapter 50

That Monday morning was as if a switch had been turned on. Val glided around the kitchen in her matching shorts and tank top humming. Her hips swayed to the tune in her head as she turned off the stove and removed the sizzling skillets with pancakes and bacon.

"Wow, what happened to you?" Karen questioned, entering the kitchen and easing down in a chair. Creases trekked across her forehead.

"What do you mean? I'm feeling good is all."

"Yee-ah, that's what I mean."

"I got a loan," Val said, batting her eyes while placing three strips of bacon on a plate.

Karen slapped her hand on the table and leaned forward. "Get out. How much?"

"Not much, but it's enough to carry me till I get my new job," Val chirped, flopping pancakes next to the bacon then placing the plate in front of Karen. "The money will buy extra food and pay off some bills until I start working." She handed Karen a fork and a glass of milk, and beamed when Karen's face formed into sheer glee, her eyes sparkling.

"You got a job, too?" Karen said, slicing her pancakes before biting into them.

"Well, not exactly . . . not yet at least. I received a call. It wasn't *what* they said that convinced me, it was *how* they said it: 'Hello, Miss Williams. Hope you are well,' yada, yada, yada. Then they said, 'You will hear from us later this week with our decision. If you have any additional questions, don't hesitate to contact the office.' I read between the lines. And to my ears, the decoded pleasantries meant, I have the job." She sat at the table looking self-assured.

Karen dropped her fork and stopped chewing. "Val, you mean they ain't said it outright . . . you didn't hear them say 'you got the job?'"

"No, but they will."

Val hopped up when the kettle on the stove whistled. She poured water and dunked a slice of lemon along with a tea bag into a cup. She also felt Karen's eyes burning a hole in the side of her face when she slid back into her seat.

Karen wiped her mouth on the back of her hand. "Val, I don't mean to sound negative, but you can't go by that."

Val understood Karen's skepticism. She sympathized with her inability to comprehend what she had come to know. So she leaned over and rubbed Karen's arm. "Oh, Keekee. Don't worry. I'll be fine. We both are going to be fine. Look, we've hit rock bottom. It can't get any worse than this. It's up hill from here on."

Karen shook her head. "Well, I'm glad you're in good spirits. You had me worried over the weekend." She pushed her plate away and stood. "I better get going. I have a few errands I need to run myself before I go to work. Let me know if you want me to run you anywhere when I get back tonight."

Val loved Karen's transformation. She sounded thoughtful and mature. She watched her rinse out her dishes and come back to wrap her arms around her neck. Her gentle touch warmed her soul.

"See ya."

"See ya," Val said, turning her head to watch her leave. Just as she'd disappeared, seconds later, she reappeared, mouth open with a quizzical expression.

"Forget something?" Val asked, twisting her body to look around.

"No, I just had a question that's been on my mind. I know it may sound silly, but . . . why do you keep that?"

She pointed to Val's right hand.

"What, my ring?" Val asked, looking down and flipping her hand over.

"Yup. Why do you keep it? It's a broken toy ring."

"Well, first of all, it's not a toy. It's a costume ring that belonged to Mama." Val glanced at the piece of jewelry again before staring at the floor. She continued in a sober reflection. "She told me not to bother it but I didn't listen."

"Who, Mama?"

Val nodded twice. "It seemed, at the time, so beautiful. But Mama said I'd never look as pretty as that ring. I didn't know if she meant it or if she was teasing. But she never laughed afterwards. I snuck the ring out of the box and wore it to school. Back then, it didn't fit properly, of course. I showed it to my English teacher, Mrs. Rumsfeld. Remember her?"

"Yeah," Karen replied, rubbing her temple. "I used to sleep in her class all the time, though. She didn't like me."

Val shook her head and continued. "She used to praise my work and said I could be anything I wanted to be. Anyway, when I showed her the ring, she made a big deal about it and how beautiful it was, but said the ring didn't hold a candle to how beautiful I was."

Val looked away with a swift shudder. She hadn't thought about the woman in years. Her teacher's words meant everything. Her kindness had proven rare. Val dabbed at both eyes. "Silly, huh?"

Karen shook her head and walked away. Seconds later, Val heard the door open and close. She felt funny inside, though. Not because the light had faded from Karen's eyes, or the fact she conjured up a delicate memory, but something didn't set well with her. The uneasy feeling finally settled, but resurfaced two hours later when a bang at the front door sent her mood spiraling downward once again.

Chapter 51

The woman behind the counter at the drugstore grumbled as Karen struggled to hold her cell phone between her shoulder and ear while digging in her purse to pay for deodorant and mouthwash. Hershel was on the line.

"Hersh, hold on a minute," she said, giving a tart smile to the cashier.

"You know, most people use an earpiece," the cashier snapped.

Karen glared at the woman then rolled her eyes, thinking the young lady should have applied as much energy into finding an acne product for her pimply face as she did giving unwanted advice.

Once she had her items and receipt, she resumed chatting with Hershel.

"Hey, I'm back."

"Good. So, have you given much thought with helping me out regarding my art show?"

"I don't know about that, Hershel. Won't Jessica be pissed off?"

"No . . . she shouldn't be."

"Hershel," Karen snickered, "you know that won't fly. Will she or won't she?"

"Look, it will be fine."

"Yeah, if you say so," Karen added, stepping into her car and starting the engine.

"So, you coming over tonight so I can show you what I want you to do?"

"I don't know. I'll hafta let you know."

"Okay, well . . . enough about my show. What's going on with you? You and Val all right? Surprised you haven't mentioned anything about your crazy sister."

Karen punched out her lips, taking immediate offense to Hershel's offhanded remark. It was her own fault, for sure, because she had dogged out Val at every turn.

"Well, I can call her that, but you can't, okay? And she's doing okay besides the fact she lost her car and her job."

"W-what? That's rough. Sorry about that . . . and sorry if I offended you."

"It's okay. I think I understand her a bit better, you know, since we had time away from each other. I've learned some things I didn't realize before. I'm going to try harder to get along with her instead of beating her down."

"Wow, is this Keekee? Hello? Hello?"

"Dang, fool, leave me alone."

"I'm kidding. I'm just impressed with how you're choosing to see your sister."

Karen allowed Hershel's last comment to linger. She knew she wouldn't tell him anything about the letter until she discussed the situation with Val first. "Look, Hersh, I'm at work, 'bout to clock in. We'll talk. I'll see you tonight about your art show. We can go over some things like you said. "

"And help me set up."

"And help your big head set up."

"Thanks."

There'd been talk of possible interviews for a new head

nurse; while the other CNAs were eager to chatter about the prospects, Jessica stared hard at Karen whenever she walked by. Karen questioned whether she still deserved the "ice treatment" because it seemed Jessica's attitude was overkill. The kicker occurred when she loaded up Mr. Hamilton's tray and Jessica strolled in her direction. Karen thought about speaking but didn't feel like dealing with the rejection. So she kept walking. Lo and behold, Jessica bumped her shoulder hard without saying a word. The knock was enough to spill the drink onto the tray.

"Excuse me," Karen called out being smart. She almost dropped the tray altogether. But what she wanted to say was "excuse *you*." Although her blood pressure rose, Karen tried to understand Jessica's behavior. After all, losing a mother made her want a deeper relationship with Hershel. Maybe that's why Jessica acted like a lovesick maniac. She didn't want to lose Hershel, especially after losing her mother and being adopted and all. Yet, Karen felt her tolerance dwindling. The two of them couldn't communicate or stand being in the same room, let alone attend Hershel's art show.

When she turned the corner and entered Mr. Hamilton's room, he sat on the bed watching TV with one leg crossed over the other.

"Mr. Hamilton, my man. What's up?"

He laughed a bit, the slack skin under his chin shaking. "Oh, nothing much, h-how're you?"

"I'm just fine. And judging by how cozy you and Ms. Blout been, I'd say you doin' all right yourself."

"Yes, yes, I suppose so," he said uncrossing his legs. "She's a bit too light for my taste. I prefer your skin tone. But she's a sweet woman just the same," he said and headed for the bathroom. *I'm scarda you*, Karen mused. Now that fascinated her. Yet, it came as no shock because he'd hit on her with his white, wrinkled self. Nonetheless, Mr. Hamilton didn't come off as though he truly liked women-of-color. But then again, what do they look like?

They don't walk around with signs stapled to their chests. A person's eyes may give off a hint or two that they prefer someone thin, tall, pretty, hippy, sexy or black. But unless they say it, you never, ever know for sure.

Karen thought about Mama and how often she had made the wrong assumptions. If a white person was dry to her, "Oh that prejudiced white boy just plain ol' hateful against black folks," she would hiss. Her mistreatment somehow represented the entire race. Karen had taken on the same mindset without even realizing it. She had misjudged Val, not understanding the shame and abuse she'd gone through for years and why she cherished that broken ring. Karen had Hershel figured all wrong too because he cared for her as a friend, but his heart, the deep part, didn't belong to her. She thought Mama was a saint. Now she wanted to curse her for what she did to Val. She had gotten it wrong with Ms. Blout, thinking the woman was white.

Karen heard the toilet flush, which brought her back to the present. She cleaned up his room while her head remained in a fog. When she left out of his room, she had Ms. Blout to tend to. The old woman lay in bed, looking up at the ceiling. Karen sucked her teeth when she first entered her room. *Dang, now who am I gon' talk to?*

"Hey, Ms. Blout. You doing okay?"

She didn't answer.

Karen leaned over and checked on her. Her eyes stayed fixed.

"You not gon' eat anything? I have your food here." She touched the old woman's shoulder.

Ms. Blout snatched her arm away and stuck out her bottom lip.

"Okay, I understand. It's all right." Everyone was entitled to a funky mood every now and then. Karen had witnessed this behavior before and knew to leave her alone for the time being.

She shrugged her shoulders and cleaned the room as usual, glancing periodically at the old woman. Later that evening, after her shift ended, Karen checked on her again. It wasn't like her to lay down during that hour. This time the old woman sat in her chair looking through pictures.

"Hey, Ms. Blout. I come by to check on you before I head out. You doing better?"

The old woman looked up in a sluggish manner and said, "Oh, not too bad. How are you?" She released a pleasant grin, the wrinkles around her mouth deepening. She smiled the way one greets a stranger at a bus station or at a bank because they made you aware you were next in line.

"Whatju doing?" Karen kneeled beside her.

"Are you here for my class?"

Karen blinked. She released a grainy, "No."

"Well, I certainly hope you take my class. I love to see my students embrace history."

"Ms. Blout, it's me . . . Karen. I came back to see how you were doing. W-whatju got there?"

"Karen?"

"Yes, Karen."

The old woman tilted her head. "You said your name was Karen?"

"Yes, Ms. Blout, Karen."

"Oh."

"What do you have there?"

"Just going over these beautiful pictures of my daughter." Ms. Blout's veiny, wobbly hand moved toward her.

Weary, Karen released a heavy sigh. She thought about how brilliant Ms. Blout's mind must have been in her heyday, and now to see it slip away made her feel hollow inside. The old woman didn't have a daughter. Karen focused on the subject in the photo and her curious eyes grew big. It was Ms. Blout as a young girl. She must've been seventeen years old or so, younger than Karen. *She was beautiful*, Karen thought. Ms. Blout looked almost as attractive as Lena Horne.

Sharing her problems with Ms. Blout made no sense. It would've been selfish to do so. She didn't need to hear about Val losing her job, her searching for Frank or Val's mental issues. The old woman had enough struggles of her own.

"I had another daughter," Ms. Blout blurted out.

Karen looked up, her eyebrows knitted close. "Oh yeah, who was she?" she asked half-heartedly expecting a truthful revelation.

"She died though, very, very young. Her name was Karen."

Allowing her to embrace the lie, Karen replied, "I'm sure you miss her quite a bit."

"Yes, she was on a path to greatness."

Karen's head hung down as she listened to the old woman babble for another twenty minutes about her imaginary children. Now she wanted to sap her up with love because Ms. Blout should have been in her family, should have been her granny. Karen gleamed into the old woman's tiny eyes and licked her own lips, thinking the poor woman was having a bad spell. She kissed her forehead, after that, she walked out of the room and out of the building. During her drive over to Hershel's house, she thought about Val. Karen ached for her when she shared her story about the ring. She understood all too well, what it meant to have someone believe in you. She got it. A looming thought plagued her thoughts: some things you can't fix no matter how bad you want to.

Chapter 52

The rapid pounding at the front door gave Val a sense of urgency. She exhaled before turning the lock and when she opened the door, a round man and two other men stood on the porch. The round man shoved an eviction notice under her nose. Val angled back and started sobbing out loud with her hands clasped to her mouth.

"No, no, please." She stepped aside as the three men forcibly came inside her home. The home she was being evicted from.

"You've been given several notices to vacate the property ma'am. We're here to remove your items."

"Please, don't. Can't you give me more time?"

"I'm afraid not," the round man said.

Val's chest heaved up and down. Did she receive the notices? She couldn't remember. She couldn't think straight either. Now she felt the men looked at her as though she had been a fugitive wanted by the FBI. It became a tag that followed her every time she lost a notch in what society considered those who were doing well. Can't pay your bills, folks will talk to you like you need to lick the bottom of their shoes. Late with the mortgage payments, congratulations, you're now a second class citizen.

The men whizzed by her with chairs and tables, placing each item on the front lawn. She whirled about in a fog before stepping outside, still disbelieving what was happening. Her tear filled eyes were now bloodshot. She met the inquisitive stares of neighbors who either ventured outside or simply lifted their blinds to get a better look. Even Old Man Sammy came out and stood on the sidewalk saying, "Umph, umph, umph." He also began supervising the men, telling them where to put the furniture and scolding them if an item landed too hard. Val, unable to do a fraction of what Old Man Sammy did, remained in a remorseless haze. She didn't know what her next move would be. She landed on the concrete steps of the porch and placed her head in her hands. It hadn't occurred to her, until then, to call Karen and break the news.

Chapter 53

Karen, who'd glanced around for Jessica's car, relaxed her shoulders then rang Hershel's doorbell when she didn't see it. She did not want to stand around picking her nails and fake-smiling while acting oblivious to Jessica's attitude.

"Hey, Hersh-Hersh," she said when he opened the door wide. He wore a torn, wrinkled shirt with track pants. Karen looked him over. "You been asleep?"

"Naw, I'm just tired, come on in." He walked ahead while glancing back at her. "See you decided to keep on your party attire," he teased.

Karen rubbed her hand over her uniform top and chuckled. "Oh, yeah. I didn't feel like changing."

"It's cool."

"Where's your girlfriend at?"

"At home. Her dad was under the weather so she's doctoring him up with honey and tea, medicine and whatnot," he revealed, entering the living room where boxes and unassembled easels were arranged about the floor. "Careful," he warned, swinging his arm in a half circle. Karen had to step over the items.

"Uh-huh. Don't have me in the crossfire when she decides to run up in here all Rambo style," Karen joked, throwing a firm hand on her hip.

"You need to quit." Hershel uttered then wiped at his face with both hands.

"No, you know I'm telling the truth."

Hershel landed on the sofa with a thud. "I wish you two would come together. After all, that's how I met her through your friendship."

"You are right, my man. But don't get it twisted. Me and Jessica weren't friends, only coworkers," Karen said, scooting next to him.

"Fair enough. Hope you two reconsider though."

"Don't count on it. She hates me."

"She doesn't hate you, drama queen."

"Auugh-ite, if you say so," Karen said, lifting one doubtful shoulder.

"On that note, let's get to work. This is all the stuff I have laid out that will need to arrive early."

"Your show is what day again?"

"The weekend of The Fourth of July."

"Okay. Go head . . . continue," Karen mumbled, placing a fist under her chin. She leaned forward while Hershel talked.

"I have glass cleaner, paper towels, markers, silverware, saucers, wine glasses, CDs, CD player, and labels."

Karen held her hand up. "Hold on. What in the world do you need glass cleaner for?"

"It's for removing fingerprints off the framed art and pedestals."

"All righty, then. Go on." Karen made an inverted smile.

Hershel talked about painting and textures for at least ten minutes. "What I need from you is to arrange the playlist from this stack of music. I trust your judgment because we have similar taste."

"True, true."

"After that . . . I . . . hold on, my phone is ringing."

Great, Karen thought. Jessica couldn't last twenty-minutes without busting up their conversation. She sighed as Hershel left and went into the next room to talk. Karen glanced up at him, aware that their relationship had shifted. She now had to be mindful of his time and respect his privacy. Hershel was moving on with his life. So, where did that leave her? Were they drifting apart? Was this his last attempt to save their dwindling friendship?

"Hey," Hershel said, reentering the room. He came over to her and placed his hand on her shoulder. Karen noticed he had a goofy look on his face. Or was it gloom?

"What?" She knew he would regurgitate Jessica's name.

"It's Val."

Karen made a sour face. "Val? My Val?"

"Yes."

"Why would she be calling you?"

"She said she tried your phone but it kept going to voice mail."

Karen frowned and quickly realized she forgot to turn her phone back on when she had left work. She reached for Hershel's phone but he clutched it tight as if he were about to give her instructions. "I need to brace you, Keekee. Val said . . . well, apparently they put your things out, yours and Val's."

"They?"

"You all have been evicted from your house. Your belongings are on the front lawn."

Karen stood, but her legs felt like cooked noodles. Her wide eyes turned red. And her breath seemed to have lodged in her lungs. "Oh, no, no, no."

"I offered to help," Hershel said. "I told your sister she could store the furniture and everything else here at my house. I have plenty of room in my basement. But, meanwhile, we need to get over to your place and start getting your stuff. Val's outside now, in the dark."

He handed her the phone.

"Val, it's me. I-I'm on my way. We're both coming." She ended the call and gave the cell phone to Hershel.

He grabbed her and pulled her close, saying, "You know it's going to be all right. This is just a rough patch."

She took in his scent, her best friend who went out on a limb for her without question. His kind words tugged at her, reshaping her emotions.

"Yup," was all Karen could pull from her lips. She felt warm and numb with humiliation. They had to help Val, she thought, staring shakily at the floor near the cleaning supplies.

"Hey," Hershel snapped his finger at her head. "Stay with me. There's no time for a pity party. Do that later. We have to go help Val and get your stuff."

"Okay, right, right. 'Cause Val doesn't have a car anymore. Did I tell you that?"

"Yeah." Hershel stopped moving about and looked her in the eyes. "You told me."

Karen appreciated Hershel taking charge. He raced to the basement and came back up with a couple of large folded boxes and a roll of heavy duty black garbage bags to help with moving the loose items. He thought it best to drive separately in order to load up more items, which would result in fewer trips, he added as he headed out the door.

Karen could hardly see out of the windshield through her watery eyes. She and Val had been hit with one thing after another and the bad news didn't seem to let up. On top of that, she didn't know if this would send Val over the edge, seeing how she'd lost her passion for life. More than ever, Karen needed to keep both eyes on her to make sure she didn't try and off herself. But where would they stay? A hotel? A shelter? They were both flat broke with no savings whatsoever. With all of the thoughts whirling in her head, another big concern remained front and center: the computer and her research papers. In no way would this halt her plans with finding Frank, no matter where they had to stay.

When she and Hershel pulled in front of her house, Val looked pitiful sitting on top of a night stand with her head bend over into her folded arms. When they stepped out of their vehicles, they both walked up slow, their steps sympathizing with what had happened. Karen went over to Val and hugged her tight. She knew Val must've cried up a storm. In fact, even in the dark, her face revealed dried lines of white ash.

Broken down furniture, loose papers and personal items were all thrown about their front yard. Some of the notepapers started flying in the street from a passing breeze. A few neighbors peeked out from lighted windows to be nosy, as far as Karen was concerned. She stared back at them and rolled her eyes hard enough to make the right side of her head hurt. Karen thought back to Val's statement that they'd hit rock bottom. She couldn't have been more wrong.

Hershel insisted Val sit in his car to get herself together. But she was just as persistent and started to help load the vehicles. And after several trips back and forth, everyone was spent with exhaustion. Still numb, Karen glanced about the lawn, realizing that a lifetime of memories had been tossed across their front yard like trash.

Karen thanked Hershel countless times. He waved her off, saying, "Oh, it's nothing. You both will be all right." Even Val obliged him with a firm hug, topped off with a kiss to his cheek. Once back at the house, and in a typical Hersh-Hersh fashion, he started gathering linens and towels and making up rollout beds in the basement, insistent they stay with him until they got on their feet.

Chapter 54

Once Saturday morning daylight broke, Val awoke with abdominal pain. In fact, she had stirred all night with unrest. A sunken realization emerged: she wasn't dreaming. Her nightmare was a living reality. She exhaled, lifted from her new bed and began exploring the basement. *Not bad,* she thought, feeling sadder she and Karen were homeless as she spied how neat and clean everything was. The basement, an area broken up in sections, had a converted den slash sleeping area, with a bathroom and shower combination in the next room. Another sleeping spot was off the area with a washer and dryer. The burgundy sofa, which was positioned in front of the wide, flat screen TV, was also a pullout bed. That's where Karen slept.

    Val leaned her head against the doorframe and stared at her through the cracked door. Funny, the way she looked reminded her when Karen was a toddler and wanted to sit in her lap to take a nap. She had finally learned how to say her name, sorta. She couldn't say 'Karen' but 'Keekee' came out just fine. And so, Val rocked her until she fell asleep. Karen snored so loud Mama came tearing in the room like someone yelled "fire." The loud snoring eventually turned into sleep-talking and sleep-giggling. She was adorable. *Now look at us; this is all my fault.* Val's shoulders rounded with the reflection. She bit the inside of her bottom lip and turned away since she had no idea how to fix the mess they were in. *Too bad*, she thought. Too bad Karen and Hershel weren't an item. How that didn't happen eluded her because they'd known each other for years. Maybe that was it. Perhaps they were meant to be friends opposed to lovers.

She gathered her toiletries and underwear from one of the garbage bags and tiptoed to the bathroom for a bath. She needed it. She felt stinky and dirty from the inside out. After she filled the tub with warm water, she checked under the cabinet to snoop and found Epson salt. She sprinkled a little in the tub, staring at the dissolving crystals. She eased her body into the water. It felt warm and soothing as it enveloped her hips, thighs, feet and toes. If ever there was a sanctified moment, this was it as far as Val was concerned. She inched down more into the water, her stomach then breasts now submerged. It intoxicated her. The rising mist reached her nostrils like healing vapors. She moved further down until her head dipped under the relaxing bathwater, only her nose exposed. She could stay there . . . she would give herself permission. Stay . . . stay . . . stay.

"Val! Val!" Karen yelled.

She sprang up, nearly jumping out of the tub. The water shifted like a seesaw and splashed onto the floor against the swift movement of her body. "What is going on?" She didn't hear Karen come into the bathroom.

"Val, are you . . . you, you . . ."

Val cupped her hands over her breasts. "Am I what?" She then swiped a wet hand over her dripping face and repositioned it over her bosom.

"Are you, you trying to take your own life?"

Val studied the horror on Karen's face; she was genuine with her fear, and shaken, judging by her quivering chin.

"I'm taking a bath, Keekee. You took this to a whole new level of homicide. What's with you?"

She backed away a bit. "It's just that—I thought because you were in here so long, something was wrong."

Long? What time was it? All she did was wake up, look around and take a bath. Wait, she thought about Karen, Karen as a baby, a baby in Mama's house. Did she get locked in her thoughts? Or was she trapped in wanting to escape? The water no longer warmed her; it chilled her skin and her lips turned pale.

"Just because I spent a little extra time in the bathroom doesn't mean I'm, you know, trying to do-myself-in."

"Well, I'm sorry if I'm trippin', but I'd been calling you and calling you. You never answered. What was I supposed to do?"

"I think you're overreacting. An hour or so in the bathroom doesn't call for alarm."

Karen lifted her head to the ceiling and slapped her left hand against her hip. "Val, it's almost noon. You've been in the bathroom for more than four hours."

"Okay. Look, I can't keep track okay. Maybe I wanted to get away, away from all this chaos I've gotten us in!" Now she yelled. She wasn't even in her own house and already acting a fool. But right then, she and Karen shut their mouths, unable to stand against to the loud and angry voices coming from upstairs.

Karen looked at her and placed a finger to her mouth. She eased the door open and listened. After a minute, she turned back to face Val and mouthed the names Hershel and Jessica.

"What?" Val asked, whispering back.

Karen shut the door and skidded over to Val. "I said, it's Hershel and Jessica. His girlfriend. You know, the one I told you who works with me."

"Oh," she said, eyeing the murky tub water.

"Val."

She lifted her face and eyebrows to Karen. "Hmm?"

"You don't have to keep your hands over your tits. We got the same thing you know. Unless you have an extra one I don't know about."

The off comment made Val's jaws swell. Before she knew it, she laughed out loud with both hands to her cheeks. Karen hooted, too. They cackled long and hard as if it were some cathartic force running through them. Val chuckled to the point she began to cry. Karen settled and came to her side, handing over a big towel and patting her damp shoulder.

"It's okay," she whispered.

"I'm sorry," Val muttered, securing the towel around her.

"I don't want to hear another word. You didn't do anything wrong. You tried your best and things just happen. You gotta pick yourself up and keep it moving. Ms. Blout once told me it's a part of life, the ups and downs and whatnot. Sometimes it happens even when you do your best to avoid the crap."

Val nodded. It made sense. She tilted her head toward Karen and stared. She was saving her. Karen, eyes eager and filled with all the hope the world had to offer, wanted the best for her. Val knew, that no matter what they would be hit with, she would not get down on herself, or feel defeated, ever again . . . if she could help it.

Chapter 55

After she sat a bit with Val and got herself cleaned up, Karen ventured upstairs when she thought Jessica had left. She moved with caution when she topped the stairs. "Hey, Hersh-Hersh? You here?" She strode into the kitchen and found a note on the counter, which read: *Hey. I didn't want to bother you all. There's plenty of food and I left fifty bucks if you need to get something. By the way, there's an extra key to the house in the first kitchen drawer. I'll see you when I get home from the art gallery-Hershel.*

Karen smiled to herself and knew she would never be able to replace his kindness, not in a million years. In a snap decision, she pulled out her phone to call him. While he never picked up, it didn't stop her from leaving a message.

"Hey, Hershel. Dang boy, how much you gon' do for us? A place to stay, food, money. You adopting us or what?" she laughed into the receiver before swallowing down an emotional lump. "But seriously, thanks for everything. What would I do without you? I'll see you when you get home. Oh, by the way, you and Jessica okay?" She ended her call thinking about the last remark. She could guess what they argued about. If Hershel was her man she sure as sugar wouldn't want another woman staying under the same roof with him . . . she'd better be bucktoothed with no arms and have a club foot. Even so, Karen had her own concerns today. Although it was her day off and she needed to get together with Val to figure out their next move, she decided to put her plan into action. She was going after Frank.

Karen's anxiety climbed with each step she took up the walkway. Pieces of concrete crunched below her tennis shoes, and when she approached the first step, she noticed the untidiness of the brick duplex with a rake and bucket lining the front porch. Perspiration formed on her upper lip. "I sure hope they don't suspect anything," she said under her breath while pressing the doorbell. After her third attempt, a heavy woman with hair rollers came to the door. Karen tried not to compare people to animals, but she swore this woman resembled a bull the way her nose flared out and both corners of her mouth turned upward. She looked like she wanted to charge. *Dang, glad I'm not wearing red.*

"Yes," the woman said in an annoyed pitch.

"Ah, yes. Hi. I'm Michelle with Wonder Words Singing Telegram. I have a message for a Frank."

Karen thought her knees would fail her any second because the woman didn't blink. She studied every inch of Karen's face, looking for a reason to go off on her for showing up on her doorstep.

"We ain't ordered no damn singing telephone."

"Telegram, ma'am, telegram."

"We ain't ordered nothing. Why you here again?"

"I told you, there's a message for Frank Spivey from Jeff. Jeff Moore."

"Jeff? I don't know no Jeff neitha'. Who is he?"

"I have no idea. I'm only here to deliver the message."

"Humph."

"Is this Jeff gay?"

"I don't know, ma'am."

"Humph. What man sends another man a singing telephone ifen he ain't gay."

"Telegram, ma'am."

Karen wanted to run away, but held to the lies. She owned them. She'd earned them when she came up with fake names, searched the Internet for stationary, badges with logos, and, most of all, when she labored over lyrics for this fool who was supposed to be her father. She placed three orders with an online company, item number 28887, a stun gun; item number 28895, a pocket knife, and item number 29993, pepper spray, supersized with a holder. Karen felt like a superhero, vigilante and cop, all rolled into one. She prepared for the worst. Now she had to figure out how to get away from this woman who was practically blowing smoke out of her nose.

"Well, that shows how stupid yo' company is. Frank ain't been living here for over eight months now."

"Sorry for the inconvenience, ma'am." Karen then acquired the Japanese custom and bowed a bit, stepping back on the first step.

"Yeah, that no good, good-for-nothing, slob decided to hook up with my back-stabbing-two-faced-so-called best friend," the woman added while opening the door wider to accommodate the width of her hips. "Well, they were made for each other. They did me a favor if you ax me."

Karen wanted to chuckle with her inside joke: 'ax' as opposed to 'ask.' "Sorry again."

The woman continued talking. "Yeah, I used to pick that dirty trick up every time, using up my hard-earned gas money. She's the one who lived near Henderson Park. So, since we walked there all the time, I figured it only made sense for me to do the picking up."

Karen's eyes widened with an accusation of contradiction when the woman said 'walking'. The only walking she looked like she did was from the refrigerator to the pantry. Karen wanted to bolt.

The woman then stepped out onto the porch. "Oh Frank, that bum. Couldn't leave things alone—had to mess things up by going to the park, too. Humph. The only workout he got had nothing to do with walking. You get my drift?"

"Uh, yes, I do." Karen bowed one last time before sprinting away and wasting no time pulling off in her car. She kept her pad and pen on the passenger's seat, and crossed off the name on the list for that particular address. She couldn't believe she'd mustered up the nerve, on her day off at that, to play detective. When she lost her nerve, she thought about the pictures of Val and how degraded she looked. Those pictures were like an electromagnet.

She forced herself to go to the next address on the list, repeating the same process, except, this time she was Tina. A scarred-faced man came to the door wearing an undersized towel and a colossal grin.
Karen knew right off, this man, in no way, could be her father. Not because he couldn't wear the title of creep, but because the man wasn't much older than she. Frank, by now, would be in his late sixties. Karen had to think of another lie on top of the planned ones.

"Hi, is Sharon Stevens here?"

"No, but you can leave me the message." The man tugged at the knot on his towel.

Ugh. "Sorry for the mix-up." Karen sprinted.

"Come back any time."

I don't think so, weirdo. "That's okay. Bye."

With only two more houses left on her list, Karen decided to visit them both. When she turned onto the street of the third house, a stray dog darted in front of the car almost causing her to ram into a tree. The neighborhood, a depressing stretch of dilapidated homes, spooked her. She second-guessed her actions and sat in her car, checking her watch one last time. She looked over at the rundown ranch where the third Frank Spivey lived. *Come on, you can do this.* Karen pulled a stick of Dentyne gum from her purse. After a few firm chews and an attempted bubble, she spit it out and swallowed. *Can't turn back now.* Exiting the car and strutting up the dirt walkway, she had no choice but to knock on the door because of a missing doorbell. Soon after, a little boy, perhaps eight, opened the door, grabbing its side. Karen gasped at the bruise on the boy's jaw and wondered if he had gotten into a fight or if it had come from his parents.

"Well, hello, little guy. Is your daddy home?"

The boy, with wide eyes and cracked lips said nothing.

"Is Mr. Spivey home?" Karen asked, bending down.

Before words could escape the boy's parting lips, an adult pushed him aside and barfed up a string of cuss words Karen thought were impossible to connect. The male's voice made her jaw tighten with uneasiness. When the man showed his face, he looked at her with bloodshot eyes. She studied his features and stepped back because she knew he couldn't have been her father either. At least she hoped not. A small part of her wanted to find her father and have him say "I'm sorry for all that I've done, and that I'm proud of how you turned out," but that was fantasy thinking.

"Oun-no. I-I think I have the wrong house."

"Well, let's see if you do. I heard you ask for me."

Karen didn't know how she'd get out of this one. Then, she heard another male voice in the distance yell out: "Hey, Frankie, what's up, man? Are you in the game or ain't you?"

The third Frank Spivey's head snapped back and he bucked his eyes. "Look, girl, I ain't got time to be messin' with you."

"Sorry, I have the wrong Frank." Karen trekked away without another word. Even the old relic gained record speed when she pulled off. Clenching her stomach, Karen felt sick, but took solace in knowing the last person on her list had to be her father. She wondered what she'd do once face to face with him, looking into his eyes; eyes that looked at a young girl with sick, lustful yearnings. Karen pulled over in front of a storefront pawn shop. She hung her head and cried. Her pearl-formed tears flowed heavy and long. Was she crying for an absentee father? Or, did she take on Val's pain of having to fend off a pervert with no one to protect her? Karen wanted very much to believe people could change.

This is it, she told herself as she pushed the doorbell. Her head pivoted around the nice looking Ypsilanti neighborhood with double-garage doors. But, no matter how nice the block seemed, she planned to cut loose on Frank and raise the white flag on any responsibility for what might come out of her mouth.

Interrupting her thoughts, an old woman opened the door before she pushed the buzzer a second time. She wore a hairnet and had large dentures.

"Oh, hello. I'm Lucy with Wonder Words Singing Telegram. Is, eh, Mr. Frank Spivey here?" Karen coughed for no apparent reason.

"What do you want with him? He's been dead for five years now."

"Are you sure?" Karen asked, figuring the woman had to be mistaken.

"Pardon me?"

Karen felt bad for the question. Of course she was sure. But how could that be? She had reached the end of her list. What now? The devastating blow sent her to the nearest Dollar General. She bought a pack of Dots, Skittles and Pringles potato chips, and sat in her car, in the parking lot, substituting tears for salt and sugar. Now, more than ever, she wanted to find Frank, her father, who she felt still lived in Detroit. How could she have missed him? Did he change his name? Karen had this cockamamie idea she'd save Val by vindication, which would have been Frank's knock down, his demise. But she couldn't do him in if she couldn't find him.

Chapter 56

With Karen and Hershel gone, Val felt compelled to cook and clean . . . and think. Earlier, she'd resisted the urge to hold herself in pity. She remembered the promise she had made and centered her attention on solutions, not hopelessness. Right then, like a seamless roll of masking tape, a new idea flowing from the one prior, hit her as she mopped the kitchen floor: the crusty feet woman. She was involved in real estate. Perhaps she could provide a place for her and Karen to stay. Val scratched her head trying to recall the woman's name. Another thought occurred to her to check her purse for the woman's card. She dropped the mop handle and quick-stepped to the basement for her purse. When she located the handbag among her belongings on the floor, she dug to the bottom and pulled out several pieces of paper. Among them was a card.

    The woman's name was Jane. Jane Flanagan. Maybe she could help them? Or, maybe not, Val thought, remembering she'd been so repulsed by the woman she asked to have her seat removed. "No, not now," she told herself aloud. "Time out for second-guesses. If she can't help, at least I tried." Val thumped the card with her middle finger and decided to call.

"Hello?" the voice on the other end spoke hurriedly.

"Miss Flanagan, you may not remember me, but I met you at the airport."

"The airport?" she asked.

"Yes, the uh, Phoenix Sky Harbor International Airport. I sat next to you briefly." Val punched her hip, hoping she didn't say too much.

"Oh, yes, I remember. You were the nice petite lady."

"Why thank you. Anyway, I'm hoping you can help me. My . . . sister and I need a place to stay."

"Let me stop you right there. I don't have any vacancies now, and won't until November. If you can wait until then, great."

Val exhaled, "No, we can't wait that long. We need to move ASAP, some place that's not too costly."

"Well, let me think. Hmm," Miss Flanagan replied after a few seconds. "I do know of another friend who mentioned an area for low income if you're interested."

"Yes, we are," the words rushed from Val's lips. She didn't have time to feel ashamed.

"It's not the Ritz, but if you are in a bind, it will serve its purpose."

Val jotted down the information and repeated it back. "Thank you so much." She hung up and smiled broader than she'd done in quite a while. They were going to be okay.

Chapter 57

The Fourth of July holiday had passed and now, with Saturday laid out, Karen practically dared the cops to ticket her as she drove fifteen miles over the speed limit. Hershel needed his items for the art show and fast. "Karen, don't over sleep. I need you to bring my stuff on time," he reminded her earlier, with a soft knock on her bedroom door. She did the complete opposite. Now she drove hunched over the steering wheel zooming through lights like a lunatic.

When she entered Royal Oak Township, she drove down North Main Street toward the *Expressions Art Gallery*, which was also one block away from the *Main Art Theatre*. She parked in front of the gallery and turned on her hazard lights. Karen entered the building hurriedly, calling out for Hershel to help unload her car. Once that was taken care of, she drove off to find a parking spot on University Street.

When she stepped back inside the gallery, Hershel had already begun hanging paintings on the folded stands, which were strategically placed throughout the floor. On the sly, Karen eyed how fabulously important he looked wearing a white buttoned down shirt, highlighting his chest, and a gray vest with white pants. To top off his look, he added a brimmed hat. Karen hadn't planned to stay, especially when she saw Jessica come around the corner and give her a cutting look, after which, she retreated to a back room. Karen's stomach muscles tightened. This was the one and only reason she hadn't planned to stick around. Jessica.

By 10 o'clock, a tall, thin, middle-aged man, who appeared to be of Nigerian descent, came through the door first. His eyes looked up at the banner featuring Hershel as the artist. His theme was: Freedom. The small gallery had a posh feel with its marble pedestals and thick crown molding along the floor and ceiling. Plus, Hershel's art looked amazing on the walls. A couple of his pieces put her in the mind of a black version of Joan Miro's work. At least to Karen it did. Of course, Hershel had to teach her who the artist was. Still, she marveled at the paintings, along with the Nigerian man, gasping with fascinating approval because everything made such a bold statement, so much so, the gallery had a palpable energy, all due to Hershel's art.

Karen never felt more proud of her best friend. Hershel was on fire. And because Hershel sold a few of his paintings to the GM corporate location down town, he had a bit of clout. The attraction of the Ren Cen alone brought out folks from all walks of life with its shops, restaurants, private clubs, and the Marriott hotel. That particular Marriott was also one of the tallest hotels in the United States. That, she knew on her own. And that was how Hershel started a friendship with the owner of the gallery: Adolfo Esposito. Of course, Karen didn't care to know about the owner. Out of boredom, she started cracking her knuckles.

"Hersh, I'm gon' leave now."

"Don't go. You just got here," he said, his eyebrows gathering.

"I know, I know, but . . . well, you know," she blinked sympathetically.

"Look around a bit, I'll be right back. I need to take care of something in the back with the catered food and drinks."

"Okay." Karen moseyed around another room, gazing at the art. Without a moment to react, Karen was blindsided when Jessica grabbed her shirt from the front, gathering it in her fist. All the gaiety was sucked from the room.

"Hey, hey," Karen spit out, all the while, trying to avoid a scene. Aside from Hershel and the Nigerian-looking man, the caterers were setting up and a jazz band member started arranging the equipment where they would play.

"I don't want you here. You don't belong here." Her words sizzled with fury.

Karen had never seen her look this way. Her eyes were narrowed like a panther stalking its prey. Before she could answer, she felt Jessica's other hand deliver a hot smack to the side of her face. She must have anticipated a reaction from Karen, since she then grabbed her arm.

"Stop it!" Karen hollered. She snatched her arm free, drawing her fist back in warning. What she felt next made her heart sink. Glass broke and something fell. She couldn't look. Even though Jessica's large breast had nearly knocked Karen's tooth out, she was wild and all over the place, ranting. Karen grabbed her by the back of her collar, some of her hair caught between her fingers.

"Let go," Jessica snapped.

"You stop it. I ain't done nothin' to you." Karen figured they must've looked ridiculous, blowing their breath on each while going around in circles. People started coming into the room, including Hershel. His eyes doubled in size and his arms started fanning the air before they clung to the sides of his head.

"Break it up. Come on, now," he said in a deep, authoritative voice, which sounded as if it were reverberating from beneath the floorboards. Hershel stood between them. "What the hell happened?" He whirled around. Then he stooped and grabbed his broken picture from the floor.

The tall Nigerian-looking man walked out shaking his bowed, bald head.

"Hershel," Karen reached for his shoulder as he knelt.

"Don't touch me. I'm upset with both of you. After this is over, we're all going to have a nice, long talk."

Karen pulled at the front of her shirt and gave Jessica a look of fury. She didn't remember landing one blow. How did two young women get to this point? She felt embarrassed. "Hershel, it wasn't my fault." She pivoted her head from Hershel to Jessica.

"I don't want to hear it, Keekee. Don't say another word to me."

Karen zeroed in on the chaos. What took seconds to destroy, Hershel spent hours in strategic preparation. *Another talk*, Karen fumed as she exited the gallery. At least Jessica was in trouble as well. For a split second, she wondered would Hershel want her and Val out of his house for what had just happened.

Although it seemed foolish, Karen tried to gauge Hershel's seating position in comparison with who he sided with more. He sat in a chair closer to her; she sat on the sofa, and Jessica, the furthest away, sat on the loveseat. Hershel sat for the longest, wordless, and holding his clasped hands up to his lips. For some odd reason, Karen wanted to laugh when Hershel's hands squeezed his lips. They resembled that of a fish. He already had full lips. This didn't help.

When he stood and began pacing the floor, Karen and Jessica's eyes followed him.

"First of all, I don't care who started what," he said, tilting his head at the both of them.

"B-but," Karen started in.

Hershel snapped a stop-sign hand in the air. "Naw, I don't wanna' hear it, Keekee. The two of you had better come together . . . and quick. Jessica, you're going to have to accept the fact Karen and I are best friends. We've been friends since childhood. This friendship is not going to end because you're in my life, I'm sorry."

Karen felt satisfied and tossed Jessica a smug stare after she smacked her lips.

"And you," he said, looking at Karen. "I would think you would be happy Jessica and I are together. After all, you introduced us. I can't figure that out to save my life." Hershel raised his hands then allowed them to fall to his sides.

Karen lowered her head. She never intended for them to get together. He was supposed to be with her.

Hershel started moving closer to Jessica. When he sat next to her and held her hand, Karen's heart pounded in her throat. "I didn't want to break the news to you like this but . . . Jessica and I are engaged."

Karen's lips parted as she shook her head. "Excuse me?" She thought he said they were engaged.

"You heard right," Jessica spoke up, inching closer to Hershel.

"I proposed over the holiday." He lifted her left hand and Karen saw the beautiful diamond ring. In Karen's mind, it practically sung out with brass instruments playing in the background. Her mouth went dry. She thought she had made peace with the notion of them being together. Somehow, her moving into his house made her cling to the thought of him coming around and realizing he should be with her instead of Jessica. All this talk from Hershel about their friendship not ending . . . yet, where could she go from here? He was moving on with his life and she didn't have a clue as to her next step.

She scrutinized Jessica's broad smile. It looked as though her face was on the verge of cracking. Karen cleared her throat and added, "Why would you do this? You haven't known her that long?"

"Excuse you?" Jessica asked.

"I've known her long enough."

Karen ignored Jessica and spoke up again. "Why does this seem like you jumped to this decision? Did you do it to keep her quiet about me moving in here?"

"We love each other. Why can't you get that through your head?" Jessica barked.

Hershel took his hand and rubbed down on the front of his neck. "Okay, okay you two. Look: I had planned to propose anyway, Keekee."

"Sure you did," she mumbled. The battle was over, Jessica won. Now all she had left were fading memories and thoughts of what could have happened between them. She felt more alone in that moment than she had ever experienced in her entire life. She stood and extended her right hand to Jessica. "You win." Jessica, although hesitant, shook her hand. Karen then shook Hershel's hand and said, "Congratulations, I'm happy for you."

"Yeah right."

"No, really. I want you to be happy Hersh. You deserve it. I'm sorry if I caused you problems. You too, Jessica."

Karen lowered her head and descended into the basement. She laid her face onto her pillow. In a way, she wished she could have started out as friends with Jessica. They did have a few things in common. They both had losses in life, for certain. Jessica probably would be good for Hershel. But for Karen, everything was going wrong. She didn't find Frank, she lost Hershel, and she didn't have a clue as to what her future held.

Chapter 58

Val looked up and down Schaefer Street until she located the cheap rental property. The house, a jarring contrast to how picturesque the day turned out, had chipped dark green and pink paint, in addition to several broken steps. Val looked over at Karen. Her nose was crinkled.

"Dang, what a dump," Karen said.

"You can say that again. But, let's not judge it until we've seen the inside."

"Whatever, I don't think it's gonna' get any better."

They both stepped with care from the car and up the walkway of the broken concrete. The front banister wobbled when Val grabbed it, and because there wasn't a doorbell, she knocked. No answer. She knocked a few more times and still no answer.

"Let's just go," Karen suggested.

Val threw up her hand. "We can't 'just go,' we told the woman we'd be here to see the place."

"Well, we held up our end, so now what?"

The front door opened. A woman with purple streaked hair stepped out. "Hey. Y'all the Williams, right?" the woman asked in a lazy tone.

"Yes," Val spoke up, forcing a lilt to her own speech.

"Follow me. I'll show you around."

They walked closely behind the woman, each room, hollow and squeaky, echoed the woman's listless words. Loose floorboards that lifted in spots and cracked plaster on the walls didn't escape Val's perception of the rundown place either. When they entered the kitchen, and right when the woman stated the appliances were included with the monthly rent, a mouse peeked out from the eye of the stove, ran down the side, and scurried across the floor into a hole in the corner of the room.

"Oh, Jesus," Val screeched, jumping back and holding her chest. She thought about Mama's house. Granted, they didn't have the best furniture; while repairs and updates were in order, they certainly hadn't stooped to the poor conditions of this home.

The woman looked at Val as if she'd over-reacted. Karen turned around a full ninety- degrees and started coughing uncontrollably. Val suspected that was hysterical laughing in disguise.

They all stood by the front door at the end of the tour. The woman asked, "So, how soon you think you can move in here?"

Val's eyes widened. "Uh, well, let me think on it, and I'll get back to you."

The woman twirled a strand of purple hair in her finger and said, "By the way, we don't allow no pets."

Val pressed in her lips and bobbed her head at the woman. At every account, she did her best to look beyond Karen's twisted face.

When they stepped out of the house, the woman closed the door without so much as a grunt.

Back in the car, both women laughed until they sighed.

"Are you kidding me?" Karen said.

"That was pretty awful." Val threw her head back on the headrest of the car.

"Uh, yeah, you think?" Karen bucked her eyes. "You should let me pick the rest of the houses," she added, eventually turning the key in the ignition.

"What do you mean? We're moving in this one."

"Na-uh. I'll stay in a shelter before I move in that joint."

"Well, you might have to eat your words. Besides, you have a better idea?" Val asked, drumming her fingers on the armrest.

"Well . . . Hershel continues to say he doesn't mind us staying there."

"Look, that's fine, but the little money we've been giving Hershel is not covering the cost of the extra lights, food and gas he's using to house us. Besides, our staying there is making his girlfriend uncomfortable."

"Fiancé."

"What?"

"He decided to get engaged to her."

Val stared at Karen's profile. "You okay?"

Karen fanned out her lips then shrugged her shoulders. "Eh, sure."

"Keekee, I know it may seem like you missed out, but you'll meet a great guy when the time is right."

"Eh."

Chapter 59

That Monday afternoon, Karen did a double-take when she looked up from the busy desk at the nurses' station. Jessica, whose cold stare appeared calculated, walked toward her, sure-footed as all get-out. They hadn't seen each other since the talk Hershel gave them. In fact, Karen remained in hiding most of the weekend, avoiding Hershel altogether. Now that Jessica was a few feet from her, she tightened her fists and resigned to losing her job right then and there if Jessica tried to attack her again.

"Hey."

Karen hesitated, nonetheless, responded with a firm, "Hi."

"I have something to tell you."

Karen figured Jessica was trying to *make nice* by informing her of the hired head nurse. "I know, I know, Mrs. Daniela Hall's the new hired manager. I saw them showing her around when I punched in." Karen allowed her eyes to wander because Jessica stood there, silent. It wasn't the reaction she thought she'd get.

She spoke up again saying, "So, do you think she'll be nicer than Margaret?"

Jessica didn't answer. Instead, she grabbed her

arm. Karen glanced down at her limb then back at Jessica. But this seemed different. Even though she wasn't smiling, she didn't appear angry. Everyone else came off as fine with the new transition and not at all bent out of shape. Was there something else? Did it involve Hershel or the two of them?

"You don't know, do you?"

"Know what?" Karen's eyes searched for answers.

Jessica shook her head then guided Karen over to the empty dining area, flicked on the row of lights and sat her down.

Karen waited.

"Ms. Blout died in her sleep last night."

There was no preparation or warning beforehand; nothing to cushion the harsh blow that made Karen's heart thump so hard her chest ached. She leaned in, blinking hard. For a moment, she doubted Jessica. "D-don't play with me." Her voice trembled.

Jessica rubbed Karen's bent back. "I'm so sorry, Keekee."

"What, what happened?"

"She stopped breathing."

"Augh, I hate this," she cried, waving a helpless arm in the air and allowing it to flop on the table. "I don't believe this."

"I know you feel awful, but you can't beat yourself up."

Karen sniffed hard, but the droplets came down anyway and landed on her shirt. "She wasn't just any patient. She was more like a grandmother. The type of grandmother I should've had."

Jessica nodded.

Karen didn't care that Jessica witnessed her vulnerability even though she seemed truly concerned. Her focus remained on Ms. Blout. Now that the tether was broken, she would no longer be able to draw from the old woman's reassurance. Karen didn't care that the woman made up stories about people she had known or thought she knew. She missed her.

Jessica tilted her head and said, "I am sorry. It was obvious you two had become very close."

"Now, what am I gonna' do?" she asked herself while wiping at her watery eyes.

"You'll go on. We all do somehow."

"I need to get away." Karen stood and walked away with her head hanging down.

"Say, Karen," Jessica said.

She looked over her shoulder, eyes fixed on the floor.

"I really am sorry."

Karen exited the dining space feeling certain Jessica's apology had more behind it than Ms. Blout's death.

Karen spoke to the administrative head and punched back out. There was no way she could finish out her shift. As she headed for the exit door, she saw Daniela look her way.

Chapter 60

After she raked over Karen's sleeping image, Val, as a joke, placed the key's on Karen's cheek. As of late, she'd been allowed to drive Karen's car and take care of personal business. This time it included picking up mail from their old house and buying a light bulb for the basement bathroom.

"Val, stop playing around." Karen swiped the car keys from her face.

"Wooph," Val fanned her own face.

"What?"

"Think you may want to get cleaned up? Get the crust out your eyes and brush your teeth?"

Karen wobbled her head. "Naw. Nope. Don't believe in it no more."

Val grinned and turned her eyes to the ceiling. She was going to be okay. "Look, when're you going to get up? You've been dragging around here for a week and . . . ever since the funeral, you haven't been the same."

"You think?" Karen rubbed her eyes.

"Why do I feel there was a silent 'duh' in there somewhere?"

"I wasn't thinking that. It's that I really miss her. Plus, I gotta take a test at Wayne State, remember?"

"Oh, right. Well, moping around here won't solve your problems. If what you've told me about Ms. Blout is true, I'm sure she'd want you to continue on and fulfill the aspirations she had for you. Well . . . more like the ones you have for yourself. Like you said, you're planning on furthering your education. Right?"

"Sure."

"Sure, what?"

"Sure you are right, and sure, I'm tryin' to further my education. I just hope I pass this doggone test."

"Of course you will."

"You *sure* 'bout that?"

Val gazed up long enough to check out Karen's crusted-eyed face twisted up in doubt. "Here." She handed Karen two envelopes. "These are addressed to you."

She held onto the envelopes until Karen eased upright in bed and retrieved the mail. She flipped one envelope over to show Val when her eyes narrowed. "Look, from the law office, Lang and Associates. What now? What did I do? Look, I can't read it. Val . . . you read it." Val opened the envelope with her thumb and began to read:

> I, GERTRUDE ROSE BLOUT, residing at Wayne County, Michigan, being of sound mind, do hereby make, publish and declare this is my Last Will and Testament and to revoke any and all other Wills and Codicils heretofore made by me.
>
> ARTICLE 1
> 1.1.   I direct payment of my debts, funeral expenses and expenses for administration of my estate.

ARTICLE 2

2.1. I give the rest of my possessions located at CHASE BANK, to, KAREN WILLIAMS.

2.2. If any beneficiary shall fail to survive me by 45 days, it shall be deemed that such person has predeceased me.

I, GERTRUDE ROSE BLOUT, do hereby declare to the undersigned authority that I am 18 years of age or older, of sound mind, and under no constraint or undue influence willingly sign and execute this instrument as my Last Will and Testament in the presence of the following witnesses, who witnessed and subscribed this will at my request.

Val and Karen had a matching set of enlarged pupils.

"Ms. Blout must've left me something in her will," Karen said, snatching back the letter.

"That's great, Keekee. I'm happy for you," Val said, touching Karen's leg and rocking it.

"Well, I wonder what possessions she would have in a bank? Wouldn't it be money?"

"She probably has valuables stored in a safe deposit box." Val reached for the letter to read it again.

"Oh my God." Karen kissed her hand then flung it in the air. "Thank you Ms. Blout. I love you, I love." Karen leaned over and kissed Val's cheek, looking at the letter again. "But I thought you had to meet with attorneys when you're in somebody's will?"

"That's only in the movies." Val relaxed her shoulders, happy that Karen sprang back to life. "Funny how God places people in your life. They can be right up under your nose and sometimes go unrecognized." Val let go of a chuckle and reflected on Brady.

On occasion, when she went off to bed, she felt his presence, his touch on her shoulder or back lulling her into a serene sleep.

Karen snapped her fingers. Val assumed it was meant for her but when she did it again, she knew something was up.

"That's it," Karen said, throwing her legs out to the side of the bed.

"What?"

"I can't say now, but I promise you, I'll tell you soon?"

"Tell me what?"

"You'll see."

Val unrestricted her lips since Karen looked happy, truly happy. And that made her smile inside, even though job offers had dried up, along with their dwindling funds. Somehow, she held onto hope that they would find their way out of all this mess.

Chapter 61

The thought came to her like a Clapper device turning on the lights. Karen figured Val must have thought she was a couple brain cells short from acting normal the way she hopped up and started getting dressed without washing her butt. Well, she did have sense enough to brush her teeth and wash her face. Furthermore, she realized she knew the whereabouts of Frank. It was the first woman she'd talked to who provided the answer. Now, with the blazing sun highlighting weeks of dirt on her windshield, Karen drove to Henderson Park with a mission.

     Glancing at her rear-view mirror, she observed the thickening traffic behind her. She veered right when she reached her exit, all the while anticipating what she'd do if she ran into Frank at the park. As soon as she arrived, she got out and glanced around the area as if any second, Frank would jump out and yell "Here I am." She wandered toward the walking trail, wondering what areas Frank usually ventured to. If necessary, Karen was prepared to knock on every residential door near the park. But in no way, did she plan to go back to the woman who spoke of Frank and her back-stabbing friend.

Over the next few days, she drove back out to Henderson Park, sometimes before work, and on occasion, late at night when her shift ended. With little luck, she maneuvered around the outskirts of the park, eager still, to cross paths with Frank. This particular Thursday, she rushed out to get to work. But as she exited the park, a man in a dented beige Buick with a thin salt and pepper beard stared back at her as he entered the park. Karen did a double-head turn before driving off. There was something about him. Could he have been Frank? She turned her car around.

    She bent close to the steering wheel, searching for the Buick. When she spotted it in a nearby parking lot, Karen drove on a short distance then circled back to the same area. Out of her passenger's window she watched the man get out, flick something from his hand, like a cigarette, then walk to a nearby bench adjacent a walking trail. Attempting to look inconspicuous, she shuffled some items around in the trunk of her car before slamming it shut.

    Karen's next move surprised even her as she sauntered over near the man on the bench, under the light post.

    "Phew." She plopped down on the bench next to the man then bent to tie her loose shoe laces. That was intentional. "It turned out to be a nicer day than I thought it would be."

    The man grunted.

    She didn't expect that. She had nothing else. That was her big icebreaker. She quietly eased up and pretended to head for the walking trail.

    "You ain't been around here much, huh?" the man asked, raising a hand to his eyes to block the sun.

    Karen turned toward him, surprised he spoke. She absorbed the pitch of his voice, the depth of his eyes. Could this man actually be her father?

"Never seen you walking these trails before," the man added.

"Um, I-I've been coming off and on," Karen lied. She inched in closer to the man, the sun, in an instant, became her halo from his vantage point. The back of her neck hairs stood up and a chill crept over her; this was Frank. She began to shake. She had to know. She had to ask.

"What's your name, sir?" She stepped even closer.

"It's Buddy," he said, lowering his hand and squinting one eye.

Karen tried her best to mask her perplexity because she felt certain she had the right person.

"Well, actually, that's what my beer-buddies call me," he chuckled. "My real name is Frank."

Her heartbeat quickened while her knees grew weak. She sat back down before she fell down.

"H-how often do you come out here?" she asked.

"Oh, a few times a week. I like the, eh, fresh air." He gave her a once over and sniffed. Karen had so many questions, yet, she didn't know what to say next. She stood again and did a fake stretch left then right.

"Well, I better get going."

"You never gave your name," Frank said. "You gon' make me guess it?"

"It's Sandy," Karen lied a second time. "See you later."

"You bet." Frank whistled as she departed.

Karen gave a half-smile as she jogged away, feeling his eyes on her every step. Many thoughts came rushing at her. *Dang.* She was going to be late for work, too.

That weekend, later in the day, she returned to the park and found Frank at the same bench.

"Hello, there," he said, sounding delighted.

"Hi." A plastic grin etched across Karen's face. She turned to him and said, "I already know who you are."

She figured that would stop him in his tracks. She sat beside him.

"Come again?" he said, turning his head in her direction and pushing his tongue against the inside of his jaw.

"My name's not Sandy. It's Karen."

Frank blinked.

"You know my family."

Frank was stuck on mute or something because he didn't say a word; he started looking around like he didn't want to get caught.

"Dottie . . . Val . . . the Williams' family." She could feel her heart pounding so hard she thought for sure it was audible. By now, she knew Frank knew who she was. "I'm . . . your daughter."

He grabbed his heart and swayed from side-to-side. Right then, Karen wanted to place her fingers around his throat and squeeze. She could have easily cut him with her pocket knife if she wanted to. He made her into a bastard child, worthless and unwanted, often feeling shame around others who asked too many times, "Where's your father?"

Val's face flashed before her eyes and the horror she'd endured at the hands of this man who sat beside her, shaken, looking dumbfounded by the news he'd been given. Karen felt warm about her neck and head.

What was he thinking? Was he happy? Stunned? He sat there, staring and sniffing like he had done a line of coke. She wanted to smash that damned face of his with a nearby rock she spied by a tree. Her hands folded into fists as she tightened her jaw.

Why won't he say something? She then cupped her hands over her reddened face and began to sob. Why did she do that? She wanted to kill him, not breakdown and cry.

"Hey, hey. Shh, shh. It's all right," Frank said, while pulling her into his chest.

Moment of Certainty, page 303

Karen looked up into his eyes and searched them. Even as the day gave way to the night, she held out for a slither of hope, for the truth. While her insides were in turmoil, she wasn't about to let Frank off so easy. But his response shook her to the core.

Chapter 62

It didn't make sense to place clean clothes and papers back into boxes and garbage bags, but Val respected Karen's wishes. "Why can't you unpack your belongings?" she had asked before she knew the true reason. Karen insisted that by the time she unpacked, they'd be moved out. Val let her be. Maybe it gave her something to cling to, she thought as she popped the large plastic bag open wider and put in Karen's important envelopes and notepads. She tied it back closed and pushed it to the corner of the room with the other storage items. Val stuck out one hip and stared at the corner of the room. Too bad she couldn't tie up her feelings in that way.

As of late, Frank had been sneaking in her room, laughing and touching her. Was it him? She could smell his scent. Or was it Brady? She couldn't remember now, if Brady's presence still protected and soothed her from her demons throughout the night. Maybe it was anxiety that kept her tossing because the money was drying up and she hadn't yet found a place in her price range.

Val drew comfort from Hershel's pleasant glances and nods as he moved about the house. He usually made it a point to come down and let her know how good her dinner dishes were or to thank her for taking on some cleaning task. Once, Jessica ventured to the basement to say "Hello." It made her feel relaxed. It was where she spent most of her time, within the cooling brick walls and floor fans; alone with bills and a notification that she would no longer receive unemployment benefits.

Chapter 63

She'd longed to hear Frank apologize for his disgusting treatment of Val. Karen's throat tightened. As much as she wanted to present a strong front, her next words tumbled out and fell flat. "It was hard," was all she managed to say before she became a blubbering mess.

"There, there," Frank twisted his body toward her and drew her close, hugging her tight.

Karen sobbed into this man's chest for what seemed like forever. She couldn't speak. Nor did Frank require her to. He held her and rubbed her shoulder. She wanted to talk more but her words remained lodged behind a thickened tongue. She wanted clarity from his perspective as to what happened when he stayed at Mama's house. The fact that he offered her comfort made her think that he would be straight with her and tell the truth.

"Like I said," she added, wiping her face with her hands, "it was hard."

"What was?"

"Seeing how tore up all this made Val. How it, it just messed up her childhood. You coming onto her and all." Karen looked away feeling sickened and victimized by his filthy acts. When she pulled away, Frank loosened his grip and stood. He spanned the park then turned back to her. "You know that was a long time ago. She shoulda' gotten over that by now and so should you."

Karen's back became erect. "Excuse me?"

"Look, I ain't got time to babysit no old feelings. And ifen you lookin' for a handout . . . money or somethin' 'cause you think I'm yo' daddy, then, you got another thing comin'."

"W-what? A handout? I want you to know how you ruined my, my mother's life!" Karen yelled out, spit spraying from her mouth.

"Look, that girl, Dottie or you, don't mean nothin' to me. You best to get outta my face."

Karen's heart pounded in her chest so hard her entire body thumped. She scrutinized Frank, his arrogant stare, almost gleeful she was in emotional agony and shaking. She could end it right now and cut him in the jugular. She fingered around in her pocket for the small silver knife until she held it snug in her hand, her thumb rubbing at its smooth edges.

When she thought he couldn't say anything more cruel, he hissed, with a devious grin, "Hey, look, don't be fooled. Val . . . yo' mama, loved it; every bit of it." He placed a hand to his groin area.

Karen flicked her head back away from him and toward a flock of birds flying by. She thought about the photograph of Val holding her. And she remembered Ms. Blout saying, in life, you have to pave your own way, and most times, you got to forgive, even if it's for yourself, no matter how bad somebody hurt you. Everything faded into the background. Karen held her head down and noticed an ant hill a short distance from her foot. They had scurried about building and preparing. For what, she didn't quite know, but the evidence of their labor impressed her. She exhaled and got up to walk to her car.

She heard Frank's acidy voice call after her. "Hey! Hey girl, you hear me! Whatju gonna' do now, huh?"

At first her sluggish feet seemed to belong to someone else, but her steps soon turned purposeful. She neared her car with one thought on her mind: she was loved. Nothing or no one else mattered.

But a swift idea came to her and fluttered her brain into a haze. Before she knew it, she'd whirled around and marched back toward Frank. His nasty remarks boomed louder with each step she took.

Signaling to him, she continued in his direction, as he kept grabbing his jewels. She moved closer until she stood inches from him. She breathed in his disgusting presence like taking in the stench of old garbage.

"One last thing," she said, narrowing her eyes.

He raised his hands near his shoulders, and released a crooked grin. "What's that, baby?"

"This." Karen put every ounce of energy she had into her right knee and thrusted it into Frank's groin with a force his ancestors possibly felt. "How ya' like your balls now!" she yelled.

She watched Frank hit the ground with a thunderous thud, jerking and twitching about in a fetal position. All he needed was his thumb in his mouth. She spied a young couple walking by. The woman yanked at the man's sleeve and they both stopped, then, she pulled out her cell phone. Karen didn't know if the young lady called 911 or videoed Frank's ridiculous manner. Either way, she didn't care.

She strode away, her slender hips swaying left and right. She'd allowed the old Karen to take over, and that, aside from Frank's girlish wails, gave her immense pleasure.

Chapter 64

That Monday morning, Val heard Karen in the bathroom brushing her teeth before the alarm clock went off at 7:45 a.m. Val didn't want to face her. She couldn't allow her to see the fear in her eyes, not when she was upbeat about taking her test at the university. But she had to tell her about the glitch in the system, her checks stopping cold. She had nothing coming in. There was no savings, no stash, no 401K, nothing. When Karen came out of the bathroom Val said, "You're bright and ready to rock n' roll huh?"

"Yup. Good morning." She chuckled and did a hip twist.

"Maybe we can do lunch or something, you know. To celebrate your test-taking."

"Eh, well, we'll see. Let's not break out the party favors just yet."

"You're funny. It's okay. It'll give us a chance to talk . . . about everything."

Chapter 65

Karen decided to wear a striped blue and white shirt, and a white buttoned down sweater with her jeans to look more conservative, although she'd worn her hair blown out straight and a little spiked at the top. Still, she looked bookish and marveled at her appearance, confident she would make a good first impression. When she stepped into the counselor's office, her armpits were wet from nervousness; however, her nerves calmed when she laid eyes on the counselor whose wide smile looked as if it weighed more than the woman's petite frame. Karen carefully avoided saying "Yeah" and "Uh-huh" and the biggie, "Ain't." She relaxed in the tiny, separate room from the counselor's office, and took a deep breath before she took the admission test. Some questions were quite easy, while others challenged her intellect.

    She drummed her nails on the desk and marked "B" or "C" for some of the unfamiliar answers. She heard once, that the odds were better with a C when you didn't know the answer to a multiple choice question. The math portion made her head ache but she at least felt certain her answers were correct. When it came to the essay portion, she took her time. She wrote about Mama, Val, and her struggles growing up, although she left out the drama about Val being her real mother. She jotted down the lessons she had learned even though she understood them late in life. Handing over the completed essay, Karen began biting her bottom lip. She hoped to sway the woman in her favor. She wanted to attend the school and dreamed about walking from class to class. She could taste it.

Ms. Blout's spirit must have reached down and touched her because she didn't fret her scores after that. She knew she had passed. The petite counselor came in quietly and sat across from her with the test results. Karen tried to read into her poker face.

"You scored very well on the math portion," the woman said. "The multiple choice, though, not so well."

While Karen's shoulders slumped, she sensed this situation was going to work in her favor. And when the woman's smile broadened as she shuffled her essay papers, Karen knew she had triumphed.

"I must admit, your writing was quite moving," the woman said, dabbing at her eye behind her eyeglasses. "Because of your life experiences, and overall scores, you are admitted. Welcome to Wayne State University."

Karen didn't remember her feet touching the floor. She couldn't help but marvel at the fact she would soon be a part of the most cultured area of the city; the Detroit Institute of Arts, the Fox Theatre, Comerica Park, Ford Field, and the Michigan Science Center. Sadly, she hadn't cared about any of those places six months ago. *But things are different now*, she thought, as she wandered around the campus, venturing into the Purdy/Kresge library.

Karen felt smarter holding the heavy text books. When she flipped through the pages, she remembered the first time Ms. Blout wanted her to read to her. The woman was quite clever. Karen closed her eyes and whispered, "Thank you, old woman. Thank you."

After she left the library, she perused novelty items in the bookstore, and smiled at students coming and going, with the sentiment *that* would be her. Thirty-minutes or so, she noticed a tall blue-eyed young man staring at her. She pretended not to see him as she glanced over the sweat shirt she held one last time before placing the item back on the shelf. He made his way near her, slow and cool-like.

"Sure you don't want to reconsider?"

Karen released a nervous smile.

"I love your hair, by the way."

"Thanks," she said. "I-I like yours, too." She glanced at the sandy coils of dreadlocks that hung below his shoulders. On the sly, she combed over the form of his forehead, cheekbones and lips. He was indeed, a good looking white dude.

"Like I said, if you reconsider, we'd have matching sweats."

Karen blushed, eyeing the stranger, then the shirt, then the stranger. "So, what's the deal with you? You the store monitor?" Karen threw her right hand on her hip. She couldn't stop flirting with him. Why was she playing around with this man? Here she was, starting out on the wrong foot with her education.

He tilted his head back and laughed. "Yup, that's me. He shifted his army-style backpack on his shoulders and extended his hand. "I'm Jeff. And you are?"

"Karen," she said, deliberately peeling herself from the juvenile name *Keekee*.

"Karen," he repeated. "Nice to meet you." She separated her hand from her hip and shook his.

"Nice to meet you, too." She smiled and began leaving. "See ya 'round."

She almost skipped to her car, all the while thinking: this was a good day. She had tested well and was now a student at the university. On top of that, some cute white guy hit on her. Karen never had a white guy flirt with her. Sure there was Roy from the neighborhood, but no one took him seriously. He tried to talk to every girl in-the-hood because he was treated like any other brotha. He and his family were the only white folks that couldn't afford to move out into another more suitable color-coordinated zip code.

Karen whipped around in the direction of a distant voice calling her name. When she saw it was Jeff, her stomach flipped. Did she look cute even though the wind began to kick up? Once he reached her, he flicked his hair like the white girls with long hair usually did. His thick coils glistened in the sunlight.

"Hey. I'd like that."

Karen scrunched her face. *Is he on something?* "You'd like what?"

"To see you around some time. That was the last thing you said to me."

She blushed and looked away, focusing for a split second on the passing pedestrians.

"May I have your number?" he asked.

"Wow. You don't waste time."

"I don't have time to waste."

"Okay, sure." Karen recited her digits after Jeff opened his cell phone. He nodded at the phone as if checking to make sure his entry was correct.

"Say, are you new here?"

"Yes, I am. How did you know?"

"Because," Jeff said, slow while walking backwards a few steps, and adjusting his backpack again. "I would have noticed you. See ya." He walked backwards a few more steps before turning to walk forward.

Karen slid into her car, disbelief and glee spread across her face. She thought about Ms. Blout and how proud she would have been. She remembered the old woman telling her that love can find you anywhere and with anyone. She also recalled what Val said just days ago when she told her Hershel was engaged. "When the time is right, you'll meet someone," or something like that. And she was telling the truth. When Karen thought about trying to give her heart to Hershel, she knew that he already had it, but there was now room for a special love of her own.

Chapter 66

Beans and Cornbread. Karen's restaurant pick turned out to be a wise choice as far as Val was concerned. Every item on her plate, the black eyed peas, yams, and the broiled chicken, was cooked well.

"Mm, this is what I'm talking about," Karen said, digging her fork into a small heap of juicy collard greens.

Val nodded. "I must admit this was a good selection. Excellent call suggesting we eat here."

"Well, the food is good, but it's not better than your cooking."

Val's face beamed to the point her eyes became slits. She needed it with all the bad news she had been hit with. "Why thanks, Keekee. I appreciate that." She smiled before shoving a piece of yam into her mouth. "This is all for you. I'm very proud of you. I knew you'd pass everything."

Karen lifted her fork in the air, executing a type of seated curtsy. "Thank you, thank you."

Val wanted to postpone delivering negative news, especially since Karen glowed like a bulb. She couldn't remember the last time she had seen her this upbeat.

Maybe she could soften the news, Val wondered as she chewed and stared at Karen.

"What? Why you burning a hole in my face? I got a booger in my nose? Food on my face?" she sniggered.

"No, it's not that," Val chuckled, too. She lifted her napkin, but didn't wipe her mouth. "It's just another hurdle we . . ."

Karen's cell phone rang. "Hold on, Val." Karen lifted a finger then dug in her purse to retrieve her phone.

Val nodded and sipped her lemonade, pivoting her head about the restaurant. She allowed the circulating chatter from patrons to fill the space at her table. Maybe she shouldn't say anything about her checks. But she had to; otherwise Karen would think she was keeping secrets. It wasn't fair. Why couldn't she conjure up one pleasant event or uplifting news?

"Hello? This is she." Karen smirked, covering the phone with the tips of her fingers, mouthing "This is Jeff."

Val had no idea who she was talking about.

"Jeff, you have a slight accent. How did I miss that? Oh. Where are you from? London? Get out. Well . . . no. I'd love to . . . someday. Yeah. Well I'm at a soul food restaurant . . . *Beans and Cornbread*. What? Get out. You have?"

Val smiled to herself and pushed her plate away. A waitress came to the table and said, "Do you want me to take that?" referring to her plate.

Val nodded and placed her elbow on the edge of the table after the woman left with her empty dish. She allowed her chin to slip into her opened hand. *This Jeff must be important*, she thought as she continued to wait for Karen's call to end.

Karen blushed. "He sounds cute," she whispered to Val, covering the phone again. "Especially the way he says 'mom' which comes out 'mum'."

Val lowered her lashes then allowed them to pop up at Karen.

"No, I haven't," Karen said, now talking back with Jeff. "But have you? No, no, no, a Canadian who looks Puerto Rican with coarse hair doesn't count." She giggled. "I can cook . . . cook for you? . . . Why? I don't know you well enough to start pulling out all my goods. Oh . . . well, it's not gonna' happen on this phone conversation. What? I can't do that either . . . oh, I bet."

Val's eyes enlarged to the size of the plate she had eaten out of. She tilted her head at Karen and her raised finger.

"Yeah, uh-huh . . . yes, I said," Karen chuckled. "Fair enough. 'Au revoir right back at ya. Bye."

In Val's opinion, it sounded a bit beguiling.

"What?" Karen said, lifting her face after she saved Jeff's number to her phone's *contacts.*

"Mm, what have we here? A sprouting romance?"

"You know what," Karen replied, playfully smacking Val's hand.

"Come on, do tell."

The waitress came back and looked at Karen who shook her head regarding her plate.

"His name is Jeff and he's from London."

"I heard."

"I met him when I took my test . . . well, after I took my test. I was looking around in a bookstore and ran into him. He's nice."

"Good. I'm happy for you. So . . . tell me all about him. What does he do, what does he look like?" Val leaned forward.

"Well . . . he's a student at Wayne State and he has dreadlocks and blue eyes."

Val parted her lips before speaking "Blue eyes? He wears contacts? Does he look funny-looking with them?"

"Uh-uh. These baby blues are the real thing."

"What makes you so sure?"

"Cause . . ." Karen released a delicate rock from side to side, ". . . he's white.

"Oh, my. So, you're talking to a white guy?"

"Yeah. Why? You have a problem with that?"

"No, of course not. I'm surprised to see you've opened up your options."

"Actually, it doesn't seem like he's white. I mean, well, he's kinda like me. We fit each other. And he's never talked to anyone black before. Well . . . he has friends, but, you know. He ain't never dated one before."

Val nodded, and added, "Take your time. Enjoy dating, but don't rush into anything."

"Yeah, yeah." She rested her back against her chair and added, "Enough about me and my future husband . . . what were you going to tell me?"

Val lifted her brows and smiled. "Well, I have more bad news. My checks stopped coming."

"Why?"

"There's gotta be a glitch or something. I've tried calling the office but I haven't received an answer. I emailed my representative. I plan to go to the office."

"Sorry to hear that, Val. But . . . maybe Ms. Blout's money will help out, at least a few bills . . . something."

"I doubt it. We need Jesus, the Lord . . . God all Mighty to come down and give us a break." Val's eyes went skyward.

"I'll make a deal with you," Karen said.

"Sure, maybe. What is it?"

"I'll go to church with you if you, if you . . . you know, see a doctor."

"A doctor? I don't feel sick, I'm fine. I may be depressed but that's about it."

"That's what I mean." Karen raised a single eyebrow and pressed in her lips. "We all need someone to talk to, Val. There's no shame in that. Somebody better than me, could set you on the right path. You'd be able to get everything out in the open."

Val looked in Karen's eyes and saw the wanting, the hope that she would agree to her suggestion. In truth, she didn't want to get everything out in the open. She didn't want Frank pestering her more than what he'd already been doing. She wanted to forget. But because of the light in Karen's eyes, she said, "Okay. I'll go."

It took the administrator at Chase Bank forty-minutes before she came back to her cubicle where she and Karen waited. "Here you are. You're all set." The woman handed Karen the key to the safe deposit box. Val felt sorry for her as she had to pay one-hundred-sixty-five dollars because Ms. Blout didn't think to leave an extra key with a trusted relative, nor could the original be located. Karen told Val she could recoup back the money from what Ms. Blout left her.

    Val didn't want her to get her hopes up, although she prayed for a miracle. Val stared at Karen as she licked her lips while turning the key into the metal box. She also entertained the fantasy of seeing stacks of cash, but knew that was foolish. Still, she dreamed and wanted it for Karen. Karen glanced at Val's gleaming face, then, lifted the lid to the box in a slow, deliberate manner. Karen's shoulders drooped when she saw there were only three letters, a holey, brownish pouch, and a wooden necklace of some sort, wrapped in a dingy plastic bag inside the box.

    "Dang." Karen sucked her teeth. "I was hoping for more than *some* bag, necklace and *some* funky ol' letters," she said, sounding disappointed.

    "Oh, who was that person who was 'I love you, and thank you' when you got wind of the will."

    Karen rolled her eyes. She wasn't amused by Val's teasing.

    "Let me see," Val said, scrutinizing the items. "Keekee, these must be worth some money. Look." She pointed to the back of the envelopes which all had official seals on them."

"Hmm. So, what? And this raggedy necklace, what could that be worth?"

Karen opened one of the letters and read it carefully, but stopped abruptly when she saw who the letter was from. "Look . . ." she flung the opened note in front of Val.

In unison, they both said "Frederick Douglass" then grabbed each other's hands.

"Naw, naw, this can't be real." Karen's voice and eyebrows were now elevated.

"Well . . . it does have the seal."

"You mean to tell me Ms. Blout wasn't crazy after all? She really did know what she was talking about when she claimed she knew historical people?"

"Apparently so," Val chuckled.

"Okay, so now what?"

"We get the items appraised."

Chapter 67

The following day, they went to an appraisal shop. A beautiful chime rang when they opened the door to *Nostalgia Antique Appraisal Services*. Val convinced Karen to go before work so she wouldn't procrastinate. Maybe there would be enough money to pay a few bills. Val could only hope. Karen seemed doubtful.

"May I help you?" asked a serious looking gentleman.

"Yes," Val said, speaking for Karen. "We'd like to get these items appraised. My sister became a recipient of them due to a friend's death."

"Have you been here before?" he asked in a nasal-like voice.

"No," they both said in unison.

"Well, let me tell you a little bit about us. We've been in business for over twenty years, and all staff members are certified appraisers and affiliated with the International Society of Appraisers."

Val blinked at Karen, then back at the gentleman.

"So, not to worry, you are in good hands because we are all well-trained in appraisal law, concepts, ethics and procedures. Once we've completed our applied expertise and research, you'll receive a formal typed-written document detailing our findings and the value of your items. On top of that, the education of the company's president ranges from a number of fine arts, estate appraisals, classification of woods and the Detroit Institute of African arts. Her credentials go on and on," he said. "Any questions?"

"No," Val and Karen said.

"Well, now, let me see what you have."

Val eased the sack onto the counter as if its contents would break with a force superseding what she'd displayed. She pulled out the letters first.

"Hmm," the man said, inspecting the envelopes, then the letters.

"Is it the real thing?" Karen asked.

"Yes, from the looks of it," the man confirmed, still looking them over with care. He then wrote in a notepad.

With ease, Val pulled out the pouch, the wooden necklace, and waited for the man to stop writing. When he observed the two items, his eyes darted up at her then Karen, then back at the items.

"Excuse me for a moment," he said, retreating to the back with the items in hand.

Val and Karen hunched their shoulders and waited. Minutes later when the man returned, he had someone with him.

"Hello." The woman with long earlobes and expensive looking diamond stud earrings extended her hand to Val and Karen. "I'm Mrs. Simpson. How did you come to get these items?"

Val shifted to look at Karen.

"I received them from a will. If there's a problem, I have the papers right here from the attorney," Karen said.

The woman and the man stared at Val and Karen, neither of them smiling. Val felt so anxious it was as though her emotions were hanging on the edge of a cliff.

"We'll be right back. Please be patient. Thank you."

"What was that all about?" Karen asked.

"I don't know."

"You think it's something bad?"

"It's hard to say. But let's be positive."

Karen hummed and looked upward. "Know what I'm humming?"

"No, what?" Val asked.

"Me and My Shadow."

Val snickered. "You remember that after all this time?"

"Yeah, you sung it to me ever since I was three. I guess I followed you around a lot, huh?"

Val's face lit up. "I suppose. You were an adorable kid. Just following after your big sister."

She blinked when the light in Karen's eyes dimmed. She sighed heavily and stared. Val hadn't seen that look in a while. It made her heart ache to see it now. The two employees reappeared, which made them perk up.

"Sorry about the wait," Mrs. Simpson said, placing the items back on the counter.

"Is there a problem?" Karen asked.

"No, not at all. But let me ask you; are you aware of what you have here?"

The woman patted the counter.

Karen looked away in embarrassment and bucked her eyes at Val. Val spoke up.

"Eh, we believe these items are from Harriet Tubman."

The woman looked intently before smiling. "Well now. I think I have some news that's going to make you very happy."

Chapter 68

Six months later . . .

"Dang, Val. Hurry up," Karen called out, turning her head toward the stairs. "As slow as you are, Jeff and Brady will beat us there." It made her smile to know that a few months back, Brady had started calling Val for casual chats, a couple of them had extended to lengthy conversations. They even took in a movie together. Now they were all going to church with her; Val, Brady, and her man, Jeff.

"Hold on. I have to put my lipstick on."

Karen shook her head after the reply then shoved her gloves into her coat pocket. She nestled onto one of the comfy loveseats, stretching her legs out in front of her, as she glanced around Val's place, with its traditional and modern décor.

The beige loveseats from Joss & Main faced each other, while the brick fireplace at the head of the room made a bold statement. A European ottoman rested in the center of the floor, with an elegant Persian rug underneath. Artwork from Hershel hung on the wall with bronzy abstract color-splashes. In fact, every time Karen stepped foot into Val's high class condo, she felt tranquil, not only because of how it looked, but it smelled good with the scent of Asian Spice.

"Hey. Thanks for waiting," Val said, sounding a bit winded after she'd descended the stairs. Val walked into the room where Karen sat as if she were sashaying down a runway.

Karen batted her eyes at Val then sprang from her seated spot, looking her over from head to toe. "Uh-huh. Folks get uppity when they move out to West Bloomfield Hills, the suburbs for rich folks. Keep you waiting and what-not and don't think anything about it," she teased, throwing her hand on her hip. "You look pretty, though, in your dress and ankle boots," she added, and kissed Val's cheek.

"Thanks." Val glanced down at herself, brushing a hand across her thigh.

Karen folded her arms and took a step back. "I'm digging that spunky new haircut."

"You like it?"

"I love it." Karen leaned in and took her right palm and patted Val's free-flowing curls. "I love your makeup, too."

"I'm using the one I purchased from our last shopping trip . . . from the time my bagged items set off the store alarm. Remember?"

"Oh, yeah. I remember." They both exchanged a light chuckle. Karen turned and pointed to the wall opposite the stairs. "I see you got Hershel's other painting you'd been eyeing."

"Yes, beautiful isn't it?"

"It is." Karen tilted her head, admiring every inch of the art. "Ol' big head is cleaning up between the two of us," she snickered. "I bought another piece from him, too."

"You said you wouldn't."

"I know. I gave in."

"Well, it's such a shame, putting all that fine art in that little bitty dorm room. I still say you should consider staying with me." Val's eyebrows lifted as she nudged Karen's shoulder.

"I know, but I wanted to have the full college experience."

"Like I've been saying, you have the best room, especially the way you've hooked it up."

Karen put a hand to her chin and cocked her head to the side. "True."

Val gave her a measured look then grabbed her coat from the closet. "Okay. I'm ready. Let's get this show on the road."

Karen helped Val slip into her coat while she exited through the door first. She waited while Val locked up, fumbled with putting her keys away, and struggled to hoist her handbag's strap over her shoulder. Karen rolled her eyes, figuring service would be close to ending by the time they arrived at church.

Walking side by side, they stepped out into the bleak, wintery morning. Light, fluffy flakes cascaded, some landing on their heads and outerwear. The wet, salt-covered pavement crunched beneath their feet.

"Everything's going okay, though, right? In school, I mean." Val grabbed her coat collar close as they trudged through the parking lot. "I know the first year can be rough."

"Yeah, but I'm doing well. I like my classes, and my roommate is cool, aside from the fact she snores something awful. Other than that, she's quiet. She doesn't bother me, and I don't bother her. Did I tell you I decided on a major?"

"No, you didn't."

They both stood by Karen's new black BMW and got in when she clicked the door locks. For the longest time, she had kept her clunker, against Hershel's pleas to junk it or donate it. She'd finally ended up giving the car to a woman Hershel knew who was thrilled to pass it on to her teenage son.

"So, what major *did* you decide on?"

"Education," Karen said, sliding on her gloves once she'd settled inside and fastened her seatbelt. She started the car and drove off.

"Ah, seems you're following in someone's footsteps." Val allowed her left elbow to relax on the armrest.

"I suppose. All that talk about history from Ms. Blout started sinking in." Karen shifted her eyes toward Val. She gave a quick grin when Val turned to face her because she was finally able to show she'd done something with her life, which made her want to burst against the breeze of her happiness. They had made it through some tough times. Now they were going to be all right.

Turning left, she drove onto Thirteen Mile Road, passing a stretch of bare trees with coiling branches, and a huge construction sign advertising the building of a furniture store by the summer. Karen knew she would bring up the letter to Val. She didn't want to enter church, any church, having that on her conscious. Yet, finding the right time to do so, made her wince.

"Did you start your new job?" Karen asked, turning on her wiper blades. They swished back and forth a few times before she cut them off.

"In a week. I'm pretty excited. I'll be working with an old coworker, too. And I'll be her supervisor. Humph. Funny how life turns out."

"I'm happy for you, Val. If anybody deserves a break, it's you."

Karen knew Val had made a beautiful transformation, but also part of her healing included seeing a doctor. Without giving it another thought, she pushed out her concerns. "How're the sessions going with Dr. Johnston?"

Val's head swiveled so fast, it made Karen blush. "My sessions?"

"Yes. You are still going, right?"

"Well . . ."

"Val."

"I've attended two."

"Out of thirteen? Please tell me you'll consider going through with this."

Val lifted a hand in the air. "I will, I will."

"You will or you are?"

"W-what's the difference?"

"Just continue seeing Dr. Johnston. That's all I ask. It's for your own good. Look, I'm holding up my end of the bargain by going to church. You should finish all of your sessions."

Val snapped a firm hand to her temple before thrusting it out.

"Okay, be funny." It wasn't the outcome Karen had hoped for, but at least Val had made an attempt. And that made her heart gush with possibilities.

She tried to lighten the mood by giving her updates on Hershel's wedding plans. Val grinned, but the glimmer in her eyes had dimmed.

Karen knew she'd brought up a touchy matter. She could only imagine how depressed Val must've felt sitting in the doctor's office, having to recount painful events of her childhood, and that same past, threatening to grind away at her adult life. She wanted to see Val heal, though. Karen cared for her so much, and knew without a doubt, she would do anything for her.

But Val didn't spring back until the church's steeple came into view. Karen eyed Val pat her folded hands onto her lap, grinning with anticipation. "Can't wait to see Brady, huh?"

"Does it show?"

"It couldn't be any clearer if his name were stuck to your forehead with glittering letters."

Val tossed her head back and chuckled. Perhaps it was the way she appeared when her eyes, once again, lit up. Maybe it was the fact Karen's right shin still hurt from bumping it while exercising the day before. Either way, it made her think back to a time when she was young. She'd fallen off her skateboard, injuring her knee and outer thigh. Shocked at the sight of her own blood, she screamed out like someone snatched off the head to her Strawberry Shortcake doll.

It was Val, always Val, who had raced to her rescue and grabbed her close, carrying her inside to the nearest bathroom to clean her off and bandage her up, although Karen was still a tattletale, stating to Mama that Val didn't watch her good. Still, Val gathered her in her arms, pretending Karen was an infant after a feeding, and singing in soft octaves, "Hush little baby, don't you cry, Mama's gonna' buy you a cubiloop." Replace that with "boobilop, zupatutu, or yakakaboom." Val had tried her best to make her laugh. And it worked. Through the stinging from the rubbing alcohol and the taste of her own salty tears, Karen managed to laugh. "I ain't no baby," Karen told her. Val continued rocking her and said, "Oh, yes you are."

"No I not."

"Oh, yes you are."

"I not!"

Karen now wondered if that song had been a vehicle for Val to tell the truth. It was a good memory, and it made her want to open up right then and there.

Both women stepped from the parked vehicle, and walked out into the cold toward the entrance of the cathedral, although Karen's footsteps were unhurried. She wanted to talk.

"Say," Karen started in. "I forgot to tell you the Charles Wright Museum of African American History sent me complimentary invites to their Pathways to Freedom tour."

"Pathways?"

"You know, the story of slavery and how they came here."

"Oh, yes, right."

"Since I have clout now as a contributor, wanna go with me?" Karen joked.

"Sure, why not."

Just yards from the entrance, Karen could no longer put off talking to Val about the uncovered truth.

"I must say I'm impressed you followed through with attending church," Val said.

Karen bit into her bottom lip. "I'm nervous, though. But I need something steady in my life."

Val smirked and grabbed onto Karen's arm as they walked up to the carved, double doors. "How'd you get to be so wise?" Val asked.

"Oh, just trying to play catch-up with growing up."

Val looked pointedly at Karen and said, "Mama would have been proud of you."

Karen wiped at her nose, and swallowed down a lump, overwhelmed by Val's words. *Who cared what Mama would have thought*? She wondered how Val managed to fix her mouth to say the words. She nudged Val and signaled for her to stop walking. She took in Val's gleaming face then led her to the side of the church. Val followed like an obedient pupil.

"I have something to tell you." Karen's shoulders shuddered from the cold as she blew into her cupped hands.

"Okay. What is it?"

Karen's mouth turned downward but she had to say it. "I know about the letter. I know about your secret . . . Frank, everything. And . . . and I know that you're my real mother." Karen inhaled so deeply it caused her to gasp. Her heartbeat raced with each struggling pant.

Val held her eyes to the ground. Her breath puffed out into the wintry air.

"Val . . . you hear me?" Karen moved in closer.

"You know, huh?" she said after a few seconds.

"Yeah," Karen sighed, relieved that she'd finally released the news that had turned her life into a whirlwind. "I've known for some time, but I didn't know how to tell you."

"Humph," Val said, now gazing up at the sky, snowflakes sticking to her mascara-covered lashes. "You know about the others?"

Karen's eyebrows crunched in when she jerked her head. "Others? W-wait . . ."

Val cut her off. "I don't know if God can forgive me."

"Of course he can forgive you. What happened to you was not your fault. Val . . . what do you mean by *the others*?"

Karen's mind felt chained by Val's words. What was she trying to say, exactly? And had she ever even read the letter?

"I couldn't let it happen. I just couldn't. I had to, don't you understand? I had to do it."

"Okay, okay, it's all right," Karen said, rubbing Val's shoulders with short strokes. The friction from Val's coat against her gloved hand became an extension of her emotions. "What did you do?"

"I've always tried to be good. Honest. Always."

"Yes. Yes, you have." Karen tried to understand, but nothing was making sense. She searched Val's eyes for clues. Her eyes had become a window of salvation for her, but now, they refused to give way to what was locked behind her thoughts. "Val, what did you do? Please . . . tell me."

A child raced past them, with an adult following, a parent, perhaps, promising to knock him into next week if he didn't slow down. Val watched, smiling at the youngster who dashed around in the snow. She bobbed her head toward the woman who marched after him.

Karen waited, now feeling light-headed. Her thoughts were like tiny fairies, fluttering about, and her heart pounded wildly. She waited. She waited. She waited.

Val tapped each foot to the cold ground then said, "I had to do to Mama what she'd done to those other babies . . . my babies. I had to, right?"

Karen's eyes widened as she swallowed hard, violently ingesting Val's words and spitting them out to fit her own understanding.

"You're saying you had other babies?"

Val's voice barely topped a whisper. "Yes."

Karen blinked away the moisture in her eyes, fearful of what she might hear next. "You hurt Mama?"

Val dipped her chin.

"Did you hurt Mama, Val?"

Val began bobbing her head fiercely.

Every facet of Karen's being felt reshaped. *But Val couldn't hurt any living thing.* Karen's bottom lip dropped open. She couldn't tell if her trembling body was from the chilly air or from what she'd just heard. She managed a slow, feeble nod; her empathy fell into direct proportion with Val's unimaginable deed.

Truths that had swallowed whole, the lies of her childhood, now left her with the knowledge of her *real* mother, and for that, she was grateful.

Val's sad, watery eyes became Karen's moment of certainty.

She knew exactly what she was going to do . . . what she had to do.

She'd always said they had their secrets.

THE END.

Moment of Certainty, page 333

Made in the USA
Charleston, SC
02 March 2016